NEW
DRAGON
CITY

BY MARI MANCUSI

DRAGON OPS

Dragon Ops

Dragon Ops: Dragons vs. Robots

THE CAMELOT CODE

The Camelot Code: The Once and Future Geek

The Camelot Code: Geeks and the Holy Grail

New Dragon City

NEW DRAGON CITY

MARI MANCUSI

LITTLE, BROWN AND COMPANY
New York Boston

Little, Brown and Company
Hachette Book Group
1290 Avenue of the Americas, New York, NY 10104
Visit us at LBYR.com

First Edition: October 2022

Little, Brown and Company is a division of Hachette Book Group, Inc. The Little, Brown name and logo are trademarks of Hachette Book Group, Inc.

The publisher is not responsible for websites (or their content) that are not owned by the publisher.

Dragon icon copyright © Studio77 FX vector/Shutterstock.com

Library of Congress Cataloging-in-Publication Data
Names: Mancusi, Mari, author.
Title: New dragon city / Mari Mancusi.
Description: First edition. | New York : Little, Brown and Company, 2022. | Audience: Ages 8–12. | Summary: Five years after dragons decimated the world, a chance encounter with a young dragon leaves twelve-year-old Noah questioning everything he thought he knew.
Identifiers: LCCN 2021058477 | ISBN 9780316376686 (hardcover) | ISBN 9780316376891 (ebook)
Subjects: CYAC: Dragons—Fiction. | Toleration—Fiction. | Fantasy. | LCGFT: Fantasy fiction. | Novels.
Classification: LCC PZ7.M312178 Ne 2022 | DDC [Fic]—dc23
LC record available at https://lccn.loc.gov/2021058477

ISBNs: 978-0-316-37668-6 (hardcover), 978-0-316-37689-1 (ebook)

Printed in the United States of America

LSC-C

Printing 1, 2022

To Diana. Mother of dragons and best of friends.

CHAPTER ONE

The library? Again? Really?"

Maya raised her eyebrows at me as we stepped out of an old hotel and onto the sidewalk of what used to be known as Times Square. The sun was shining high in the sky, and the air was warm and sweet, with only a hint of ash to it, thanks to a light breeze. A perfect April New York City day. I slung my empty backpack over my shoulder, then leapt onto a cracked cement barricade, jumping off the other side.

"What can I say?" I gave her a devilish grin. "I'm out of books again."

"Of course you are," she groaned, dodging a parked car

with a smashed windshield as we abandoned the sidewalk to head down Forty-Second Street. Maya always liked to tease me about my obsession with reading and my super-power of finishing books at lightning speed. But I knew, deep down, she didn't really mind our frequent trips to the New York Public Library. For one thing, it was a supercool building, with huge marble lions standing guard outside and endless stacks of books once you walked in, just waiting to be borrowed.

Maya liked books, too, even if she didn't have much time for reading, after putting in long hours helping out with her family's shop. Her mother had one golden rule. Work first, play second—and that included reading.

My mother, on the other hand, had been a teacher back in before times and always made reading a priority. In fact, she'd built a tiny library filled with our favorite books down in our family bunker when we'd first gone underground five years ago. When we had left the bunker three years later, there were still books I hadn't gotten a chance to read yet. Mom had wanted to take some of them along with us, but Dad insisted we save the room in our packs for more essential supplies like food and water. Which made sense, of course. My dad was always the practical one. But I knew it had made Mom sad to leave her precious collection behind. To know they would remain there forever, gathering dust, unread.

"Fine. We'll hit the library," Maya agreed. Then she wagged her finger at me. "But seriously, Noah, no more than three books. The last time we went you picked out so many books you had no room left in your pack for actual supplies."

"As if you didn't fill half your pack with chocolate that day!" I shot back with an impish grin.

She rolled her eyes. "It was Valentine's Day! We needed it for the shop!"

"For the shop! Right!" I gave her a teasing look. "And you wouldn't dream of eating *any* of it yourself, now would you?"

She shoved me playfully. I scurried away, dancing down the empty Forty-Second Street, my steps light as I leapt over piles of trash and other debris. It really was a beautiful day out. Great scavenging weather.

Maya and I were gatherers, along with some of the other kids in our group. We'd go out into the city and search for stuff like canned food and batteries and medicines and other nonperishable items and bring them back to our home base to barter with. It was kind of like a treasure hunt. You never knew what you might find abandoned from the world before. One time, I found this amazing, limited edition Zelda figurine in an old comic book store. The box said there had only been a hundred made, which meant it had probably been worth a ton once upon a time. But now it was free for the taking.

Mom had never liked me scavenging. She worried it could be dangerous. You never knew if a floor had become unstable, rotted away over the years. *You'll break your leg,* she'd say, *and who will fix it if you do?* After all, while there were still hospital buildings, there were no doctors left to run them. And while there was still medicine, much of it was years past its expiration date. Which meant something as simple as a scratch from a rusted piece of metal could be a death sentence. Something Mom used to love to remind me of.

But Mom was gone now. And Dad didn't worry about silly things like—

SCREECH!

A sudden shrieking sound tore through the air, stopping me dead in my tracks. My eyes snapped to Maya beside me to see if she'd heard it, too. She stood still as a statue, her brown face lifted to the sky, her eyes wide and searching. My heart skittered in my chest.

Was that…?

Could it be…?

I swallowed hard, trying to will my hands to stop shaking, all thoughts of books and bright spring days vanishing in an instant, as my mind raced with panic and fear.

It couldn't be, right? There was no way. It was way too early. Way too early for—

SCREEEEECH!

4

Maya's mouth dropped open. A fraction of an inch, but it was enough. Enough to confirm my greatest fear. A moment later, a dark shadow crossed over us, blocking out the noonday sun. Another moment, and my ears began to pick up the thrum of leathery wings, snapping at the air. Like the beat of a deadly drum.

Thrump.

Thrump.

Thrump.

Yup. It was a dragon all right. I didn't even have to look.

It was all I could do to remain motionless, barely daring to blink as fear burned through me like wildfire. If we stayed perfectly still, the dragon might miss us. They had poor eyesight and we were wearing black, our bodies blending into the charred city in a perfect apocalyptic camouflage.

But if we moved—even a muscle—it would see. It would come.

We would die.

What was it doing here? My mind raced with questions. It was only April. We should have had a month before they came back from their winter hibernation. Plenty of time to pack up and head down to the underground subway tunnels as we'd done the last two years. But if they had already returned...

We had to warn the others!

Sweat dripped down my face, stinging my eyes, but I didn't dare reach to my face to swipe it away. Instead, I glanced upward, hoping the quick flick of my pupils would not register as movement. The dragon circled, high above, swimming through the sky with impossible grace. It was a big one, I realized with rising dread. Possibly full-grown even, with silver scales that flashed blindingly in the sunlight. Even from here I could see the twines of smoke twisting from its ugly snout. And I knew if I were to somehow touch its belly, I would burn my fingers on its brewing fire.

I'd almost forgotten how terrifying they were up close. I hadn't seen a real-life dragon in years. Not since shortly after we'd emerged from our family bunker and met up with a group of survivors who had charted the dragons' hibernation cycles. They taught us when it was best to lay low and when it was safe to come back up for air.

Today should have been safe.

You just have to wait, I reminded myself, trying to wrestle my heart back under control. We'd been lectured countless times on what to do if we ever ran into a dragon. But all the lessons seemed to flee from my head as my stomach swam with nausea. *It'll fly away and you can run back to the hotel. We'll pack up quick and get down below before the rest of them return.*

It hadn't seen us.

It was about to leave.

For a brief moment, it appeared as if I was right. The dragon snorted loudly, a black cloud blooming into the air, filling my nose with smoke. As I watched, still holding my breath, it dipped its head, changing its pattern. No longer circling. Preparing to fly away.

But then Maya sneezed.

The dragon's head snapped back in our direction, its beady eyes locking onto us below. Its snout started quivering madly, as if it had caught our scent. My stomach heaved. A horrified gasp choked from my throat.

We'd been spotted.

We were as good as dead.

"Run, Maya!" I cried, diving into a nearby alley. My feet pounded hard against the pavement, making far too much noise as I tried to dodge piles of garbage and burnt debris. My breath came in short gasps as I ran, and my ears strained as I tried to listen for Maya, praying she was behind me but not daring to turn back to look. I could sense the dragon was still above us, attempting to track us down. The tall buildings gave us some cover. But it wasn't enough. It would eventually find us. And when it did, we were toast. Literally.

Suddenly, I came to a dead end. A chain-link fence, rising high and blocking our path. I whirled around, heart in my throat, eyes darting from building to building, praying for an open door. A collapsed wall.

Something.

Anything.

Maya ran up beside me. But she didn't pause.

"Come on!" she cried, throwing herself at the fence. She was small but strong, easily scaling it like an alley cat. I started after her, but I was so winded, I could barely catch my breath. My mind flashed to all the times my father had scolded me for skipping his daily workouts in order to read in my room. At the time, it hadn't seemed like a big deal....

Now it might cost me my life.

I shook my head. I needed to focus. On my fingers, clawing at the metal. My toes digging into each chain link as I pulled myself upward.

Upward.

Upward.

Finally, I reached the top, throwing myself over. I hit the ground too hard, nearly eating it as my feet slammed down on the concrete. Maya caught me before I tumbled, giving me a worried look. I could read the question in her eyes.

What do we do?

The dragon roared into view, flying lower now, so low I could see its razor-sharp teeth and blackened tongue as it opened its mouth in another scream. The dragon didn't need to worry about scaling fences. Dodging debris. It only had to lock its eyes on us and unleash its deadly fury.

I squeezed my eyes shut, unable to watch.

"It's unlocked! Noah! It's unlocked!"

My eyes flew open. Maya was standing by a door, holding it ajar and gesturing wildly with her hand. Without a second thought, I dove through it, into the dark room beyond. I didn't like going into abandoned apartments—where the smells of smoke and death still lingered, even after all these years. But at this moment? It was our only hope.

Once inside, Maya slammed the door shut. She turned to me. "The bathroom! Quick!" she commanded.

I didn't need a second invitation. Running through the apartment, we attempted to avert our eyes from things we didn't want to accidentally see. We dove into the bathroom, which luckily contained a large claw-foot tub—not every NYC apartment did. Jumping in, we huddled together and tried the tap. A trickle of water leaked out.

Yes! Another bit of luck.

The front door exploded, flames rushing into the apartment, greedily eating up everything in their wake. The dragon was trying to smoke us out—so it could grab its prey for dinner. But we forced ourselves to stay put, crouching lower in the tub, splashing ourselves with water, praying it would be enough protection. The temperature in the apartment rose sharply, and I broke out into a fierce sweat, my eyes itching from the intense heat. I splashed more water on my arms, trying to cool myself down. The smoke began to seep into the bathroom, and I couldn't help but start to cough. Maya handed me a towel drenched in water, and I put it to my nose.

"What is it doing here?" she whispered, tears streaming from her eyes—probably only half due to the smoke. Somehow it made me feel better to realize she was as scared as I was. "They're not supposed to be awake yet!"

I nodded grimly. But I had no answer. She was right—everyone knew dragons hibernated in the winter months and didn't wake until late May, long after we humans had vacated the city streets and taken cover down in the subways below.

So why was this dragon awake in April? And did that mean others were, too?

There was a large snort, sounding vaguely annoyed. I glanced over at Maya and caught hope reflected in her eyes. The dragon couldn't figure out where we went. It was growing frustrated. Maybe it would give up and leave. Maybe we'd survive this after all.

Maybe...

Suddenly the ground seemed to shake as the dragon pushed off on its mighty back legs, thrusting itself into the sky. My ears once again filled with the sound of its thrumming wings. But this time I was relieved to hear the sound.

It was leaving. We were safe. At least for the moment.

"Come on, let's get out of here," I whispered, scrambling out of the bathtub and offering a hand to Maya. She took it in her own, and I realized she was still trembling. But then, so was I. Shaking like a leaf, more like.

We rushed out of the apartment. My legs felt wobbly, like they were made of Jell-O. As I stepped back into the alleyway, I dropped the cloth from my mouth and released the cough I'd been holding in as my eyes scanned the sky above.

It was empty. Just the sun and a few puffy clouds. A perfect April New York City day.

The dragon was gone.

For now.

Maya glanced at me. "That was close."

"Too close." I swallowed hard, my eyes fearfully lifting to the sky once again. It might have been gone, but I was no fool. It would return. And when it did, it would not be alone.

Which meant we had to get out of here. Now.

"Come on," I said. "Let's go tell the others."

CHAPTER TWO

No one could have predicted the dragon apocalypse.

Sure, we'd all been warned by Hollywood about all sorts of potential doomsdays looming on the horizon. Zombies? Seemed legit. Plague? Been there, done that. Giant meteors crashing into the earth and throwing the planet off its axis, bringing about spectacular and certainly Oscar-winning special effects? About as American as the Fourth of July.

But massive, fire-breathing beasts of legend swooping down on the earth and decimating everything in their wake? No one had that on their bingo card. And when it happened, no one was prepared.

Well, except my dad, of course. He had been prepping for some kind of apocalyptic disaster since before I was born. And when the beasts finally did come, we simply did what any self-respecting prepper family would do. We retreated underground to my dad's bunker in Cold Spring, New York, to wait it out, eating canned food and reading books and watching old movies on something Mom called a DVD player. I had my own room, which was small but cozy. And there was even a gym with a weight bench so we could stay in shape. *Don't want to get soft in here*, my dad would lecture every time I tried to get out of a workout to finish my latest book. *In the end, only the strong will survive.*

This may sound kind of cool in theory, but trust me, the whole thing totally blew. I mean, imagine not being able to leave your house for three straight years—not even to go for a walk. From age seven to ten, I had no FaceTime. No Minecraft. No Messenger Kids. No kids my own age to play with at all. Not even any virtual school. Just me and my parents, who were constantly in my face—no chance to escape. There were times I wondered if we'd be better off taking our chances with the dragons.

Which, eventually, we were forced to do. Three years in, we ran out of food and had to return to the surface. And when we did, we were shocked to find a whole new world waiting for us outside.

You gotta understand. When we'd first went underground, people had considered the dragons a temporary plague. The world's governments had promised they would take care of them—their armies blasting them to smithereens. We only had to wait it out, my dad had promised. Then things would go back to normal. It was funny now, thinking back to that. Thinking they'd just go away. That the world would return to what it was before.

Instead, the world as we knew it was totally gone. The dragons had taken out at least half the population (many of whom had refused to believe there actually *were* dragons, until they ended up as dinner) while the other forty-five percent, estimated by my dad, died of starvation, disease—all the good old-fashioned ways to kick the bucket after society screeches to a halt.

Which left roughly five percent of us, scattered around the country—at least that was our estimate. Obviously, there was no way to conduct a census to know for sure.

Where did the dragons come from? No one really knows. There's no Wikipedia page to look it up, after all. No scientific studies to explain how mythological creatures from fantasy novels suddenly appeared in real life and started burning the place down. Sure, there were theories before the internet went dark. Back then everyone with a YouTube or TikTok account seemed to have a hot take. A pair of eggs, preserved in a glacier since the first ice age, melted by global warming. A government plot to create biological weapons of mass destruction, gone horribly wrong. And then there were the really wacky ones that involved alternate universes, time travel, space aliens. You name it.

But in the end, it didn't matter how they arrived. Only that they were here.

And that mankind had become an endangered species.

"Come on!" Maya called, practically dragging me back into the center of Times Square. My mom had taken me here once, before the apocalypse, and I still remembered being awed by all the neon lights and larger-than-life ads projected on giant TV screens on skyscrapers high above.

Now, of course, it was all dark. The buildings scorched and empty, their storefronts with shattered glass windows, their awnings sunken and torn by heavy winter storms. Burnt-out cars and taxis lay abandoned everywhere, some with their doors wide open as if, in a last-minute, desperate attempt for survival, someone had jumped out and tried to make a run for it.

As if that would ever work...

But the most interesting part of Times Square wasn't the soot-stained buildings or the rusted-out street signs pointing to places you could no longer go. Rather, it was how nature had found a way to reclaim the once-concrete jungle as her own. With grasses and wildflowers poking defiantly through cracks in the sidewalk. Vines ambitiously climbing the sides of buildings as if in a race to the top. And then there were the city trees, once pruned to within an inch of their lives, now stretching tall and strong and free. Nature didn't care that we were no longer on the top of the food chain. If anything, she seemed pretty happy about it.

Maya stopped in front of a building on the corner. The place that used to be known as a hotel, now home sweet home for our group of survivors. She leaned over, hands on her knees, drawing in a huge breath. "We made it," she said.

"Yup," I agreed, my eyes scanning the sky for any menacing shadows. But all seemed clear.

We pushed through the double doors and dashed inside. The lobby was dark, and it took a moment to adjust my eyes to the dimness. We didn't typically use lights during the day if we could help it, so we could try to conserve as much electricity as we could. Though we did have power, thanks to the solar panels someone had set up on the roof of the hotel, it wasn't limitless. And we needed to keep the essentials—like our plumbing and water pumps—running at all times.

"Maya! Noah!"

Maya's mother stepped out from behind the counter

of the family shop, a small store inside the hotel that once sold coffee and magazines to hotel guests but now provided daily staples like warm clothes, canned food, batteries, and first aid supplies. She took her daughter's face in her hands, turning it from side to side. She'd been a corporate lawyer in before times. But these days, she liked to say, people needed bread more than legal briefs.

"What's wrong?" she demanded. "You look as if the devil himself is on your tail."

"Dragon, actually," I replied in the most matter-of-fact voice I could muster. Trying to make it sound like no big deal. As if we hadn't actually almost died ten minutes before.

Maya's mother's jaw dropped. She grabbed her daughter, picking up one arm, then the other, examining her closely. As if she was looking for burn spots or something. As if we'd still be walking and talking if we'd gotten close enough for those.

"We're fine, Mom," Maya assured her, pulling her arm away. "We hid in a bathtub, like you told us to. We didn't even get singed."

Her mother's shoulders drooped in relief, but her face was still lined with worry. "They shouldn't be back so early," she said almost accusingly.

I shrugged. "Tell that to the dragon."

She ran a hand through her graying hair. "We need

to inform the others. Will you activate the fire alarm, Noah?"

I nodded. The fire alarm was a relic from before times that used to alert hotel guests of a possible blaze, especially when the dragons first came. There had been so many fires: Entire towns were torched. Forests decimated. The air so thick with smoke that health officials would warn people not to go outside, at least not without masks. Though plenty didn't listen until it was too late.

Back then the alarm's flashing lights had been accompanied by a loud blaring sound. Since that wasn't practical when dragons might be about, Javier, our resident tech guy, had altered the programming so it just flashed a white light in the rooms and the halls. If you saw the light you knew to head to the lobby. There was something you needed to hear.

I ran to the wall and pulled the alarm, and the hotel started flashing its lights. I then found a seat near Maya in the lobby while we waited for the others to arrive. Our found family, banded together by need rather than blood. Before the apocalypse we'd been total strangers. Now we depended on each other every day.

Dad hadn't been super excited about joining up with the group at first. They'd been a ragtag team of survivors we'd met on the road after coming out of the bunker. They were headed to New York City, where it was rumored there'd be more food and shelter from the dragons than out in the fire-scorched 'burbs. Dad would have preferred, I think, to strike out on our own, go where the wind took us. But Mom had reminded him that there was safety in numbers, and I had begged for the chance to finally have kids my own age to play with after three long years of being stuck with only my parents. So he was basically outnumbered.

"What's this all about?" demanded Griffin as everyone arrived and took their seats. He was older than most of the group, a former college history professor from Syracuse, and was known to be a bit grumpy. "I was having a nice nap upstairs! This better not be a false alarm like last time."

"I wish it were," Maya's mother said, rising from her seat and looking over the group. Some had settled in on tattered chairs and couches. Others were standing or had plopped down cross-legged on the well-worn rug. Young, old, and in between. Most with nothing in common besides the will to stay alive.

I didn't see my dad in the mix, and it worried me a little. I remembered he said he was going out hunting today. One of his jobs was to try to track down any animals that may have wandered into the city over the spring. Deer, rabbits, maybe even a bear. Anything edible that we could hunt now and salt and preserve for the months we'd be spending belowground when the dragons came back. Every year things grew a little scarcer, with the dragons hunting the same prey as us during the summer months.

I glanced at the front lobby doors, biting my lower lip nervously. Hopefully Dad hadn't run into our big friend.

"Look, I won't mince words. There's been a dragon sighting," Maya's mother stated flatly, without emotion. But I thought I could hear a slight tremble in her voice. "It seems they're back early this year."

The room erupted in murmurs. Maya's mother turned to us. "Go ahead," she urged. "Make your report."

All eyes shot to Maya and me. I squirmed in my chair, feeling suddenly awkward. "Um, we were headed down Forty-Second Street," I explained. "We were, uh, gathering supplies."

I stopped short of mentioning the library side trip, not wanting to get Maya in trouble with her mom. While we were given more freedom this time of year, when the dragons were supposedly still in hibernation, we were also not supposed to just wander off without letting someone know which high-rise or city block we were scavenging that day. After all, the dragons might be gone, but there were still plenty of other dangers out there. If we didn't come back, they needed to know where to look for us.

"The dragon came out of nowhere," Maya added, her dark brown eyes flashing fire. She swiped a lock of black hair from her face. "It was full-grown. Big horns. It started chasing us. We barely escaped."

The murmurs intensified. A few of the younger children started to cry. The leader of our group, a man named Mike, rose from his seat. He walked over to Maya and me, peering down at us with steely brown eyes. Mike had been in the Marines in before times and was tougher than anyone I knew, even my dad. But when I looked into his eyes now, I saw a hint of fear.

Mike was brave. But he was also smart.

"You aren't just messing with us?" he asked in a low voice. "Because that wouldn't be a very funny joke."

"Of course we're not messing with you!" Maya cried, looking indignant. "We aren't stupid!"

"But it's only April," cried a young mother in the back, cradling her infant son. "They should still be at least a month from awakening!"

"Maybe one woke up early! Maybe he'll move on!" cried someone up front. A few people voiced their agreement. They were desperate for any excuse. Any reason not to go below early.

I didn't really blame them, either.

Mike waved his hand at the group, effectively shushing them. When everyone was silent, he spoke. "Maybe so, but can we bet our lives on it?" He tugged at his gray-streaked beard with his finger and thumb. "They were a week early last year. Now a month. It could be their hibernation patterns are shifting. Or it could be due to the unusually warm weather we've been having."

I nodded grimly. We didn't know a lot about dragons, but we did know they were reptiles and cold-blooded. Every winter they'd take to the ground in some hidden location where they'd sleep until spring. Which gave us about six months to live life aboveground before we'd be forced to evacuate underground to the subway tunnels to wait for them to leave again.

Six months. Or now, five.

Javier scrambled to his feet. "Well, then, what are we waiting for?" he demanded, looking over the group. "There's no time to waste. We need to head underground before someone gets hurt."

The room was silent. As if everyone was holding their breath. All eyes were on Mike. For a moment he didn't answer. Then, at last, he sighed.

"Agreed," he said. "We'll start packing immediately. We'll head down tonight."

There were a few groans from the crowd. Which was understandable. No one liked going underground, being stuck in hot, sweaty subway tunnels with smelly air and strict food rations for months on end. It was boring and miserable and reminded me too much of life in the bunker. Also, it usually smelled like pee.

22

And while it was certainly safer to block off all entrances so no one could get in...it also meant no one could get out. Which meant we were the ones stuck hibernating until fall. Without the benefits of actual hibernation to pass the time.

"What about my father?" I asked, glancing uneasily at the front double doors that led to the city outside. "He's still out there somewhere."

Mike nodded solemnly. "I'll send out a couple men to find him and let him know what's happened. We'll get him back here safely, don't worry." He caught my look and gave me a toothy grin. "Come on, you know your father. He's not going to let some silly dragon get the jump on him."

He chuckled, and I gave a half laugh though I still felt a little uneasy. That said, he wasn't wrong. My dad was probably one of the only people left in the world who could claim he'd actually killed a dragon. Three dragons to be precise—two before we first went underground and one just before we ran into the New York City group. But that was years ago now. And even he had admitted he'd been lucky.

What if he ran into another dragon and wasn't? My stomach churned with sudden nausea. I'd already lost my mother. Dad was all the family I had left.

He's going to be okay, I scolded myself. *Like Mike said, he'd never let some silly dragon hurt him.*

The meeting adjourned, and everyone rushed to their rooms to pack up. Maya's parents began emptying the store supplies into boxes, to be brought underground. I wondered if the early move would affect food and rations. Had we gathered enough to survive the summer?

And what would happen to us if we hadn't?

My mind flashed back to the dragon. Its beady eyes. Its fierce snarl. A shiver crawled down my back. Soon, there would be more of them. A lot more.

And if they found us, supplies would be the least of our problems.

CHAPTER THREE

Reading instead of packing. I should have guessed."

I looked up from my book, my eyes going to the hotel room door. It'd been an hour since Mike had made our evacuation official, and, like everyone else in the group, I'd gone up to the room to start getting ready to head underground. But my mind couldn't focus on the work; I'd been too worried about my dad, out there, somewhere, with a dragon lurking nearby. At last, I'd given up and cracked open my book. I'd read this one a few times before, but since we'd never made it to the library it would have to do.

I sat up in bed as I saw the tall, broad silhouette in the

doorway. "Dad!" I cried, setting down my book. "You're okay!" I ran to him, throwing my arms around him. He patted me awkwardly on the back. Let's just say he wasn't the biggest hugger.

"Of course I'm okay!" he replied gruffly, untangling himself from me and peeling off the rifle harness he'd been wearing across his body. He set the gun on the floor. "The question is, how are you?"

I grimaced, walking back over to my bed and sitting down on the edge. "I guess Mike told you what happened."

My father nodded, plopping down on the other bed. The one he used to share with Mom. When she was here, she'd always made the beds each morning, insisting that an apocalypse was no excuse for bad housekeeping. Now the blankets were rumpled, and the sheets definitely needed a wash. Dad rubbed his bearded face with his hands, then gave me a piercing look. "Are you all right?"

"I'm fine," I assured him. "We found an empty apartment and hid in the bathtub. The pipes still had some water."

My father nodded, almost absently, his eyes going to the windows. I'd pulled the blinds shut, as we'd been told to do after a dragon sighting. So they wouldn't catch any movement inside. Mike liked to tell a story about a dragon denier family in the early days who hadn't taken such precautions, believing that the dragon sightings on TV were simply fake news. That was, until a giant fiery beast flew directly into their front window, crashing through the glass and dive-bombing their living room.

"They sure believed in dragons after that, let me tell you!" Mike would say with a laugh.

My father reached out, patting my knee with a calloused hand. "Very good," he said. "That was exactly the right move."

I smiled a little at the praise. Dad didn't give it out often, so when it did come, I knew to appreciate it. He squinted as he peered at me closely. "Were you frightened?" he asked.

"I..." I considered lying, not wanting him to think I was a wimp or something. But at last I shrugged. "A little," I admitted.

Dad nodded. "You'd be a fool not to be," he said, rising from the bed. "It was a big one."

"You saw it?" I looked up at him in shock.

"Yup. Caught me by surprise on Fiftieth and Broadway, as I was lining up my sights on a deer. I got a good shot at it, though. I think I hit its wing. You should have heard it screech!" He smirked. "Sounded like a wild peacock in rut."

I shivered a little as my mind flashed back to the terrible screeching sound I'd heard earlier that day. "Did you kill it?" I asked hopefully. My eyes fell to the three black slashes he'd tattooed on his right forearm. One for each dragon he'd killed.

"Nah. Unfortunately it got away." He grabbed his rifle from the doorway and brought it over to the bed, starting to disassemble it for cleaning. Mom always hated when he cleaned his guns on the bed.

But then, she wasn't here anymore to complain.

I guess I should explain. Mom had disappeared two months ago in the dead of night. And no one had any idea where she'd gone. One evening she was here, reading me a story before bed just like any other night. The next morning, she was gone without a trace. Dad had organized a search party, and for weeks they combed the streets and abandoned buildings around town, searching for some sign of her, but they'd found nothing. It was like she'd vanished off the face of the earth.

I knew some people believed she'd left on purpose. And it was true, she and my dad hadn't been getting along. Their fights had been growing worse and worse over the past few months, and several times Mom had left the hotel for the entire day, returning late at night without saying where she'd gone. At the time, she claimed she'd just needed space. Some time to think. But now I wondered. Where had she been going? And was she still there now?

28

Still—if she'd just up and left for good of her own free will, wouldn't she have at last told *me* she was going? Or sent a message letting me know she had found somewhere safe to live? We'd always been so close. At least I thought we had. We'd spent hours together, just she and I, reading books in the bunker. Talking, sharing. How could she just up and leave without even saying goodbye?

But the alternative was almost worse. The idea that something bad had happened to her. That she'd run into trouble—there were still so many dangers out there for someone out on their own. And she wasn't the first in our group to just disappear....

But I didn't like to think about that.

And so, I chose to hold out hope. That she must have had a good reason to leave. Something important she had to do—but was sworn to secrecy about what it was. And when it was over, she would return to us. To me. And we would be a family again.

If we were here, that was...

A horrifying thought suddenly struck me. "What if Mom tries to come back here to find us and we're already gone?" I asked in a trembling voice. "She might not know about the dragons coming early. What if she's stuck out here all summer?"

I cringed at the thought. While it was relatively safe to wander around New York in the winter and spring, once

29

summer hit and the dragons came back, the city became open season on humans. If Mom was out there, she'd never survive on her own.

Last summer, a handful of our group had decided to stay aboveground for the summer, saying they'd take their chance with freedom rather than living their lives in fear. They were big men, strong with lots of guns and survivalist skills. The kind that should have been able to take care of any threats. But when we'd come out of the subway the next fall, only one of them was still alive. And the tales he told were almost too horrific to hear.

My dad stopped cleaning his gun. He stared down at his lap. "Don't think I haven't thought of that," he said in a low voice.

My shoulders drooped with relief. Okay, he had a plan, I should have known he would. My dad had a plan for everything. "So, what are we going to do?" I asked.

My father shot me a piercing look. "*You* are going to go underground with the group as planned," he said firmly. "I'm going to stay up here to find your mother."

"What?" I exclaimed, horrified. "No way. You can't! It's too dangerous!"

"I'm aware of the danger," my dad said. "But I also can't leave her out here unprotected." I heard a thread of hurt in his voice. I knew Mom leaving had gutted him. He never talked about it, but I could see the pain in his eyes when someone mentioned her name. I was pretty sure he blamed himself for her leaving—but I wasn't sure why. Had he done something? Said something? All I knew was that he loved her. And he missed her as much as I did. And every time he signed up for hunting duty, he was really out there searching for her.

"Fine." I swallowed hard. "Then I'm staying, too."

His mouth tightened. "No. Not a chance."

"Come on, Dad!" I pleaded. "You can protect me. And I can protect you. We're a family. You always say family needs to stick together."

That had been his motto, even in before times. We were the unbreakable triangle family. No matter what happened, we stuck together. The three of us against the world.

But now Mom was gone. And Dad wanted to leave me, too.

My father sighed deeply. "I'm sorry, Noah. But this is how it has to be. You're going to go with the group. With your friend Maya—I've already talked to her mother. She's agreed to look out for you. You'll have a nice summer underground with their family, and when you come out on November first, I'll be at the door waiting for you. With Mom, if all goes right."

I could see the resolve on his face. There was no way I'd be able to get him to budge. When my dad made up his mind, there was no changing it. And nothing I could say would make a difference.

My breath hitched. He was going to leave me. I was going to be alone.

"So much for *family*," I growled, anger suddenly churning in my gut. I rose to my feet and stalked past him toward the hotel room exit. I yanked the door open, then purposely let it slam shut hard behind me as I stepped out into the hall. The sound echoed loudly down the corridor. I stared at the wall in front of me. It took everything I had not to punch it, hard.

"Wow. What did that door ever do to you?"

I looked up to see Maya standing in the hallway, arms crossed over her chest. She raised her eyebrows at me. "What's wrong?" she asked. "You're not still freaked out about the dragon, are you?"

I scowled. "No. Of course not."

"Is it the packing, then? 'Cause believe me, I understand. You're just lucky you don't also have to pack up an entire store as well as your room."

I leaned against the wall. "It's not the packing," I said. "It's just…" I glanced at the hotel room door. Was my father back to cleaning his gun? Or was he gathering up my things, preparing to send me away?

"I don't know if I'm going," I blurted out, before I even realized what I was going to say.

"What?" Maya's eyes bulged. "What are you talking about?"

I sighed and grabbed her hand, dragging her down the hall and into the emergency stairwell at the end. No one ever used this back staircase that bypassed the lobby and led straight outside. It'd be safe to talk here.

I sat down on a stair, picking up a small pebble and throwing it against the wall. Maya sat down next to me, peering at me with worried eyes.

"Okay, spill," she demanded. "What do you mean, you're not going?"

I sighed, staring down at my hands. "My dad told me he's staying behind," I confessed. "He's going to keep looking for my mother."

"Oh. Wow." Maya bit her lower lip. "I'm sorry."

She didn't have to say anything else. I knew what she was thinking. If my dad stayed aboveground, he'd end up like the others. Dragon dinner.

"But you don't have to stay with him, do you?" she asked, her face etched with worry. "You can still come down with us. My mom will totally let you stay in our tent. Or we can get you your own! It wouldn't be a big deal at all."

"That's what my dad wants," I admitted. "But how can I just leave him up here by himself? Especially with the dragons back. I mean, he even shot one today. They're going to be looking for him."

Maya gave me an anguished look. "And if you're with him, they'll kill you, too. Noah, you're a kid, no offense. You can't protect your dad from a dragon."

I shook my head, making up my mind on the spot. "Maybe not," I agreed. "But I also can't leave him. He may be the only family I have left."

"Noah—"

"Look, don't tell anyone, okay?" I begged. "Especially not your parents. Once we start heading down, I'll just slip away. You can cover for me until they've closed the vault door. At that point, it'll be too late. And my dad will have no choice but to allow me to stay."

"What? You're not even going to tell him? Noah, this is crazy!" Maya protested. "Please don't do this."

"Don't you understand? I don't have a choice. And we'll be fine, I swear. You'll come back up next November and I'll be waiting for you. And I'll have all new records for you, too." Maya had a hobby of collecting old records from apartments we scavenged to play on the record player that Javier had set up in the hotel lobby. I was always trying to find the weirdest ones to play for her to make her laugh.

"I don't need records," she said, her voice cracking. "I need you alive. Promise me now, you won't do anything stupid. Promise me you'll be standing there, in front of the exit, when we come out on November first."

"I promise," I said, meeting her eyes with my own. She nodded slowly, then reached out, pulling me into a warm hug.

But even as I hugged her back, I wondered if I would be able to keep my promise. The world was about to get a whole lot more dangerous once the dragons were back. And I wasn't sure my father and I, out there alone, would stand a chance.

But I had to try. For his sake. And for Mom's.

We were family after all. And family was forever.

CHAPTER FOUR

A ll right people, we are good to move!"

The lobby erupted in activity in response to Mike's announcement, with everyone grabbing their luggage and pushing carts stacked with boxes as they moved toward the front doors of the hotel. A few volunteers barked orders, trying to get people to form some kind of orderly line. But no one was really listening, each wanting to be the first underground so they could claim their spots for the summer. While most people created makeshift camping sites by setting up tents in the halls and around the subway tracks, there were a few small spaces that used to be stores that provided more private living quarters, and everyone wanted to be first to grab them.

It was a block-and-a-half walk to the Times Square subway station entrance. Sharpshooters lined up along the road, their guns pointed to the sky in case there was any trouble. My dad was out there somewhere, too, to make sure everyone got safely underground before he took off on his own.

Our parting had been...tough. He'd hugged me really tight. Told me to be a good boy—to do whatever Maya's mother said. He promised me again that he'd bring Mom back, and he looked like he actually believed it. Meanwhile, I grilled him for details—like where would he stay since our hotel would be boarded up for the summer? He looked at me a little strangely after that, and for a moment I wondered if he suspected what I was planning. But then he shrugged and told me about the basement apartment he'd found a few blocks away. It was small, but secure. With an extra-strong door with extra-strong locks. He would stay safe, he promised. He wouldn't take any unnecessary risks.

I wished him luck. I told him I'd see him soon.

I just didn't mention *how* soon.

I dragged my suitcase into the lobby, acting as if I was loaded down like everyone else, to keep up with the charade. But in truth, my suitcase was empty; I'd stashed my clothes and other belongings in the dumpster at the back of the hotel. This way I could make a clean break and retrieve my stuff once everyone else was already underground.

"Are you okay, Noah?" Maya's mother asked for, like, the thousandth time as I shuffled behind her and Maya toward the door. She was pushing a large luggage cart, filled with both their family's possessions and stock from their store. Normally it'd take the group at least a week to move everything from the hotel to underground for the summer, especially all the extra stuff like games and sporting equipment and old records— all that we'd need to power through the dull days to come. But this time, Mike had ordered that we bring only what was necessary to survive the months underground—whatever we could carry in one trip. Which meant all the cool stuff we scavenged—all our fun entertainment—would be locked up tight in the hotel until fall.

I suddenly felt bad for Maya and the other kids. This was going to be the worst summer ever.

"I'm fine," I replied, wishing she'd stop paying so much attention to me. I knew she felt bad for me and, like everyone else, thought my father was being completely irrational for choosing to stay aboveground. She'd already assured me multiple times that she'd take care of me down below. That if I needed anything at all, I should just ask. In fact, she'd even produced two new fantasy books she'd evidently uncovered in one of the empty hotel rooms and gave them to me, saying she knew how much I liked to read.

38

Which was really sweet and all. But it was only going to make it tougher to slip out of sight when the time came.

But I was determined. And Maya and I had a plan.

The people in front of us stopped, halting us in our tracks. I groaned impatiently. I forgot how long it took to get everyone underground. There were almost a hundred people living in the hotel at this point, and some of them were old and needed assistance climbing down the stairs.

But soon they'd all be underground, locked behind a solid titanium door, stolen from a bank vault and installed by some of the men and women with construction experience. The vault had a mechanical time lock that they'd set for November first—the day it was safe to come out again. No one, not even Mike, had an override on this door, and all the other subway tunnels had been blocked up long ago. There was no way for dragons or anyone else to get in.

And no way for anyone to get out.

Some people (including my father) had disagreed with this security measure, claiming it took away their freedom. They were adults and had free will and should be able to come and go as they pleased, taking their own personal risk. But in the end, they were outvoted. If the dragons caught anyone emerging from the tunnel, the space would no longer be safe for the rest of us. Sacrifices of personal freedom had to be made for the good of the group.

Finally, we were able to step outside. The sun was

setting behind the skyscrapers to the west, casting a warm orange glow onto the abandoned cityscape. This would be the last time anyone in our group would see the sun over the next seven months, and several people released wistful sighs as they glanced upward as if trying to take pictures in their minds to remember fondly in the dark days to come. While we did have limited LED lighting installed in the tunnels, it wasn't the same as real daylight.

We shuffled forward again. We were getting close.

I glanced over at Maya. She gave me a slight nod, telling me she knew what I was thinking. We'd planned to wait until we were almost to the subway entrance before launching into my escape plan. Close enough that by the time anyone noticed I was missing, it would be too late to do anything about it.

I looked up at the sky, something uneasy worming through my stomach as we inched closer to the spot. I realized my hands were trembling, and I felt a little like I was going to puke. Was I really going to go through with this? Was I really prepared to spend the entire summer out here, with no protection? What had once seemed like a great plan, back in the comfort of the hotel, was now starting to feel like a suicide mission. And once that bank vault door closed, there would be no changing my mind.

"You know, it's not too late to back out," Maya whispered, as if she could read my thoughts.

I bit my lower lip, glancing over at the subway entrance, something squeezing inside me. She was right, of course. I still had a chance to just scrap it all and go underground like I was meant to. Stay hidden. Stay safe. Stay alive. Let my dad do this thing. Hope he was able to survive. Hope he was able to find Mom.

But in the end, I shook my head. "No," I whispered back. "My dad needs me, whether he knows it or not. I can't leave him out here by himself. And my mother, too..." I gave a helpless shrug.

She nodded, her eyes solemn. "All right," she whispered as we moved a few steps closer to the stairs. "We're almost in place. Let me know when you're ready."

I wasn't even close to ready. But I was also running out of time. It was now or never.

"Okay," I said. "Let's do this."

I watched as Maya pushed her cart forward, as if she was trying to cut the line. The group ahead of her gave her a dirty look, elbowing her to get back in her place. She pretended to lose her balance, shifting the cart toward the curb. The wheel slipped and the cart began to topple.

"Argh! Help!" Maya cried. She pretended to try to grab the cart, while instead pushing it off the edge. The cart toppled. A pile of clothes spilled out onto the street.

The people around dove into action, all trying to help at once. Someone grabbed a shirt. Another person scooped up a handful of socks. Maya had made sure there was nothing in her cart that was too important. Nothing essential needed to survive the months below. But the way she was crying out made it sound like she had spilled precious supplies. And soon a crowd surrounded her, on their hands and knees, trying to help.

And no one was paying any attention to me.

Perfect. I smiled to myself. *Almost too easy . . .*

I took a hesitant step toward the alley, looking around once more to make sure no one was watching. I took another step. And another . . .

"DRAGON! On approach!"

I froze in my tracks as the cry rang out from somewhere in line. Looking up, my jaw dropped in horror as I watched a large dragon sweep into Times Square, screeching so loudly I had to put my hands over my ears. It was big, bigger than the one we'd seen the day before, with huge, curved horns and shiny scales that caught the sunlight and scattered deadly rainbows on the ground below. Its screeching cries filled the air as its wings thumped their terrifying beat.

Thrump.

Thrump.

Thrump.

This was not good. This was *so* not good.

"To the tunnels! Run!" someone called out.

Everyone bolted, tripping over one another as they dove

for safety. Gunshots erupted as the shooters tried to take out the beast. But it was too quick, darting between buildings so fast that their shots missed the dragon completely.

Heart in my throat, I turned to the subway entrance. Mike was ushering people down the stairs, his body tense and his eyes filled with fear as he kept glancing up at the sky.

"Come on, come on!" he cried out.

But at that moment, the dragon made its move, swooping down from above with an ear-piercing screech. Everyone screamed and jumped back. Suddenly, I found myself standing all alone. Alone and unprotected. The dragon locked its eyes on me. It seemed to sniff the air for a moment. Then it dive-bombed in my direction, just as the other dragon had done just hours before.

And this time there was no bathtub to hide in.

I opened my mouth to scream, but no sound came out. I knew I should run, but my feet felt glued to the ground. The dragon was getting closer and closer....

"Noah!"

BAM! I was knocked to the pavement. Pain exploded in my leg, and for a moment, I saw stars. When my vision came back, I found Javier facing down the dragon. He must have been the one who pushed me out of its path.

"Javier!" I cried. "Run!"

But it was too late. The dragon scooped up Javier in its forepaws. He screamed, fighting desperately to free himself, but the thick, deadly claws dug into his shoulders, refusing to let go. Soon, he was fifty feet off the ground, still struggling uselessly as the dragon spirited him away.

It could have been me.

It *should* have been...

The crowd surged, screaming and shoving in a desperate attempt to get to the stairs. Friends and family trampled over one another in order to gain position. Suitcases were abandoned. Supply carts toppled over, spilling food and bottles of pills. Precious supplies were being stomped on by dozens of frenzied feet.

"Order!" Mike barked, waving his hands in the air. "We can't count you if you all dive in at once!" But no one was listening. No one cared about being counted. They just wanted to get underground before they ended up like Javier.

Suddenly I felt a hand on my arm. It was Maya. "Come on!" she begged. "Forget the plan! Just get down below!"

"But my dad!"

"You can't help him if you're dead!"

She had a point. I glanced over at the subway again. I could still make it. I could still be safe.

But my dad. My mom...

"No!" I cried, wrestling my arm away. "I'm not leaving my parents!"

Maya gave me one last desperate look, then started

running toward the subway. I watched her go, wanting to make sure she made it. I let out a breath of relief as she reached the stairs and Mike ushered her down.

She was safe.

Now it was my turn.

I dove toward the alleyway, praying I wouldn't be noticed. But everyone was too busy screaming and running and pushing one another—they didn't see me at all. It was the best distraction I could have hoped for. But also, the worst. What if more dragons came? What if more people died?

When I reached the dumpster where I'd stored my bags, I heaved it open and launched myself inside, then pulled the cover closed over my head.

I let out a breath. I was safe. At least for now.

I swallowed hard, huddling in the darkness, trying to still my trembling hands. The shouts and cries outside had stopped; hopefully that meant everyone had made it down into the subway. My mind flashed back to the scene just moments before. People screaming. The dragon dive-bombing in my direction. Javier, pushing me out of its path, only to be taken himself.

I wondered if more would come.

I wondered if Mike had locked the door.

I wondered if I'd just made a big mistake.

CHAPTER FIVE

I waited in the dumpster for what felt like an hour, just to be certain the dragon had gone away and no others would show up for round two. When I finally allowed myself to open the cover and climb out, my legs were all pins and needles, and I had to shake them out a few times before I could put any weight on them. I considered pulling my suitcase out, too, but in the end I decided to leave it in the dumpster—for now. I didn't want to drag it around with me while I tried to find my dad.

I crept down the alleyway, keeping one eye on the sky. At dusk, it was harder to make out any dark shapes swimming through the air. But it would also be harder for the dragons to see me, I reminded myself. I'd take any advantage I could get.

I stepped back into the main square. It was quiet now. No dragons, no people. Just a line of overturned carts and lost suitcases, abandoned in the rush to get underground. A sick feeling washed over me as I took in the cans of foods and precious bottles of medicine spilling out onto the street. Would they be able to survive all summer down below with only half their supplies?

Stupid dragons. I glanced up at the sky. If they'd just stayed on their schedule, none of this would have happened!

My eyes fell to a forgotten apple on the ground, and I reached down to pick it up, wiping it on my shirt before taking a bite. My mouth exploded with the sweetness and my stomach growled in pleasure as I chewed and swallowed. Apples were rare in the spring—we harvested them from apple trees in Central Park in the fall and tried to eat as many as we could while they were still fresh. Anything left over was carefully placed in cold storage in the hotel and enjoyed as a special treat during the summer months down in the subway tunnels, where there was very little fresh food to be had. Someone was going to be very unhappy their apples hadn't made it this year.

But I wasn't complaining.

I picked through the rubble until I found another

treasure—a flashlight, with good batteries, too. Then I walked over to the subway entrance, shining my light down the dark stairs. Sure enough, the bank vault door had been closed and locked in place. I wondered if anyone had noticed that I wasn't with the rest of the group. Would Maya inform them of my intentional escape? Or would she let them think the dragon had gotten me, too? Hopefully not. I didn't want her mom freaking out after she'd told my dad she'd watch out for me.

I sighed, stepping away from the stairs, feeling itchy and uncomfortable, though I couldn't really explain why. I just felt...well, really alone all of a sudden. In a way I hadn't been prepared for. In the hotel we were always surrounded by people. Even in the bunker, I had my parents with me.

But now there was no one at all.

Well, except my dad. He was out there somewhere. Maybe my mom was, too. Once I found them, it would be okay.

We could keep each other safe.

I looked around the vast, empty square. The darkness was growing stronger. I realized I needed to find shelter for the night. I had originally planned to find my dad's apartment. I knew approximately where it was from his description, but I didn't want to be wandering out in the dark. It would be much easier to find it in the morning.

Unfortunately, the hotel was now locked up tight, all the lower windows boarded up and the doors padlocked. I had to find somewhere else to go. Preferably before it got too dark.

I scanned the square again, thinking hard. There were other hotels, of course, but they wouldn't be cleaned out. There'd be spiderwebs and rats and maybe rotting floorboards that were unsafe to walk over. It would be too risky, especially in the dark.

Especially alone.

It was then that I spotted the old Broadway theater just up the street, its battered marquee still advertising a play that hadn't been performed in five years. Mike and a bunch of other adults had cleaned it out last winter so some of the kids could perform a holiday play for the grown-ups. Javier had even rigged up a generator to light the stage. I bet it was still there.

Javier. I swallowed hard as I remembered him being lifted into the sky. Screaming, flailing, disappearing from view. He'd always been a friend to me and Maya and the other kids. Never too busy to play with us or explain how something worked. He was so smart, and talented, and nice. And now he was just gone. Because he tried to save me.

Anger rose inside of me. Monsters. They were such monsters. Why couldn't they just leave us alone? They'd already destroyed the world. Now they wanted to take what little was left.

Gurgh?

A sudden sound made me stop in my tracks. What was that? It sounded like gargling—like my dad each morning down in the bunker, rinsing his mouth out with mouthwash. But who would be gargling out here? In the dark? In the middle of Times Square?

Gurgh...

Heart in my throat, I slowly turned around, though I was pretty sure I didn't want to see what it was. My jaw dropped as my eyes locked onto the dark shadow, looming a few feet above.

The shadow of a dragon.

A baby dragon, my mind corrected. I took in the creature's height as it settled down on the ground just a few feet away. *Or maybe a child?*

The dragon shook itself, its shiny, silvery scales sparkling like jewels under my flashlight's glow. It stood about the height of a small pony and its wings were still kind of stubby-looking. But what really struck me was its eyes. I'd never seen a dragon's eyes this close up before. They were like glowing crystals of amber light. So brilliant, they were almost blinding. So beautiful, they practically took my breath away.

Beautiful...and deadly.

I stared at the dragon, willing my body not to move, my heart racing madly in my chest. What was I going to do? I was out in the open; there was no place to run. No door to dive through. No bathtub to hide in until it went away.

Which meant I was dead meat. Just like Javier.

I squeezed my eyes shut, not wanting to watch. If I was going to die, I didn't need to see it. I imagined the creature's belly warming with fire as it prepared to take me out. Its mouth creaking open. Sparks crackling on its blackened tongue. Soon, it would suck in a mighty breath, then slowly exhale and—

Glurp?

My eyes flew open. The dragon hadn't moved. But it also hadn't shot fire and its belly still looked light and cool. As I watched, it blinked twice, then slowly cocked its head, staring at me with big, amber eyes that looked almost...hopeful? Like it wanted something. Something I had.

I looked down at my hands.

Or, more precisely, at the *apple* in my hands.

Shocked, I glanced back up at the dragon.

"Do...you want my apple?" I stammered before I could stop myself. It was madness to talk to a dragon. And I was sure it couldn't understand my words. Also, since when did dragons eat fruit? From everything I'd ever read, they were carnivores.

Glurp? The dragon blinked. It looked at the apple, then at me. Like a dog, begging for a treat. Its tongue slipped from its mouth, and it slowly licked its lips. It would have been almost funny had I not been so scared.

I sucked in a shaky breath, hardly able to believe what I was about to do. Somehow, I managed to get my hand to work, tossing the apple in the dragon's direction. Even as I made the move, I knew it was crazy. Surely, this had to be a trick, right? The dragon didn't actually want the apple—it wanted me. And any second now, it would attack.

I would become dragon dinner.

The apple bounced once off the curb, settling at the dragon's feet. I watched in amazement as the creature dropped its silvery head, then slurped up the apple, chewing twice, then swallowing the entire thing, core and all. When it had finished, it looked up at me and did the most surprising thing of all.

Its lips curled upward as if in a smile.

I watched as the dragon pushed off its hind legs, shooting itself into the sky, unable to believe it was actually happening. It circled once, dipping its wing in my direction as if it was waving, then began to fly away. Soon, it had disappeared over the rooftops.

For a moment, I just stood there, too shocked to move. Then, my body sprang into action, and I bolted toward the theater, shoving its doors open and dashing inside. Up the corridor, through the lobby, past the old refreshment stand. Straight to the auditorium, yanking the doors shut behind me.

I sank down into a back-row seat, sucking in a huge breath. Trying desperately to reset my reality. I was okay. I was safe. The dragons couldn't get me in here. Everything would be okay.

But all I could see when I closed my eyes was the baby dragon with the glowing eyes.

Chomping happily on an apple.

CHAPTER SIX

I *was standing in the middle of a cornfield.*

Which was weird, actually, since I was pretty sure I hadn't seen a cornfield since I was six years old and my parents had taken me to visit my grandmother in Nebraska. I remembered at the time being fascinated by the wide, open spaces stretching out from her small farmhouse in the center of the field. The seemingly endless rows of green stalks, blowing in the breeze. It seemed magical then.

It seemed terrifying now.

Thrump.

Thrump.

Thrump.

My eyes darted around the field, heart pounding in my chest. It was too open out here. I was too exposed. I needed to get back to the city, with its tall buildings and narrow streets that provided protection from the monsters above. But where was the city? Everywhere I looked, the tall grasses seemed to stretch out into infinity.

Thrump.

Thrump.

Thrump.

Suddenly, across the field, I saw a lone figure, waving frantically in my direction. I squinted, at first unable to identify them. Then my eyes bulged in recognition.

"Mom?" I whispered.

"Noah!" she cried. Her voice seemed to reverberate in my head, like when you yelled "Echo!" in the middle of a tunnel. "I need your help, Noah!"

"I'm coming, Mom!" I cried. "Stay right there!"

I started running in her direction, as fast as I could. My feet pounded the earth, my arms swinging from side to side. Soon, I was running so hard I could scarcely suck in a breath. But still I pushed forward. I had to reach her. I had to get to her before the dragons did.

I had to keep her safe.

But the more I ran, the farther away she seemed to get. Until I could barely see her at all, just a small speck on an endless horizon, the setting sun casting her in a fiery glow.

"Noah!" she cried. "Why won't you help me, Noah?"

"I'm trying, Mom!" I choked on the words. "I'm trying!"

Screech!

Suddenly a dragon swooped down, landing directly in front of me with a loud thud, completely blocking my path. It shook itself, its silver scales shimmering down its side as it folded its massive wings. It was huge, as big as a house, and its belly was burning with fire. I looked around frantically, but the field seemed to mock me with its emptiness.

No place to run. No place to hide.

No saving my mom.

No escape for me now.

I dropped to my knees, cowering, with my hands over my head. As if that would do anything to keep a dragon away. The creature took a step forward, its mouth creaking open to reveal a mouthful of scary-looking teeth. I whispered a prayer under my breath. Tried desperately not to cry. Tried not to think about Mom and how I'd failed her.

Mom...Dad...

No. I couldn't die like this. I wouldn't.

I rose slowly to my feet, forcing myself to face my

worst fear. Squaring my shoulders, lifting my chin. If I was going to die, I would look death in the face.

I locked eyes with the dragon. Then I held my breath, waiting for the fire to come.

But instead of flames? A question.

"Do you have any apples?" the dragon asked with a smile. "Do you have any apples, Noah?"

Noah...

Noah...

I shot up in bed, my body drenched in sweat. For a moment, I had no idea where I was, my heart thumping a terrifying rhythm in my chest. I sucked in a breath and tried to regain my bearings. My eyes darted around the room, my mind struggling to catch up.

I was not in a field. I was not facing down a fierce silver dragon.

I was in a bed, in a dark theater, in the middle of Times Square.

I was okay. I was safe.

At least for now.

I fell back onto the bed, relieved, memories of the night before flooding my brain. After I'd gotten safely inside the theater and had calmed myself down, I'd made my way backstage to the props room, where I knew I would find a bunch of useful stuff—including an actual bed. The last play they did here must have had a bedroom scene. The blankets were super dusty, and I'd had to re-home a few small spiders, but it was certainly better than sleeping across a row of seats in the auditorium.

And certainly better than being outside.

I had just settled in when I heard the dragons come. A few squawks at first, then more screeching as they were joined by others. I lay uncomfortably in bed, trying to picture what they were doing just beyond the theater's walls. Probably ransacking the supplies abandoned by my group. At least they had no idea I was in here.

But while I knew I was safe, it wasn't easy to sleep through their cries. Especially on an empty stomach. When I'd packed my bag, I hadn't thought about my need to eat. And now I was stuck in here with no food, no water. Not even that apple I'd given to the baby dragon.

Do you have any apples, Noah?

My mind flashed back to the strange creature I'd encountered the night before. Its pale silver scales, its eerie amber eyes. The odd way it'd acted—like no other dragon I'd ever heard of. Preferring fruit over human flesh.

Maybe it was a vegetarian, I thought with a snort. *That would be lucky, running into the only vegetarian dragon out there.*

I shook my head, forcing myself to return to the present. I needed to get up. I needed to go find my dad. Pushing myself out of bed, I headed back into the auditorium. Stopping on the stage, I stared out into the empty rows of seats, my mind flashing back to the play we'd performed here last winter. *A Christmas Carol*, it had been called, and my mom had directed it. I played the ghost of Christmas Past and Maya played Ebenezer Scrooge. When I had walked onstage, trying to act all scary and ghostly, she started to laugh and couldn't stop. I tried to keep a straight face myself, but it was too hard, and I eventually started to giggle. Finally, Mom had to call for an early intermission to get us back under control. She'd pretended to be stern—*"Stay in character!"*—but I could see her eyes dancing as she tried not to laugh herself.

Those were the good times. The times I thought maybe this would all turn out okay. That even though life was different than before, it didn't have to be bad. A new normal, you might say. As long as we stuck together as a group, played by the dragons' rules, and stayed out of their way, maybe we really could have a future. Not the one we planned, of course. But one with laughter and friendship and hope. Wasn't that all we really needed in the end?

But then Mom left. And all the laughter had died. Without her, it was like the sun had slipped behind a cloud and every morning felt dreary and hopeless. Where had she gone? And why had she left? And most importantly, why hadn't she said goodbye?

Feeling a little sick, I leapt off the stage and headed to the front doors, stepping out of the theater and back onto the street. Sure enough, all the supplies that had been left behind had been thoroughly picked over by the dragons during the night, and there was nothing edible left. My stomach growled in annoyance, and I sighed. So much for the hope of a morning bite to eat.

I glanced at the sky, making sure it was clear, then headed down toward the street where my dad had told me he'd found an apartment. I kept close to the buildings, dashing between awnings and scaffoldings, not wanting to be seen from above. When I got to the street, I did a quick scan of all the apartment buildings. At first, I thought it'd be hard to figure out which one Dad was staying in. But then my eyes caught sight of a bear trap in front of one of the stoops. Bingo.

A moment later, my dad was opening his front door. If he was surprised to see me, he didn't show it. Instead, I saw only sadness in his gaze.

"What have you done?" he asked softly, not bothering with a hello. "Why didn't you go with the others?"

I swallowed hard, something catching in my throat. I could have dealt with him yelling at me. But the disappointment in his voice was almost too much to bear. Disappointment mixed with something that sounded a lot like fear.

And suddenly I worried I'd had made a huge mistake.

"I wanted to help you," I mumbled, feeling the heat rise to my cheeks. "I wanted to help find Mom."

He sighed deeply, moving away from the doorway and ushering me inside. I stepped hesitantly into the apartment, looking around. It was small—one bedroom, one bath. A combination living room and kitchen area with a beat-up couch and a useless TV. There were tiny windows up near the ceiling, the only part of the apartment not underground, and they cast dim rays of light into the otherwise bleak space.

My dad turned to me. "Look, it's not like I'm not happy to see you," he said, raking a hand through his thick, graying hair. "You know I didn't want to leave you as much as you didn't want to be left. It's just—you know what it's like out here, Noah. It's so dangerous. I wanted you to be safe."

"I'll be fine," I protested. "I'm not a baby. I can take care of myself. Remember? I got away from that dragon yesterday. I can do it again if I need to."

Two dragons, actually. But he didn't need to know about the second one.

He grimaced. "I hope so," he muttered. "I really do."

61

I stared down at the ground, stubbing the parquet floor with the toe of my boot. I didn't know what reaction I was expecting from him. Surely, I had known he wouldn't be overjoyed to see me. But still, somehow the weight of his disappointment was heavier than I'd imagined. And suddenly I felt the strong urge to try to prove myself to him. To show him I'd be an asset, not a burden.

"I'm sorry," I said. "I know it was stupid. But I couldn't just go down there by myself. We're a family. And if Mom needs you? Well, maybe she needs me, too. We can search the city together. Look everywhere until we find her."

My father frowned, turning away. "What?" I asked, confused.

He let out a heavy breath. "There's no need for searching. I know where she is."

I stared at him in shock. "What do you mean you know where she is?" I demanded, my heart thudding fast in my chest. "If you know where she is, why haven't you gone to get her?"

"Because she doesn't want to come back," my father said simply, refusing to look me in the eye. "I thought maybe if I stayed out here for the summer, I could convince her…"

My mind raced with questions as an uncomfortable knot formed in my stomach. "I don't understand," I said, stalking over to him. "Where is she? Why doesn't she want to come back?"

He whirled around, his face stormy. "Because she's joined a cult, Noah. A cult of dragon sympathizers."

Wait, what?

"Dragon sympathizers?" I wrinkled my forehead in confusion. "You mean, people who feel bad for dragons?" But that didn't make any sense. Why would anyone have sympathy for a dragon? They'd destroyed our entire world! My mind flashed back to the dragon that had chased Maya and me yesterday. How vicious it had been. How cunning, how cruel.

No, there was no reason on earth any human should sympathize with dragons.

"They're brainwashed," my father said with a helpless shrug. "And they've convinced your mother that they're in the right. You know she's always been an animal lover. They've somehow persuaded her that dragons should be protected. Be given the same rights as people."

"But that's ridiculous!" I cried. "I mean, look what they did to Javier!" Javier had done nothing wrong—he'd never hurt a dragon in his life—and now he was dead.

Because of these monsters.

"It's also against the law to aid and abet a dragon," Dad added. "The president said so, before things broke down completely. Of course, there's no one left to prosecute them, so I guess they figure they can get away with it. But that doesn't make it just." He squeezed his hands into fists.

"I can't believe Mom would leave us for people like that," I said, still feeling confused. It was one thing to know she was missing. Quite another to know she'd taken up with criminals on purpose.

"Don't be too hard on your mom," Dad said gently, reaching out to put a hand over mine. "It's not entirely her fault. It's like she's sick, Noah. And we need to help her get well. Once she's away from these traitors, she'll start seeing reality again. We have to...deprogram her. That's what they call it, when you help someone in a cult. I got a bunch of books from the library. I'm hoping they'll help."

I pursed my lips, starting to get the picture. "You were planning to spend the summer deprogramming her," I realized aloud. "So she'd be ready to rejoin our group in the fall."

"Exactly. At least that's my hope."

"Well, then I can help!" I exclaimed, excitement rising inside me. "You can bring her back here, and I can help her get well. Surely once she's back with us, she'll change her mind. I mean, no one would choose a monster over their own family, right?"

But she already did, a voice inside me whispered. *And she didn't even say goodbye.*

My stomach wrenched. I pushed the thought away. *It wasn't her fault*, I reminded myself. She'd been brainwashed, like my dad said. Which meant she was sick.

And we could help her get well.

"So when do we go get her?" I asked.

"I'm going to head up today and scope out their community on the Upper West Side," my father replied. "See how much firepower they have, guards—that kind of thing. Then I'll work up a plan to spring her. She's not going to come willingly, that's for sure."

"Can I come?"

"No. This operation needs to be extremely stealthy. If we're caught snooping around, they'll only tighten security and make it harder for me to extract her. From what I've heard from Mike and some of the others who have scouted the area, this group is extremely protective of whatever they've got going on up there. And they don't take kindly to strangers."

I considered this for a moment. If that were true, how did Mom get invited to join their group in the first place? Were they in need of teachers, maybe? Maybe that's why she couldn't bring me—they only wanted people who could help them in some way, and I was just a kid. Not that I would have gone anyway, obviously. I had no interest in joining a cult that worshipped dragons or whatever.

But still, it would have been nice to have been asked....

"Anyway," Dad said, looking around the apartment.

"Maybe you can get the place ready for her? You know how she likes things tidy and clean."

"I can do that," I agreed eagerly, happy to be given a task. "I can make it super nice for her!" I thought about all the things my mother loved. Herbal teas, cozy blankets. And Disney! She was always talking about how much she missed Disney World. I could totally go and try to find some cool stuff for her at the old Disney Store in Times Square to make her feel like she was there. I'd make the place so nice she'd forget all about those stupid dragon huggers.

My father gave me a rueful smile. "That sounds perfect, Noah," he said. "I'm sure she'll appreciate that." He turned to the stove. "Anyway, you must be starving. We'll have breakfast together and then I'll head out."

I felt a smile rise to my lips and my empty stomach growled in anticipation. Breakfast. And even better—breakfast with my dad. And soon Mom would join us, too. I was positive that she would start to get better once she was back with people who cared about her. She would start remembering what was important.

Family. Our family. Because there was nothing that mattered more than that.

CHAPTER SEVEN

I was full. So very full.

I leaned back onto the ratty couch, rubbing my bloated stomach. My dad had prepared a feast for breakfast, which wasn't usually like him at all. He was always the first to scold Mom when she'd "waste" precious food—even on a special occasion like a birthday or Christmas. *We eat to live,* he'd always say. *Not live to eat.*

Not that I blamed him. He'd spent years calculating how much food we'd need in the bunker to survive an apocalyptic event. He'd even made detailed menus based on these calculations to stretch out the food for the maximum number of days, ensuring that while we were never quite full, we were never at risk of starving either.

But today, for some reason, he'd made an exception, opening up three cans of refried beans and scrambling up a mountain of powdered eggs. I guess it was his way of saying he forgave me for not going underground. Let's just say my dad was more of an actions-speak-louder-than-words kind of guy.

After eating, Dad rose from his seat and threw his dish in the sink. Then he walked over and grabbed his gun, slinging it over his shoulder. At the door, he turned to me. "You going to be okay here?" he asked. "Until I'm back?"

"I'll be fine," I assured him. "I'll clean the place up really good for Mom, like you said."

He opened the front door. "That's my boy! Thanks, son. I'll see you soon."

And with that, he left, allowing the door to slam shut behind him. I ran over and locked it, just in case. Then I set about fixing up the apartment. Sweeping the floors, dusting, making the bed. I couldn't wash the dishes; there was no running water in the apartment, and I didn't want to waste any of Dad's precious bottled stuff. So I put them outside in the back alley next to the empty buckets that Dad had placed along the wall to collect rainwater. Nature's dishwasher.

It was a lot of work, but I didn't mind. Anytime I started to get bored, I forced myself to picture Mom stepping through the door and looking over the place. She liked things neat. Clean. Tidy. I wanted it to be all those things for her. So she'd feel right at home. I imagined her mouth lifting in a smile as she wrapped her arms around me and held me close.

I'll never leave again, I imagined her saying. *How could I when you've made me the perfect home?*

At least I hoped she would. Because I couldn't imagine the alternative. That she'd decide to stay out there, with her traitor friends. That she would choose dragons—actual *dragons*—over her own loving family.

That she would choose them over me.

I shook my head. I couldn't think of that now. I *wouldn't*. I had to trust Dad. He had a plan. And when Dad had a plan, he was basically unstoppable. He would get Mom back. He would make her well.

We would be a family again.

After cleaning up, I took a short nap. Thankfully this time I didn't have any bizarre dragon dreams. When I woke up, Dad still wasn't back, so I read my new book for a little while, then ate the leftover canned beans.

It was then that I started feeling a little lonely again. The kind of loneliness I remembered feeling back in our early days in the family bunker when the dragons had first come. When I had been forced to leave all my friends behind and retreat underground with only my parents to keep me company. At first, I'd been able to talk to my friends over the shaky internet connection we had in the bunker. We'd even played some Roblox. They'd tell me crazy stories about the dragons, and I remembered feeling like I was missing out on all the excitement. But then, as time passed, one by one they stopped signing on. My friend list was shrinking each and every day. I tried to find out what happened to them—had they retreated to a safe place but couldn't get online? Or had they been killed by a dragon? There was no way to know for sure. And then the internet went out altogether.

Leaving me totally alone.

I looked around the apartment now and sighed. If I had gone down to the subway tunnels like I was supposed to, I could have found one of the other kids to hang out with—Maya or whoever. It wasn't as fun as aboveground, but we'd always find something to do. Like kickball tournaments or board games. Sometimes we'd just lay around and talk about what was going on. Maybe take a walk down the subway tracks for exercise.

But I had chosen to stay above. Which meant I wouldn't see another kid all summer long.

I hadn't really thought of this when I'd first decided to stay. I had been so wrapped up in the idea of being with my family I'd forgotten how lonely it had been with only my family in the bunker after the internet went down.

70

Mom had tried her best to keep me entertained, but it wasn't the same as having friends my own age.

This whole time I'd been worried about the dragon danger. I'd never stopped to consider the dangers of boredom.

I shook my head. No. That was selfish thinking. I wasn't a little kid anymore. I was an important member of a family. Like my dad used to say, the three of us were like legs on a tripod. And we needed all three legs to be solid if we were going to stand. I wasn't here for a vacation. I was here to help my dad and mom. I needed to stay solid.

I paced the apartment, feeling restless. I started to explore, to see what treasures might be hidden in the place. Opening the back closet, I discovered a pile of bear traps, just like the one outside the front door. I remembered Dad talking about laying traps to deter the dragons from the subway entrance and keep those down below safe. The traps looked small for a dragon, but I guessed they would do the job, with their sharp metal teeth clamping down on a foot or wing, snaring them where they stood. It wouldn't kill them, but it would prevent them from flying away. Until Dad came back with his rifle and finished the job.

I picked up a trap, feeling its weight. My dad had taught me how to set traps like this, though I'd never done it by myself. Still, maybe I could try them now, setting the rest of them out in Times Square. Maybe I'd even get lucky and capture a dragon or two. I imagined the look on my dad's face when he came back from his mission to find a dragon just waiting there for him to take out. He'd be so proud of me. And I would have proven myself useful. A productive member of the family.

Inspired, I grabbed a few traps, shoving them into the military-issue knapsack that was sitting by the door. Next to it was a cooler, where I found a hunk of rotten rat meat that Dad must have been using to bait the traps. Perfect.

I headed outside, dragging the knapsack behind me. I kept an eye to the sky as I walked up the stairs and out onto the street, making sure I didn't have company. But the skies seemed clear, so I pushed on, trudging the block and a half walk to the subway entrance.

Once there, I dumped the traps from the bag and began working to set and bait them. They weren't easy to use, and I'm pretty sure I almost lost an arm when one sprang backward, clamping shut with a bang. That got my adrenaline pumping! But I refused to give up, and, gritting my teeth, I kept working, until finally all the traps were in place.

Once I was done, I looked over my work, a feeling of pride settling on my shoulders. Dad was going to be so excited when he saw what I'd done—even if I didn't manage to catch a dragon by the time he got back. I imagined him slapping me on the back in approval.

Nice, he'd say. *Couldn't have done it better myself.*

I smiled, feeling pretty good. Now it was time to go shopping.

A few hours later, I exited the Disney Store, my arms loaded down with bags. I'd scored big on stuff for Mom and our new home, including a ton of fun board games and a little porcelain plaque to hang above the sink that read HOME SWEET HOME. I'd even found a doll from an old film called *Frozen* that had been super popular when Mom was a kid. Sure, she was a little old for dolls, but maybe she could, like, display it or something. I grinned to myself as I pushed open the double doors. Mom was going to love her new home.

I looked around Times Square, wondering if I should head straight to the apartment or check on my traps first. The sun was already getting pretty low in the sky, and I didn't want my dad to be worried if he got back and I wasn't home. But in the end, curiosity won out and I headed over to the subway entrance. *Please let me have caught a dragon*, I thought as my heartbeat picked up its pace. That would be the cherry on top of this already pretty great day.

Screech!

I stopped in my tracks at the sound up ahead. On instinct, my gaze shot up to the sky, but I didn't see anything. I frowned, thinking. Could the sound be coming from one of my traps? Had I really bagged a dragon on my very first try? Dad was going to freak out if I did!

I stepped closer, tiptoeing just in case. I couldn't see anything at first; an abandoned truck on the corner was obscuring my view. As I got closer, I heard the sound again. Heart in my throat, I rounded the corner....

And came face-to-face with a dragon, snared in my trap.

But not just any dragon, I realized, almost dropping my bag in shock. It was the same baby dragon from the day before. The one with the amber eyes. The one who'd wanted my apple.

The dragon's eyes widened as it saw me come around the corner. It squawked anxiously, trying desperately to flap its wings to get away. My stomach twisted uncomfortably as I noticed the sharp metal claws of the trap digging into the dragon's flesh, dark red blood crusting on its paws.

I'd caught myself a dragon all right.

But instead of feeling proud, I felt a little sick.

The dragon whimpered pitifully now, clearly in pain. It was female, I realized, remembering our lessons on how girl dragons didn't have horns. She tried to free herself again, this time attempting to bite at the steel jaws of the trap, but she couldn't manage to pull herself free. She snorted, frustrated, then looked up at me. I realized her whole body was shaking.

Glurp?

For a moment, she looked at me. Just looked at me, her eyes swirling with fear—and a little bit of what looked like accusation deep in her black pupils. I swallowed hard, suddenly uncomfortable. Did she somehow know that I had done this to her?

I turned away, feeling almost guilty. When I had first set the traps, I hadn't really thought about how much they would hurt, clamping down on a foot or wing. Or how terrifying it must be to be trapped and not understand how or why. Suddenly, it all felt so inhumane.

I tried to remind myself of Javier—he'd been terrified, too, when that dragon had carried him away. But instead, all I could think of was this little dragon the day before, the apple dropping at her feet. Her black tongue slurping it up in pleasure.

She could have killed me. Right then and there. I'd had no place to run.

But she'd chosen not to.

Instead, she'd smiled at me and flew away.

And now the tables had turned. She must have been so excited to smell the meat in the trap, I thought miserably. She must have been hungry. Starving maybe—I mean, she'd just woken up from a winter of hibernation and probably hadn't had much to eat. I imagined her flying down, her lips curled in that same excited smile. Then her shock as the trap slammed down onto her leg, cutting into her flesh. Probably breaking her bones. I imagined the moment she realized she was trapped. And all those moments afterward while she waited in terror, not knowing what would happen next.

"I'm…sorry," I stammered, not knowing why I was speaking out loud. It wasn't as if she could understand my words. "I was trying to catch one of the bad dragons. Not you."

She raised her head, her huge amber eyes meeting mine again. A lone tear slipped down her snout, splashing to the ground. But she didn't struggle anymore. She'd clearly given up trying to get away. She was now just waiting for me to put her out of her misery. Which, I guess, had been the plan all along.

But she was so little. So beautiful, too, with her silvery scales and strange glowing eyes. I shifted from foot to foot, indecision whirling through me as I tried to figure out what to do. If I left her here, Dad would have no problem killing her once he returned. He might even suggest we roast her for dinner. While others in the group frowned upon the idea of eating dragon, my dad was practical. Meat was meat. We didn't let it go to waste.

Ugh. My stomach rolled with nausea. I couldn't. I just couldn't.

I closed my eyes for a moment, thinking hard. Then I opened them and drew in a long breath, making up my mind.

"You spared my life yesterday," I said to her. "I will do the same for you. Just this once."

But...how? Even as I made the decision, I wasn't exactly sure how to carry it out. I'd have to get up close to her to spring the trap. What if she misunderstood my gesture and attacked? She was small, but she was still a dragon. I would be a goner, and quick.

"Look, I want to help you," I added, trying to sound confident and kind. Maybe she could at least interpret the tone of my voice? "But you have to trust me, okay? If you kill me, I can't free you."

The dragon looked at me for a moment, then, to my surprise, seemed to bow her head. I stared at her in shock. Could she understand me somehow? Could she at least sense that I didn't want to hurt her anymore?

Drawing in a breath, I took a slow step forward, keeping my hands up so she could see I was unarmed. She snorted softly, looking nervous, but she didn't make a move.

Okay then. Here went nothing.

I dropped to my knees in front of her, my heart pumping wildly in my chest. With shaky hands, I reached down, gently grabbing each side of the trap. I could feel her soft, warm breath on the top of my head, but she stayed perfectly still.

Using all my strength, I pulled the jaws of the trap apart. They were tight; it was tough, and for a moment I had a vision of the trap snapping backward, crushing her leg all over again. She would panic. I would die.

But in the end, I managed to pull it apart. She yanked her leg out, trying to step down on it, then whimpered in pain, holding it up again. She was still hurting, clearly.

But she was free.

I backed up quickly, just in case. For all I knew she was just waiting for this moment to attack. To get revenge for what I'd done to her.

But, to my relief, she didn't attack. Instead, she just stood there, looking at me. If I didn't know better, I'd say I saw something that looked like gratitude, deep in those odd amber eyes.

"You need to be more careful," I told her, just in case she *could* understand me. "There are a lot of traps around here. It's not safe. You might want to hunt somewhere else for now."

She nodded, again seeming to understand. Or maybe I was just wanting her to and gave more meaning to the movement. In any case, I gave her a small smile and a wave.

"Well, I've got to get back now," I told her. "But, uh, I hope your leg's okay."

I watched as she unfurled her wings. Shimmers of silver skimmed down her sides, reflected by the setting sun. She gave me one last look before pushing off on her good legs and shooting up into the sky.

I watched as she flew up to the rooftops, disappearing from view....

Suddenly a shot rang out, the deafening bang causing me to practically jump out of my skin. I whirled around, shocked to find none other than my dad standing behind me, not five feet away, his rifle pointing in the direction the dragon had flown. I gasped, horrified. Had he hit her?

He cursed loudly, which told me he hadn't. For a moment he kept his rifle pointed to the sky, but the dragon was long gone. At last he lowered the weapon.

He turned to look at me, an unreadable expression on his face.

"What have you done, Noah?" he asked.

I swallowed hard, staring at him helplessly, somehow feeling more frightened than I had been when freeing the dragon. How long had he been standing there? How much had he seen?

"I...I..."

He grabbed me roughly by the arm, causing me to drop my bags. I cringed as I heard the porcelain kitchen plaque that I'd so carefully picked out for Mom smash as it hit the pavement.

HOME SWEET HOME, shattering into a million pieces.

"Back to the apartment," Dad growled. "Now."

CHAPTER EIGHT

Dad practically shoved me through the door, slamming it shut behind us. I stumbled inside, losing my balance as my toe caught on the rug, sending me flying forward. I skidded on my hands and knees, managing to come to a stop just before my head collided with the coffee table.

Dad stomped in, looming above me. He looked twelve feet tall, his meaty arms crossed over his chest. For a moment, he said nothing. But I could read everything he wanted to say in his stormy brown eyes. I'd seen my dad angry before. But never like this. And for good reason, too. What had I been thinking? Freeing a dragon?

At last, he grunted, running a hand through his hair as he turned his back on me. "I don't even know what to say," he muttered, half to himself.

I scrambled to my feet. "Dad—"

He whirled around. "What were you thinking, Noah?" he yelled. "Have I taught you nothing at all?"

"It was just a baby," I protested, feeling the tears well in my eyes. I angrily swiped them away with my sleeve. "She wasn't going to hurt me."

"Just a baby? *Just* a baby? Do you have any idea what happens when baby dragons grow up?" He was so angry, he was spitting. "They become full-grown dragons, Noah. Full-grown, world-destroying dragons!"

"I'm sorry!" I cried, tears now streaming down my cheeks. I knew my dad hated tears—he saw them as a sign of weakness. But I couldn't help it. I didn't know what to say. I didn't know what to do. If only he could have seen the dragon. Seen how pitiful she looked, how scared. "You didn't see her, Dad. She was so sad!"

"*Sad?* Dragons don't feel sad, Noah!" Dad scoffed. "They're animals. Deadly creatures who have destroyed our entire world. Killed millions of people. Forced us to live like rats underground." He stomped over to me, eyes flashing fury. "If anything's 'sad,' it's the state of the human race—because of these monsters."

I hung my head. I had nothing left to say. No excuses

that could possibly explain away what I'd done. Mostly because I wasn't even sure why I'd done it in the first place. I knew what dragons were. I'd seen firsthand what they'd done to our world. And yet, I'd gone and acted like I was one of Mom's dragon sympathizers.

Dad squared his shoulders, his face filled with sudden resolve. "Look, it's okay, Noah. I know you got confused. It's been a rough twenty-four hours for both of us. But we can still make this right. Tomorrow morning, we'll go out and we'll find that dragon again. And this time, you'll do the right thing." His eyes leveled on me. "Okay?"

I cringed. *The right thing.* Did he mean what I thought he meant? The look on his face told me he did. He wanted me to find that baby dragon. And to kill her.

"Look, you wanted to be out here this summer," Dad reasoned. "Well, now you are. And if you're going to survive, you're going to have to learn some important life lessons, quick." He ruffled my hair with his hand. "We're going to get you blooded, son. It's past time."

"Bl-blooded?" I stammered, even though I knew exactly what he meant. It was an old deer hunting term from the before times. Hunters would take their kids out into the forest to bag their first buck. If they could successfully take down a deer, their father would smear its blood on their cheeks in celebration. It was considered a badge of honor.

But Dad wasn't talking about deer. He was talking about dragons.

The baby dragon with the glowing amber eyes.

I bit my lower lip. I didn't want to do it. I really didn't want to do it. But what choice did I have? If I was going to prove to my father I could hack it out here, I'd have to start playing by his rules. I'd have to prove to him I wasn't the soft boy he thought I was. I'd have to prove I was a man.

"Fine," I said, trying to make it sound like no big deal. Even though, of course, it was. "I'll kill the dragon. Whatever."

I could feel my father's eyes burning into me. As if he could see right through me and knew it was the last thing I wanted to do. But thankfully all he said was, "Great. That's great, Noah. You're going to love it. That feeling of ending one of those monsters? There's nothing like it in the world." He glanced down at his arm tattoos and gave a ruthless grin. I shuddered a little. Hopefully I wouldn't be expected to get one of those, too.

I drew in a breath. Okay. Past time for a subject change. "Did you find Mom today? With her...new group?"

Dad looked up from his tattoos. "Yes. I scouted out their camp this morning. They're holed up on an old college campus—Columbia University. I managed to slip in without any of them noticing me and waited until I saw your mother walk by. I know where she's living now. Which means I can go back tomorrow night when everyone's asleep and...retrieve her."

My heart stuttered in my chest. "So you actually saw her? You saw Mom? Did she...seem okay?"

"Physically, yes," Dad replied. "She looked healthy—well fed." He paused, then added, "But remember, Noah, she's still sick on the inside. She was brainwashed pretty bad by these people. It's going to take some time to get her back to her old self. Which means we have to be patient with her. We don't want to push her too far, too fast. It might...hurt her recovery." He shrugged. "At least that's what the books said."

"Of course!" I agreed. "Whatever she needs. I'll just be happy to have her back." I sighed dreamily, imagining my mom curled up on the couch beside me, reading a book. Just like old times. "I miss her so much."

"I miss her, too," Dad said, staring off into space. "It's just not the same without her." He sighed deeply, then shook his head. "Anyway, let's have some dinner, and then I'm going to give you a little lesson in gun safety. Tomorrow morning we'll head out hunting, bright and early."

Oh right. My heart sank in my chest, my earlier excitement deflating. In my anticipation of seeing Mom again, I'd almost forgotten what had to come first.

I had to kill the baby dragon.

CHAPTER NINE

Asha

Screech!

The young dragon whimpered in relief as the familiar dark figure crossed above her, coming in for a landing on the rooftop where she lay. Her mother had been gone so long, she had started to wonder if she'd ever come back at all. And she needed her—badly. Tonight more than ever.

She looked down at her throbbing leg. It had swollen to twice its normal size, and the wounds had begun to turn a disturbing shade of black. She felt too hot for the cool night and a little sick to her stomach, too. But at least she was alive. After what had happened, she should be thankful for that at least.

"Sorry I was gone so long," her mother said, loping toward her as she folded her massive silver-scaled wings to her sides. "Unfortunately, I didn't find much out there to eat." She dropped a small, dead bird in front of her daughter. The young dragon made no move to pick it up.

Her mother frowned. "Is something—" she started to ask, then her mouth dropped open in horror as her amber eyes locked onto her daughter's wounded leg. "Asha, what happened?"

Asha hung her head. She knew the question would come eventually, but she wasn't exactly excited to explain. "I smelled some meat," she murmured, feeling so ashamed. "I thought I could get some for us. You know, hunt, like you do." Of course, her mother would never fall for a trap like she had. "It was...a mistake."

"Oh, Asha..."

Her mother dropped down beside her, putting a wing around Asha's body and pulling her close. Then she lowered her head and set out to lick the wounds clean. Asha sighed in relief at the feeling of her mother's rough tongue scraping against her burning scales. Dragon saliva had all sorts of healing properties when applied directly to a wound. However, it had to come from another dragon, not you.

But her mother was here now. She would make every-thing okay.

"So you got stuck in one of the monsters' traps," her mother concluded, her voice rich with disappointment. She stopped licking for a moment and looked up at her daughter. "Asha, this is why I told you to stay here on the roof. You could have been killed!"

"I know. I'm sorry! I just wanted to do my share! To help the herd."

Her mother sighed. "And I love that you want to do that. But you're still too young, Asha. And too important to our herd to risk. You're going to be queen someday. And if anything happened to you…" She trailed off, her mouth dipping into a frown. "How did you manage to get out of the trap?" she asked. "Did Tolkyn find you?" she added, naming her second-in-command before con-tinuing to clean Asha's wounds.

Asha shrugged uneasily, not sure what she should say. Would her mother even believe her if she told the truth? That a monster had let her out?

Her mind flashed back to the scene from earlier that day. Her stuck in the trap, the monster rounding the cor-ner. At first, she thought he would kill her on sight. But then she recognized him. It was the same pup who had given her an apple the day before. And suddenly, for rea-sons she couldn't explain, she had begun to have hope.

She thought back to his gentle hands, closing around the jaws of the trap. Taking care he didn't hurt her as he worked to free her leg. But that wasn't the strangest part. Not by far.

She'd never tell her mother this, of course, but it was like she could read the monster's thoughts as he worked. Not exactly as words, spoken aloud, but more like sensations, feelings. And somehow, because of this, she found herself absolutely certain that he meant her no harm. As if he had told her this himself, whispering deep into her mind somehow.

As if they shared some sort of bond....

She shook her head. What was she thinking? Bonding with a monster? Her mother would be so ashamed. After all, humans were evil. They'd murdered so many of her kind. All her life Asha had been warned about them. How they were bloodthirsty, violent, and cruel.

Though this pup had seemed none of the above.

He'd given her an apple when she was hungry.

He'd saved her life when she was trapped.

Her mother lifted her head, having finished her cleaning. Asha looked down to see the wounds had already closed and her scales were now silver and shiny again. She rose shakily to her feet, attempting to put pressure on the injured leg. It was still sore, but much better. It would be perfectly healed by morning.

Her mother walked over to the edge of the building, staring down into the dark square below. "I thought they were gone," she murmured uneasily. "I saw them go underground yesterday and figured they wouldn't be a problem. But some must have stayed aboveground again." She turned back to Asha, her eyes somber. "We must find them. And we must destroy them. Before they try something even worse."

Asha swallowed hard. She had known, somehow, that her mother would come to this conclusion. There was a reason, after all, that she was queen of their herd. She had taken vows to protect their family of dragons, no matter what. And if that meant an all-out assault on the monsters? She would do so without hesitation.

Which was great, right? Exactly what should be done. Except...

The pup.

Would he have to die with the rest?

"One of them saved me," she blurted out. "He broke me out of the trap. He's smaller than the others. Maybe a puppy? I would be dead if it weren't for him."

Her mother stared at her, horrified. "What are you saying, Asha?"

Asha turned away, feeling ashamed. She knew she should stop talking, before she angered her mother any further. But somehow the words continued to tumble from her mouth.

"I just...Maybe we spare him?" she suggested weakly. "You know, like he spared me?"

Her mother roared, startling Asha so much that she almost fell off the roof. When she looked up again, the older dragon was standing above her—tall, mighty, fierce.

Not a mother anymore, but a queen.

"He may be small now, but he will grow," she scolded her daughter. "He may be kind, but he will become cruel. They will twist his mind and turn him against us. And when he is full-grown, he will be as deadly as the rest of his kind." She paused, then, staring Asha in the eyes, added, "A monster. A true threat to dragonkind."

Asha nodded sorrowfully, lowering her head to show her submission. Her mother was right, of course. All monsters were dangerous, no matter their size. They'd been hunting dragons and killing them from day one. So many dragons had been lost in the first war. Blown to pieces by the monsters' deadly rocks. Even though there were fewer of them now, they were just as violent. Maybe even more so.

"I'm sorry. I don't mean to be harsh," her mother added, her eyes softening as she caught Asha's look. "You just scared me, that's all. To know you were down there with them, unprotected. I would never forgive myself if something happened to you, my sweet girl." She lifted her wing, placing it over Asha's back and pulling her close. Asha snuggled against her, liking the warmth of her fire-filled belly.

"I'm sorry, Mother," she murmured. "I won't make the same mistake again. I won't trust the monsters. No matter what."

But even as she said the words, her mind flashed back to the pup. His kind eyes. His gentle hands. The way he had looked at her before she'd flown away. She didn't know why. And she didn't know how. But she did know one thing:

She did trust him. And the last thing she wanted was for him to come to any harm.

CHAPTER TEN

Noah

Get up, sleepyhead. Time to bag us a beast!"

I groaned, pulling the couch cushion over my head to try to drown out my father's loud voice. Ugh. What time was it anyway? The apartment was still dark, which meant it was way too early to be awake.

Dad, however, clearly disagreed. He grabbed the cushion and tossed it across the room. I groaned again and rolled over, burying my face in the couch. Dad slapped me on the back.

"Come on, Noah. The early bird catches the dragon!"

Suddenly, I was wide awake, everything from the night before rushing back to me. We were supposed to go out this morning and find the baby dragon I'd freed from the trap. Finish the job I started.

I fought back a cringe, suddenly regretting that I'd agreed to do this. I'd wanted to make my father happy. To prove I was good enough to stay out here with him and not go underground with the others. But in reality? It was the last thing I wanted to do.

Not that I wasn't all for getting rid of dragons. I hadn't suddenly turned into my mom or someone from her group. Believe me, I'd be thrilled if I woke up one day and found out the entire race had gone extinct.

Except…there was just something about her. Something special, though I couldn't exactly put it into words. The way she had looked at me with her glowing amber eyes. The way she had trusted me to free her from the trap. She was different than the rest somehow.

And I didn't want her to die.

"Just think!" Dad continued, plopping down on the couch next to me. His grin stretched from ear to ear. Clearly, he was in a better mood than he had been the night before. But then, hunting energized my dad, like reading did for me. It was his passion. For him, there was nothing like it in the world. "If all goes well, we'll have a feast for Mom when she gets back."

I swallowed hard, suddenly feeling a little sick to my stomach. So we weren't just out to kill her—we were going to roast her up and eat her, too. And of course we were. There was no way my dad would waste perfectly good meat. This was the apocalypse after all. We took what we could get and were grateful for it.

But then, she'd been hungry, too. She could have eaten me. Instead, she'd chosen an apple.

I rose from the couch, stretching my hands over my head. Dad grinned, ruffling my hair in that way I hated. "Get dressed. I've got a surprise for you," he said.

Reluctantly, I did as I was told, retreating to the bedroom to put on a pair of jeans and a faded Marvel T-shirt from my luggage that I'd had Dad grab from the dumpster the night before. When I came back out, Dad was holding his beloved rifle in his hands. To my astonishment, he pushed it in my direction.

"Surprise," he said. "She's all yours."

I stared down at the weapon, not taking it. "You're giving me your gun?"

"Betsy here has served me well over these past few years," he explained proudly. "But now it's time to pass her down to you. I know the two of you will do great things together!" He held it out again, looking at me expectantly.

"Um...thank you?" I stammered as I clumsily took the weapon. It felt heavy and awkward in my hands. "That's...really nice of you."

My dad's face fell, just for a second. Just long enough to let me know I'd disappointed him again. But he quickly recovered, slapping me on the back, then grabbing a second gun I hadn't noticed leaning against the wall. This one was bigger—semi-automatic, by the looks of it. He must have found himself a new toy yesterday while out scouting for Mom.

"What's this one's name?" I asked, attempting to get back in his good graces.

He tapped his finger to his chin. "Not sure. Gotta get to know her a little better first. Figure out her personality." He slung the gun's strap over his shoulder, then started toward the door. "All right, then. You ready to do this?"

I wasn't. I wasn't even close. But I grudgingly nodded my head.

"Ready when you are."

We headed out the door, up the stairs, and onto the street. It was a crisp, cool day, and the sun was now peeking through the buildings from the east. I glanced up at the sky, making sure it was clear, then hurried after my dad, whose long legs had already put him several paces ahead.

He turned toward me as I caught up. "Look," he said. "Don't be nervous. I don't expect you to take down the dragon all by yourself. It takes time to learn how to recognize the soft scales—the ones able to be penetrated by a bullet. It'll take even longer to learn to aim accurately enough to hit them," he explained. "But I'd like to at least see you get a clean shot in. Then I'll come and finish it off." He smiled. "Though who knows? Maybe you'll get lucky. Or you'll turn out to be a natural, just like your old man."

"Maybe," I said, mostly because I didn't know what else to say. I tried to picture myself shooting a dragon. Making my dad proud. But instead, my mind flashed back to the baby dragon in the trap the day before. The terror in her glowing amber eyes as she struggled to get free. Would those eyes still glow when she was dead? Or would they grow dull and lifeless, the spark stolen forever?

"First we'll check your traps," Dad continued, practically skipping in his haste to get down the street. "Though my bet is that baby of yours told all of its little dragon friends what was in store for them down here." He snorted. "Which, in a way, I guess, is good. Maybe they'll know enough to steer clear of the subway entrance for the rest of the summer. So our friends down below will be safe."

"Yeah," I agreed as we reached the edge of Times Square. Sure enough, the traps I'd laid out were still there, but none of them had any dragons stuck in them. I glanced up at the sky, wondering where the baby dragon had gone after I freed her. Did she have some kind of little dragon cave to retreat to? Hopefully, if so, she'd stay there.

"It's good that it's clear out," my dad noted, misinterpreting my look. "They won't be able to play hide-and-seek behind the clouds."

"Great," I said, trying to muster up some enthusiasm without much luck.

Beside me, I heard my father sigh. "Come on, kid," he said with a groan. "Can you at least try to be excited? For my sake if nothing else?"

"I'm excited!" I said, putting a little more effort into it this time. I reminded myself I was trying to impress my dad. To prove to him I was an asset, not a burden. "So where are we going to hunt?"

He scrunched up his face, thinking. "Let's head to Central Park," he said after a moment. "All those rocks and hills there will give us some cover to hunt in."

I nodded. That made sense. Central Park used to be a huge city playground back in before times. People would go there to exercise or play sports or just spread out a picnic blanket to lie out in the sun. There were outdoor theaters for plays and restaurants for food. There was even a zoo there at one point, though the animals who'd lived there had long ago disappeared. Sometimes you could still find a random monkey or two swinging from the trees. The ones clever enough to escape the dragons.

We headed up Seventh Avenue toward the park. My dad was in a good mood again, practically dancing as he dodged burnt-out cars and other debris. We stopped at what used to be a bodega—a typical New York City convenience store—and grabbed some packaged donuts from the snack aisle. They were three years past their expiration date, but everyone knew there were enough preservatives in them to stay good practically forever. We munched on the donuts as we walked, until we were about a block away from the park.

And then...we heard a screech.

My dad stopped in his tracks, eyes shooting to the sky. His expression darkened; I knew he didn't like to get caught off guard. He grabbed me by the scruff of my neck, yanking me down behind an abandoned taxi. Then he turned to me, a grave look on his bearded face.

"Guess we're not going to make it to the park," he said wryly.

I nodded, my heart pounding in my chest as I clutched the rifle tighter in my hands. Suddenly the reality of what we were about to do hit me full force. This wasn't like going out and hunting a deer—where the worst thing that could happen was we could miss our shot and the buck would escape. We were about to go head-to-head with an actual dragon. And if we missed, we might be the ones unable to get away.

I looked up to the sky. The dragon was circling above, its wings making thrumping noises as they beat against the air. It was full-grown—about the size of a small house—and its silver scales flashed fire in the rising sunlight. I sucked in a breath. It was horrible, but also beautiful, in a sense. Majestic. Powerful.

Deadly.

Suddenly, my dad jumped up from our hiding spot. I watched, frozen in place, as he hurled a huge rock at an old rusty red van parked across the street. The rock collided with the van's windshield with a loud crashing sound.

Screech!

The dragon whirled around, eyes locking on the van. Its belly flashed bright red, as if a stovetop had been turned on. I watched with a mixture of fascination and horror as it began to dive-bomb the van, fire erupting from its mouth, setting the van ablaze. My dad ducked back down, grabbing me, holding me tight.

"Wait for it," he whispered. "Let it burn itself out."

I nodded, swallowing hard. That was one thing everyone knew about dragons. They could shoot fire, but they had a limited supply—only what they could store in their bellies. And after that was gone? They'd be forced to wait for a reload before they could release more flames. That was the time to strike if you wanted to kill one. When the dragon was the most vulnerable and the least dangerous.

The flames rained down on the van. Smoke rose into the air, making it difficult to see. Another problem with dragon hunting—it was hard to line up a good shot when your eyes were burning from the smoke.

"Okay. Come on! Now!" Dad grabbed me, dragging me to the next car over. It was farther away from the fire, so it was easier to breathe and see. I looked up to find the dragon circling low, checking out the damage. Probably trying to decide if it had gotten whatever it was that had attracted its attention. Probably hoping it was something yummy for breakfast.

"Okay," my dad said, taking my rifle to disengage the safety. "Are you ready? It's going to land in a minute. That's when you want to take your shot—not a moment before."

"Wait, I thought I was supposed to shoot a baby dragon!" I protested, my hands shaking as my dad handed the rifle back to me. "This one's full-grown!"

"Big, small, they all die the same," Dad replied with a grin. "It just takes one shot to the soft scales on their bellies—and you'll pierce their heart straight through." He ruffled my hair. "I believe in you, Noah. You can do this."

I gritted my teeth, attempting to find my nerve. My breath was coming in short gasps and I couldn't seem to wrestle it back under control. I tried to tell myself it was the smoke, but I knew that wasn't it—not really. I was simply scared to death.

It was one thing to agree to hunt a dragon back in the comfort of our apartment. Quite another to come face-to-face with one of them and find the courage to pull the trigger. *But if I didn't kill it, it would kill us*, I reminded myself. And it definitely wouldn't feel the least bit guilty about it.

Something else tugged at the back of my mind: Maybe if I shot this one, Dad would be satisfied. I would have proven myself to him without having to go after the baby.

I raised my rifle, laying it on the hood of the car. My fingers found the trigger as I lined up the creature in my sights. It was slowly coming in for a landing, just as Dad had predicted. Hitting the ground with powerful hind legs, then looking around for its prey.

"Now!" Dad whispered.

I sucked in a breath, readying myself to squeeze the trigger. But before I could manage to, the dragon whirled around in our direction. For the first time, I could see its face up close.

Its beautiful, glowing amber eyes.

Just like *hers*.

My hands started to shake.

"What are you waiting for?" Dad demanded. "Shoot. Now!"

But I couldn't shoot. I couldn't do anything.

"I'm sorry," I said, sinking back to the ground. "I... can't..."

My dad grunted, clearly annoyed. He shoved me aside, readying his own weapon. I watched helplessly as he lined up the dragon in his sights.

His finger went to the trigger and...

ROAR!

Suddenly, a second dragon rose up behind us, larger than life. It charged at my father, easily swiping the gun from his hands with long, sharp claws. My father screamed—a terrible, horrible scream that sounded as if it had come from some kind of animal. I watched in horror as he fell to the ground, his chest blooming with blood.

"Run, Noah!" he cried, recovering and diving for his weapon. "Run! I'll meet you back at the apartment."

"But, Dad—"

"Go! Now!"

I bolted, running for my life. Behind me I could hear Dad's gun go off. *Pop, pop, pop*—like popcorn over a fire. Had he killed the dragon? But then there was the other one. Two giant dragons against one measly human.

102

Should I go back to try to help? Just then, I realized that in my haste to leave, I'd left my gun behind. There was nothing I could do to help my father. And if I went back, I'd be dead, too. And so, I continued to run, tears streaming down my cheeks. This was not good. This was so not good.

Soon I stopped in an alley to try to catch my breath, the smoke making it hard to breathe. I turned back, hoping to see my dad, praying he was only steps behind.

Instead, I saw a blast of fire coming down the street toward me.

I screamed, trying to run away, but the fire had caught up to me quickly, setting my clothes aflame. I threw myself on the ground and rolled around, trying to smother the flames as hot pain scalded my skin. I could vaguely hear screams echoing in my ears. It took me a moment to realize the screams were coming from my own mouth.

Finally, I managed to put the fire out. But when I tried to move, all I could feel was pain.

Then, everything went black.

CHAPTER ELEVEN

Asha

Asha flew low, weaving through the tall buildings, anxiously searching the ground below. Her stomach growled in hunger, and she was beginning to feel a little faint. If only she could find something to eat. Anything! She'd probably eat actual bugs at this point, if she could find any.

Her mother had taken off early that morning with several other members of their herd. Their mission? To find and dispose of the monsters who had set the traps. Asha had begged to go with them, but her mother had refused, saying it was far too dangerous. That Asha was to wait on the rooftop and not get into any more trouble. That she would return soon. And with food, too.

But she hadn't returned. And Asha was beginning to get worried.

And hungry. Oh, so hungry!

And so, she had ventured out on her own. Flying through the city, searching for anything to eat. She just hoped she wouldn't run into her mother and get in trouble for disobeying.

Where was her mother anyway? Why hadn't she returned?

"Argh..."

Asha startled as her ears picked up a sudden cry from somewhere down below. It was soft, mewing, barely more than a whisper, yet somehow it seemed to echo through her mind like a scream. At first, she thought maybe she had imagined it, but then it came again. More piercing. More desperate. Was it an animal? Was it food?

Her mouth watering in anticipation, she dropped to the ground, looking around. At first, she saw nothing. Then her eyes fell upon a small, charred lump on the ground. It took her a moment to realize what it was.

One of the monsters. And he was badly burned.

She frowned, pacing the ground, wondering what she should do. Well, she knew what she *should* do—she should pluck him up and drag him up to the rooftops for dinner. Sure, he was small and a little scrawny, but there was definitely good meat left on those bones. Enough to feed both her and her mother that evening. Enough to make her stomach stop whining in pain. Meat. Real meat!

But before she could make a move, the monster let out a loud groan, rolling over limply so Asha could better see his face. Her jaw dropped, and she let out a soft gasp as recognition washed over her.

No. It couldn't be.

Except it was.

It was the pup! The same one who had saved her from the trap the day before. He was paler now and shivering badly, his blue lips opening and closing like a fish's, but it was definitely him. There could be no mistake.

And now he was the one in danger.

She paced the ground, not sure what to do. Leaving behind good meat was unheard of in these times. Her mother would be furious if she found out. But how could she just end his life like that? He could have done the same the day before to her, but he hadn't.

Instead, he'd freed her from the trap. He had saved her life.

How could she steal his away?

She gave a loud squawk, hoping she might be able to

wake him somehow. Maybe he'd run away, and she could tell everyone that she tried and failed to catch him. Or maybe she didn't have to mention it at all. It could be their little secret.

But he didn't run away—he didn't even wake up. He just lay there in agony, his eyes closed and his face twisted. He was clearly in pain. So much pain. Just like she'd been the day before in the trap. Asha's eyes roved over his body, taking in the burns on his legs. They looked serious, and she knew before long they would begin to poison his blood.

Without help, he would die. And soon.

She stared at him for a moment, indecision whirling through her. She knew what her mother would do. What any smart dragon would do. But in the end, she found she couldn't bring herself to do it. Instead, she took a cautious step forward, nudging him with her snout. When he didn't respond, she lay down next to him and began working on his burns with her tongue. She had no idea if the power of dragon saliva helped monsters as well as dragons.

But she had to try. He'd saved her life. She would return the favor.

And so she licked and licked and licked some more, careful not to miss any spots. Just as her mother had done for her—had it only been the night before? As she worked, the pup tossed and turned, his face scrunching up in torment as if lost in a nightmare. It was strange; dragons had nightmares of the monsters all the time. Asha wondered what monsters dreamed about.

Finally, his burns began to cool. Asha stopped licking, looking over her handiwork. She nodded, satisfied that his once-charred skin was now smooth and pink again. He would live. He would be fine.

And now, she should go.

But before she could move, the pup lifted his head. His brown eyes opened....

And he leapt back, shrieking with fright.

Startled, Asha also took a step back, watching him as he stumbled over some burnt debris, almost losing his balance in the process. His eyes were wide and terrified as he waved his hands over his face as if trying to ward off danger.

"Don't be afraid," she found herself saying. "I won't hurt you."

His jaw dropped. He stared at her, an incredulous look on his face. Had he understood her words? Or at least sensed their meaning somehow? She remembered how she'd been able to understand him yesterday—how she'd somehow known that he'd meant her no harm. Perhaps their connection—whatever it was—went both ways.

She watched as he took a cautious step toward her,

peering at her with a look of awe on his face. "I can hear you," he said in amazement. "How is it possible I can hear you?"

It was a good question. Especially since, Asha realized with a start, she could hear him, too. Yesterday she could only get glimpses of his feelings. But today she could hear his words in her head, as clear as if he'd been speaking a dragon's tongue. Was it because she had healed him? Had it deepened their bond somehow?

"I don't know," she said. "But I can hear you, too. Are you all right?" she added, looking at his legs. They looked clean, unburnt. Did he even realize he'd been burnt? If so, wouldn't he wonder why he wasn't anymore?

Maybe he didn't remember. Which meant he wouldn't know that she'd healed him. Probably for the best.

His face suddenly went pale. "Oh no."

"What is it?" Asha started to ask.

But he was already running in the other direction as fast as his little feet could take him. Asha wondered if she should let him go. But she found herself too curious to just fly away. Instead, she followed at a short distance, wanting to see where he was going.

He stopped in a large clearing that was still thick with blooming smoke. He looked around, his eyes wide and frightened as they took in the scene. Asha watched as he peered under a hunk of metal, then scratched his head.

"Where did he go?" he whispered to himself. "Did he escape?"

Asha crept a little closer. "Who?"

He startled at her voice, then grabbed something off the ground. Asha recoiled, horrified, as she realized it was one of those rock sticks the monsters always used. The ones powerful enough to take down a dragon in a single blow. Would he turn it on her? She'd just saved his life! Had she made a huge mistake?

He seemed to catch the fear on her face. His cheeks colored, and he dropped the rock stick back on the ground. "Sorry," he mumbled. "I thought...never mind."

"Who are you looking for?" Asha asked.

"My father," he told her. "I left him here. He was..." He trailed off, biting his lower lip. "I think he was in trouble," he said, after a pause. "But I don't know..."

"Do you want me to look for him?" Asha found herself asking. "I can fly around the area—see if I can spot him."

The pup stared at her, incredulous. "You'd do that?"

"Sure. I mean, why not?" She shrugged her little shoulders.

Actually, there were a thousand reasons why she shouldn't be helping this pup. But she pushed them out of her head. He was upset. He needed to find his herd.

If he found his herd, he'd be safe and she could fly away, knowing he'd be okay.

Because she *wanted* him to be okay, she realized. Though she had no idea why she suddenly cared. But she did. For some reason, she definitely did.

She unfolded her wings, giving a little test flap. Then she pushed off into the air, rising above the buildings. She could feel the pup watch her from below as she started to circle the area, looking for signs of movement. But everything seemed perfectly still. At last, she gave up and dropped back in for a landing.

"Sorry," she said. "I didn't see anything."

The pup sighed, leaning against a charred wall. "Thanks for trying," he said. Then he shook his head. "I still can't believe this is happening," he added with a small laugh. "That I'm talking to a dragon. It's like something out of a fantasy novel."

Asha cocked her head. "A what?"

The pup shrugged. "Sorry. Of course you wouldn't know what that is." He paused, then added, "Do you know what reading is?"

Asha shook her head, not familiar with the word. "I don't think so."

"It's like...stories. But someone wrote them down on paper. So everyone can enjoy them. I have a ton of books back at the hotel...." He trailed off. "Oh my gosh, I can't believe I'm talking to a dragon about reading."

Asha couldn't believe she was talking to a monster about...well, anything. What would her mother say if she saw her now? Just hanging out, chatting away...

Her mother...

Asha glanced up at the sky. "I'm sorry, but I need to go," she said reluctantly. "My mother will be worried if she finds out I'm gone...."

She clamped her mouth shut, a little horrified, as something suddenly occurred to her. She'd been so concerned with the pup's burns, she hadn't thought to ask why he'd been burned. Or, more importantly, who he'd been burned by.

What if this was her mother's work?

What if she'd just undone it?

"I have to go," she said again, uneasiness rising inside of her. "And you should go, too. It's not safe out here for a monster."

"A what?" His eyes widened. "What did you just call me?"

"A...monster?" Asha felt her cheeks heat up. Maybe she shouldn't have said that. He might think it rude.

Instead, he burst out laughing. "A monster," he repeated. "That's kind of funny."

Asha frowned. "Why is that funny?"

"Because..." He stopped laughing. "That's exactly what we call you."

Asha felt indignant. "Why would you call us monsters?"

"Uh, maybe because you destroyed our entire world?" The pup shrugged. "I mean, not you personally, maybe. But your fellow dragonkind. You rose up and started burning it all down."

Asha scrunched up her face, confused. "But that's not how it happened!" she protested, feeling rather offended at the accusation. "You monsters hunted us. You slaughtered us with your rock sticks. I mean, maybe not you personally," she added, echoing his words. "But your herd."

"Rock sticks?" The pup frowned. "Do you mean guns?" He picked up the rock stick he'd dropped and held it out to her. She nodded.

"Yes. Guns," she confirmed. "They use them to kill the dragons."

"Because the dragons tried to kill us first," he countered, without missing a beat.

Asha huffed, smoke puffing out from her nostrils. That was definitely not how it had happened. Right? At least that wasn't how the elders of her herd had explained it to her. This pup was very confusing. And she probably shouldn't be talking to him in the first place. If the elders caught her—if her mother saw her...

"I'm sorry, I've really got to go," she said. "I hope you find your father."

"Thank you," he replied, glancing around the square again, as if the man would magically appear. Thankfully, however, he did not, for Asha was not certain what he would do if he saw his son talking to a dragon. She had an idea it would be similar to what her mother would do if she caught her conversing with a human. The pup paused, then added, "I'm Noah, by the way."

For a moment, Asha didn't understand. Then it hit her—he was giving her his name. Monsters gave themselves names, like dragons did? She hadn't even considered this. But she supposed it made sense.

"Nice to meet you, Noah," she said, feeling a little awkward. "I'm Asha."

"Asha," Noah repeated, as if tasting the name with his tongue. "I like it. It fits. Asha, the apple lover."

Asha felt a smile creep to her mouth. She dipped her head in farewell, then pushed off on her hind legs, springing into the sky. She could feel Noah watching as she flapped her wings and gained altitude. *He was nice*, she thought. So different than the other monsters, with their rock sticks—guns. She was glad she'd been able to help him.

Maybe someday she'd see him again.

Maybe he'd have more apples.

Suddenly, a large shape swooped down in front of her. For a second, she thought it was her mother and she began to smile in relief. But that smile faded quickly when she realized it was actually her aunt who'd approached her, a solemn look on her silver-scaled snout.

"Asha," her aunt said. "There you are. We've been so worried."

Asha blushed. "I'm sorry! I didn't mean to take off like that. I was just hungry and—"

"Come with me, child," her aunt said, not looking her in the eye. She turned and started to fly away, her powerful wings thrusting her forward. Asha, with her much smaller wings, had to struggle to keep up, while uneasiness rose inside of her. Her aunt was acting strange. But why? And where was her mother? Why wasn't she with her aunt as she had been that morning?

Was her mother all right? Surely, she was. After all, she was a mighty queen. No monster could take her down.

Monsters...

That's exactly what we call you.

CHAPTER TWELVE

Noah

I watched as Asha disappeared, shaking my head in a mixture of amazement and disbelief. Seriously, what had just happened? Had I really had an actual conversation with an actual dragon? How wild was that? And she'd been nice, too. Even if she did have some twisted ideas about humans.

You monsters hunted us. You slaughtered us with your rock sticks.

"Only 'cause the dragons struck first," I muttered under my breath, looking down at my own "rock stick," then up at the burnt-out square. I saw the van the dragon had set fire to, still smoldering a little. The rusty old cars we had ducked behind.

But still no sign of my dad.

I swallowed hard, my mind racing. I wasn't sure whether I should be relieved that I couldn't find my father or even more frightened by his disappearance. After all, like humans, dragons did not tend to waste good meat. But then Dad could have escaped, right? Like I had. He was a survivor, after all. He knew dragons better than anyone. There was no way he'd allow himself to be beaten by some beast.

Two beasts, my mind nagged. *Two giant beasts*.

I tried to think back to what had happened, but my brain felt all foggy and thick. I knew there had been two dragons. I knew Dad had told me to run. Which I had, right? But then what? Had I fallen? Hit my head? For a moment, my mind flashed back to a horrible vision of dragon fire blasting down the street. A searing pain up and down my legs as I tried to drop and roll. The feeling that this was it—that I was about to die.

I shook my head, feeling a little dizzy as I tried to remember more, but there was nothing else. Only blackness. Until I woke up and saw Asha. How long had I been out? And what had happened while I was?

I looked down at my legs. It was then that I realized

the bottoms of my pants were missing. The blackened fringe at the ends made it look as if they had been burned away. But my actual legs looked completely fine. No red spots, no blisters, not even a stain of black ash, which didn't make any sense. No way would my pants shield me from dragon fire.

This was too weird. Way too weird.

Then I realized something else. When I'd picked up my gun, back when Asha was still here, I hadn't seen my dad's among the rubble. And another look around confirmed it—my dad's fancy new rifle was nowhere in sight. While a dragon could have taken a body away, it wouldn't have also scooped up a weapon. Hope rose within me. Just a little, but it was enough.

I sucked in a breath, trying not to cough as the smoky air filled my lungs. Then I grabbed my own gun, just in case, and headed down the street. My dad had told me to go back to the apartment. That he'd meet me there. Perhaps he had already arrived and was waiting for me. Perhaps he was as worried about me as I was about him.

As I walked down Seventh Avenue, I kept an eye to the sky and my body close to the buildings in an attempt to avoid being seen from above. While I did have a gun now, I had basically proven that I was unable to effectively use it. In fact, if I had just shot the dragon instead of wimping out, this whole thing might have turned out differently. Dad could have taken out the second dragon, piece of cake.

I felt a lump form in my throat. What if something had happened to him? It would be all my fault. After all, he'd only been out there in the first place to teach me a lesson. He'd put himself in danger to protect me. Because that's what you did for people you loved.

Instead, I'd run away.

"Please be okay," I whispered to myself. "Please, please be okay."

"Dad!"

I burst into the basement apartment, out of breath from sprinting so many blocks. I leaned over, hands on my knees, trying to catch my breath. Then I looked up, hoping to see my father standing there, a big smile on his bearded face.

You made it home! I imagined him saying. *That's my boy!*

But the apartment was empty. My father was nowhere to be found. The place looked exactly how we'd left it that morning. No one had been here since.

But that doesn't mean anything, I scolded myself. *He might have gotten stuck somewhere, hiding out until the dragons left. Or maybe he went back out to look for me when he came home and didn't find me here. Maybe he even went up to get Mom. So she'd be here when I got back.*

But the thoughts didn't reassure me, and I paced the apartment for a while, up and down the small living room, unable to slow my racing heartbeat. Every few seconds I'd look at the door, imagining it opening. Imagining my dad stepping inside.

But it remained closed. Dad did not appear.

My stomach growled. I hadn't eaten anything but a stale donut all day. I forced myself to walk over to the kitchen area, rummaging through the cabinets for something to cook for dinner. I figured I could pass the time by getting everything ready, and then when Dad did show up, we could eat. He'd probably be starving by then, and he'd be grateful to have a nice, warm meal waiting for him.

I found a can of beans and started heating them on the old portable gas burner Dad had set up on the counter, next to the nonworking stove. Maybe if we ended up staying here for the summer, we could rig up a generator and actually cook and read like we did at the hotel. Once Mom was back, we'd probably be doing a lot of reading. In fact, maybe I could even get her to read to me out loud—I used to love when she did that back in the bunker. We'd read all seven Harry Potter books and the complete Lord of the Rings series. I'd especially loved the part about Smaug, the evil dragon under the mountain in *The Hobbit*. It was funny; in books, dragons were always obsessed with treasure. I wasn't sure the real-life ones cared about anything but food.

Speaking of reading...I walked over to the couch and picked up my book, then sat down to read. But I found I couldn't concentrate. Instead, I kept glancing up at the door every few minutes, certain I'd heard a sound outside.

The beans were boiling, and I reluctantly took them off the stove. A few minutes later I gave in and ate my share.

An hour later, I went back and ate what I'd left for Dad.

Because he still hadn't come back.

And I was beginning to worry...big-time.

CHAPTER THIRTEEN

Asha

Asha followed her aunt through the familiar forest of metal and steel, worry still churning in her gut. What was going on here? Why did her aunt seem so concerned? She'd tried asking her several times what was wrong, but the older dragon didn't answer, acting as if the wind was drowning out Asha's words. But Asha saw her ears prick ever so slightly at each question. She knew her aunt had heard her just fine and was purposely choosing not to answer. Which made Asha worry even more.

They finally alighted in a large field in the center of the city. It was a place that had always made Asha curious. Why was it here, in the middle of everything—this giant patch of green grass and trees? The monsters had all but covered the rest of their land with rock and metal and steel. But here, it was as if some kind of magic had stopped them in their tracks—forcing them to leave the land as nature had intended it.

No dragons lived here, of course. It was far too open, too unprotected from those who might wish to do them harm. But it was also about the only place in their territory large enough for all the dragons of their herd to gather together at one time.

And they had all gathered today, Asha noted with rising concern, as she and her aunt settled down onto the grassy ground below. In fact, it looked like the entire herd was standing in the field as if waiting for something to happen. Big dragons, small dragons, babies. All standing together, solemn and still. Asha swallowed hard, heart thrumming in her chest. Because there was one dragon that was clearly not present among the others.

Her mother.

After landing, she took a cautious step forward, toward the group, realizing suddenly that all eyes were on her. Eyes filled with what looked like sorrow—or worse, pity. Asha stopped in her tracks, scared and confused. Half of her just wanted to take off again, to fly away and refuse to listen. Because she was pretty sure, at this point, that she didn't want to hear what they had to say.

But you couldn't run away from the truth. That was something her mother had taught her long ago. You could try, but it would always catch up with you. Better to face it head-on. Then you could find a way to deal with it.

So Asha stood firm, squaring her shoulders. Lifting her head and meeting their eyes with her own. Desperately attempting to act like the daughter of a queen, even as her body betrayed her with uneasy shivers.

It was then that her uncle stepped out from the herd. He turned to address her, his amber eyes large and solemn. "Hello, little one," he said. "We were worried about you. It is good to see you safe."

"What's going on?" Asha demanded, her voice cracking on the words. She couldn't stand the suspense any longer. "Where is my mother?"

The dragons murmured among themselves, causing her heart rate to spike.

"Tell me!" she demanded. "I have a right to know!"

"I am sorry," her uncle said, lowering his head. "Your mother was killed in the line of duty, defending her herd. She was slaughtered by two of the monsters."

What? Asha shrank back in horror. "No!" she cried, the denial tumbling from her mouth before she had a chance to stop it. "That can't be true! My mother is the best fighter we have! She would never allow herself to be killed by any of them! She's probably just missing. In fact, maybe she's still out hunting and—"

"I was there, Princess," interrupted Tolkyn. The large, old dragon stepped forward, giving Asha a steely look. He was her mother's second-in-command and the biggest and toughest in the entire herd. "We were hunting the monsters together. I had stopped for a moment—I had a piece of glass stuck in my paw. When I caught up to your mother again, she was under attack." He paused, hanging his head. "I did my best to save her. But it was too late. The monster's rock stick had struck a soft scale and pierced her heart. I tried to bring her to see you—her last wish was to talk to you one more time. But when we arrived at your roost, you were nowhere to be found. She died on that rooftop moments later. Her last words were of you." He steadied his gaze on Asha. "She loved you dearly, my princess."

Asha felt tears well in her eyes, but she refused to let them fall. Instead, she allowed anger to rise inside of her, displacing her grief and fear. "You had a duty to protect her!" she lashed out at Tolkyn. "How could you let her die?" Even as she said the words, they didn't feel real. She had just seen her mother that morning. Felt her leathery wing cuddling her close. Her warm snout kissing the top of her head.

Could she really be gone?

"I tried, Princess," Tolkyn insisted, looking close to tears himself, which was strange to see in a huge dragon warrior like him. Someone so brave and strong. "I was able to take out one of them," he added. "Unfortunately, the other—the smaller pup—ran away before I could get to him. I tried to blast him with my fire, but I don't know if I managed to wound him. I couldn't leave your mother to go track him down. At the time, I believed she still had a chance to survive."

Asha's heart stuttered in her chest. "Smaller pup?" she repeated hesitantly, a sickening feeling worming through her stomach. No. It couldn't be. Could it?

"Yes. A father and son, perhaps," Tolkyn explained. He sighed deeply. "I am sorry, Princess. I have failed in my duty to protect our queen. I ask you now to strip me of my title and duties. I have proven myself unworthy to serve the herd."

He kept talking, but Asha could no longer listen. Her head was spinning too fast, her mind flashing back to the scene earlier that day. To little Noah, lying on the ground, terribly burned. She'd felt so bad for him. He'd looked to be in so much pain. Just as she'd been, struggling in that trap when he'd freed her.

But was Noah an innocent victim?

Or had he helped kill her mother?

Pain and confusion rose within Asha, threatening to consume her. No. Noah had been so kind to her! He'd saved her life. There was no way he could do such a thing. There had to be some mistake.

He wouldn't have hurt her mother. He couldn't have!

But what if he had? What if he was just like the others, as her mother had tried to warn her about?

She bowed her head, confusion and guilt running rampant through her. Oh, why hadn't she stayed in the roost? At least then she could have been there to see her mother one last time.

Instead, she'd let her die alone.

"I know you're grieving, Princess," her uncle broke in. "And we want to give you all the time you need. However, there is a pressing matter that must be discussed."

"What is it?" Asha asked dully, not really caring. What did it matter? What did anything matter now that her mother was dead? The tears slipped from her eyes, and she didn't bother to try to stop them this time.

"As you know, your mother was our queen. Our leader. And as her only daughter, you are her chosen successor."

Oh. That. She'd known this, of course, on some level. But in her grief over her mother's death, she hadn't put it all together. To realize what had to come next.

"But...I can't be queen!" she stammered, hardly able

to form the words. "I'm not...old enough," she added weakly. Though what she really wanted to say was she wasn't smart enough. Brave enough. Fierce enough. All the things that made her mother a good leader.

All the things that Asha was not.

"I agree that the timing is not optimal," her aunt replied. "Yet there is no one else."

"And what if I don't want to be queen?"

"You *are* queen. What you want plays no part in that truth," her uncle replied, a little sharply. Several other dragons snorted in agreement. Suddenly Asha felt childish, ashamed. Her mother would not have approved of her behavior.

Her aunt gently nudged Asha's head with her snout. "Do not fret, dear one. And remember, you are not alone. We will be here for you, every step of the way. We will help you in any way we can."

Asha nodded slowly. "I understand," she forced herself to say. "And I will accept my role. I will do my best to serve the herd as my mother did."

Her mother, who had been so wise and strong and good. Asha was just a child. How was she supposed to make decisions for the herd?

Especially when she'd made such poor decisions for herself.

But she couldn't mention that to them. They were

looking to her to be their leader. They needed someone they could trust.

"That is good to hear, my queen," her uncle said with a small smile. "And we will hold a proper coronation in due time. However, right now, we need your command."

"My...command?" Asha repeated, confused.

Tolkyn stepped forward. "Say the word, my queen, and we will avenge these monsters. We will find this young pup and make him pay for what he did to your mother."

Asha gulped. Find...Noah. They wanted to kill Noah.

"But what if he wasn't a part of it?" she cried before she could think the words through. "What if he was just in the wrong place at the wrong time?" She knew she was grasping at reeds in the grass. But the alternative—to believe gentle Noah, who had saved her life, was a murderer...

She felt the dragons staring at her in disbelief, and she cringed inwardly. If they only knew—if they ever found out she'd saved a monster's life—well, they would certainly not want her to be their queen. In fact, they might see her to be as guilty as they believed him to be.

"It does not matter whether he was the one who pulled the trigger," her uncle declared. "He was there. That makes him as guilty as the other."

"Search your heart," her aunt added. "You know this is what your mother would have wanted."

Asha hung her head. Of course, her aunt was right. If Asha gave Noah mercy now, she'd lose the respect of the herd. She'd never become the strong queen her mother had been. And without a strong queen, the herd would perish.

One monster's life to save an entire herd of dragons.

It was the only way.

"Very well," she declared, lifting her chin. "I give you permission to hunt this monster down. But do not kill him. Instead, bring him to me." She swallowed hard. "I will deal with him myself."

CHAPTER FOURTEEN

Noah

I didn't sleep well that night. I tossed and turned, every little sound making my heart race and my whole body tremble with fear. Even when I did finally collapse into a shallow sleep, I was tormented by terrible nightmares. Dreams of dragons and Dad and destruction.

When the sun finally peered in through the small, high windows the next morning, I woke to find the apartment still empty. The front door still closed, Dad still not back. And as I wandered through the kitchen like a ghost, preparing breakfast, I started to accept the truth. I wasn't stupid. I wasn't naive. He'd battled two giant dragons. It was unlikely he'd won.

It was unlikely I'd ever see him again.

I thought about crying, but the tears refused to come. I just felt empty inside. Hollow. I tried to eat my canned beans, but I was too nauseated, and eventually I shoved them away. I tried to think about what I was going to do, how I'd survive out here if Dad didn't come back. But my mind was too tormented to form any kind of plan. Instead, it chose to flash back to our days in the bunker. Dad teasing me about reading, telling me I should come do a workout with him instead. Mom, being goofy and silly and all up in my space, even as I begged to be left alone. Back then, in the tight confines of our living quarters, all I'd wanted was an escape from them.

What I wouldn't give to have them in my face now.

To have our triangle back.

Me.

Dad.

Mom.

My head shot up. Mom! Oh my gosh, Mom!

In all my grief, I'd almost forgotten one important fact. That Mom was still out there somewhere in the city. Alive. Okay. Dad had seen her just yesterday. She was at a place called Columbia University. Along with her dragon-worshipping cult.

I could go to her. I could find her. I didn't have to be alone.

But does she want you there? A voice inside me nagged. *She left you, remember? Maybe she doesn't want to see you anymore.*

No. I shook the voice away. This was Mom. I didn't know why she left—maybe she was sick like Dad said. But that didn't mean she didn't still love me. That didn't mean she wouldn't take me in if I needed her to. Sure, I wasn't super thrilled about the idea of meeting a bunch of dragon huggers.

But it beat being alone.

My mind made up, I started rummaging through the apartment, looking for supplies. I wasn't sure exactly where Columbia was, but I was pretty positive it was a far walk. I needed to make sure I had enough food and water for the trip. I stuffed everything into the military-issue knapsack I'd once used for the bear traps, then wrote my dad a note, just in case he returned.

I'm okay. I went to find Mom.

I set the note on the table, then slung the bag over my shoulder and headed out the door, taking one last look at the empty apartment before I left. Would I ever see it again? I wasn't sure.

It didn't matter, though. It was just some random building, not a home. A home was where family was. And one way or another, I was going to find that again.

Discovering the location of Columbia University was easier than I thought it would be. I just walked into an old tourist shop in Times Square and grabbed a crumbling New York City map that had survived the past five years. Then I spread the map out on the cracked glass counter and traced the roads with my fingers until I found a pretty straightforward path. All the way to 116th Street.

Which, unfortunately, wasn't close. In fact, it was almost four miles away. Back before, this wouldn't have been a problem. The map noted a subway route that practically took you to the college's front gates. Unfortunately, there were no more subways. Or running taxis. Or cars. I could go by bicycle, but it was dangerous with all the debris in the road. If I fell and got hurt, there would be no one to come help me. I would be a sitting duck for a dragon.

Which left me no choice but to walk the entire way.

I headed up Broadway, which seemed to be the most direct route. I stayed close to the buildings, keeping an eye on the sky again. Every time I caught a glimpse of a shadow above or heard a screeching cry, I would duck into a store or alleyway to hide and wait for them to leave.

Of course, this made things take even longer. In fact, at one point I had to wait almost an hour inside an old gym as the dragons circled outside. As I forced myself to lift weights to stay busy and pass the time, I wondered if they were randomly flying around or purposely looking for us—for me. Wanting to seek revenge on the humans who had shot them from the sky. Before now, I had assumed dragons were just like other animal predators, with simple instincts driving them to hunt and eat whatever they could—with little thought behind their actions. But after meeting Asha, I was no longer sure. And her words had stuck in my brain.

You monsters hunted us. You slaughtered us with your rock sticks.

At the time, I'd argued that dragons had struck first. But that hadn't been the case yesterday—my dad had purposely attracted the attention of the dragon to lure it into his sights. It hadn't even been the same dragon we'd been looking for. Just a random creature out and about, in the wrong place at the wrong time.

I shook my head. I couldn't think about that now. It was too distracting, and I had to be paying attention if I wanted to stay alive long enough to reach Mom.

Once I'd determined the coast was clear, I kept moving up Broadway, ducking behind cars, scrambling over debris. I tried to make it like a video game, imagining myself as the main character attempting to make it through a level without losing all my hit points. Which was actually kind of fun, and before I knew it, I was only twelve blocks away from the university.

But then I heard the dragons again. Argh. I looked longingly up the street.

So close, yet so far.

Sighing, I ducked into an old, abandoned restaurant with a ripped yellow awning hanging haphazardly above a patio full of tipped over tables and chairs. The sign told me it had been called *Serafina* in before times, and it looked as if it had been quite fancy—maybe French cuisine? My stomach growled. What I wouldn't give for a croissant right about now.

Once inside, I looked around the darkened restaurant. A few tables were still set, complete with fancy china plates, cloth napkins, and silverware. As if they expected customers any minute now. Except for the fact that the napkins were moth-eaten and the china plates were covered in rat droppings.

"Can I interest you in some fine cockroach?" I joked to an empty table, remembering the games Maya and I used to play when out scavenging. "How about some lovely—"

I stopped short when I caught a flicker of movement out of the corner of my eye. I whirled around just in time to see two figures standing over by what used to be the kitchen. Two human figures. Shocked, I stumbled backward, knocking over one of the china plates. It went crashing to the ground, shattering on impact. Outside, a dragon screeched. Hopefully I hadn't alerted it to my presence.

Our presence.

A man and a woman approached me, grinning widely. The woman was missing quite a few teeth. The man had a long handlebar mustache and a scraggly beard. They were both dressed in ratty clothes that had clearly seen better days and smelled as if they hadn't bathed in the river for months—or longer.

I gulped. It had been so long since I'd seen other humans outside our group, I wasn't sure how to act. We knew some were out there, obviously. Our group was certainly not the only one who took shelter in the city when things had gone bad. According to Mike, some of the others were just regular people, like us, trying to survive an apocalypse one day at a time. But others? Well, they had gone a bit...feral from the isolation. And there was no telling what they would do.

If you ever see anyone, run, Dad would say. *It's not worth taking the chance.*

But I couldn't run now. Not with the dragons outside.

"Hey! Kid! Where did you come from?" asked the woman with the missing teeth. Her voice was gruff, gravely, as if she was chewing on rocks. A nervous shiver rippled through me. This felt wrong somehow. Really wrong.

"Um, just passing through," I squeaked, not sure what to say. I backed up a bit, till my body was flush with the door. My heart pounded in my chest. I was trapped. Between them and the dragons.

"C'mere, boy," called Mr. Mustache. "Let me get a good look at'cha."

"Don't worry," added Mrs. Snaggletooth. "We don't bite."

They laughed heartily at this, as if it were some great joke—one I wasn't in on. My body broke out in a cold sweat, and my hands were shaking violently. There was something off about them. A weird glint in their eyes. They looked...hungry.

Really hungry.

"L-look, I'm sorry to barge into your space," I stammered. "I just...I needed to get away from the dragons outside. I'll be gone in a second."

"What's your hurry?" asked Mr. Mustache. "We don't get many visitors here. Why don't you stay awhile?"

"Stay for dinner," his female friend added a little too cheerfully, and the two of them started to crack up again. My throat went dry. Something about the way she said *dinner*... I shoved my trembling hands behind my back, hoping I didn't look as scared as I was starting to feel.

"Sorry. I really need to go," I apologized, my hand grabbing for the doorknob. But a dragon's sudden screech made me rethink that idea, and I yanked my hand away.

No. I couldn't go.

But I couldn't stay, either.

The man lunged at me. I screamed and leapt backward, managing to crash through the door and tumble outside, onto the sidewalk. As I scrambled to my feet, I glanced up at the sky, hoping the dragon had flown away. But no, there it was, still flying above in large circles.

It looked hungry, too.

"Are you crazy?" cried Mr. Mustache from behind the door. "What are you doing?"

"You're going to get yourself killed!" added Mrs. Snaggletooth. "Get back in here!"

But I couldn't. Because, I realized, I didn't trust them any more than the dragon. Instead, my eyes darted around the street, looking for some other building to enter. Some safe place to hide. But everything looked boarded up, locked up tight. The dragon let out a loud cry above me, and I realized it was starting to come in for a landing. I had to get out of there. Now.

But I had no place to go.

I sucked in a breath, then crossed the road, diving behind a burnt-out car. I tried the door, but it was locked. A large shadow crossed above me, blocking out the sun for a moment. The dragon was getting closer. Had it seen me yet? If not, it would soon.

I dashed down the street as fast as my legs could take me. I thought back to Maya and my dragon escape just days before. We'd managed to get away from the dragon then—maybe I could do it again. If I could just find a place to get inside. I tried a few more doors, hoping for something unlocked, but came up empty. It was just me and open sky.

And a huge dragon coming in for a landing.

I gasped as the creature dropped down in front of me, landing only a few feet away. Its amber eyes locked on me and it snorted loudly, a plume of smoke blooming from its massive nostrils and steaming my skin. Desperate, I tried to back away but only managed to smack into a brick wall. There was nowhere left to go. I closed my eyes, unable to look. Was this it? Was this really—

"Sonja! Down girl! It's just a kid!"

My eyes flew open. To my shock, there were now two people flanking the dragon—though thankfully not the same ones from the restaurant. They were both dressed in clean clothes and looked as if they ate regularly. One of them was about my dad's age, with a beard and a balding head, wearing a red-and-white plaid shirt and a pair of slouchy jeans.

And the other was... Javier?

I gaped as our tech guy—the one who had been carried away by a dragon just days before—casually walked up to the deadly creature in front of me and gave her a scolding tap on the snout. The dragon immediately bowed its head, and if I didn't know any better I'd say it looked almost sheepish. Like it knew it had done something wrong.

"Javier?" I croaked, my voice barely audible. "Is that really you?"

He turned, surprise and disbelief clear on his face. "Noah?" he asked, incredulous. "What are you doing out here?"

"You know this boy?" the second man asked, giving me a curious once-over. "Is he one of ours?"

"No. But his mother is," Javier replied. "He's Diana's kid." He gave him a knowing look. "You remember."

"Oh!" The man's eyebrows shot up. I frowned, confused. What was he remembering?

And did he know my mom?

"Do you know where my mother is?" I blurted out, hope now rising inside of me. I still couldn't believe Javier was standing there in front of me—and with a dragon. I thought back to that moment in Times Square. Was this the same dragon that had taken him away?

How was any of this possible?

The balding man reached into his pocket and pulled out a walkie-talkie. He pressed the side button and spoke into the device. "Echo One to Echo Three. Please inform Diana I need her to meet me down at the fire station on One Hundred and Thirteenth. Immediately."

"Ten-four. I'll send her down," came the crackling reply.

The man slipped the walkie back into his pocket, then nodded at me. "Come on, kid," he said. "Let's get you to your mom."

CHAPTER FIFTEEN

Noah

Mom!"

About fifteen minutes later, I was hurtling toward my mother, throwing myself at her with so much force I nearly knocked her over. But she steadied herself, then grabbed me in her arms, squeezing me back just as tight. It was funny; I'd almost forgotten what a good hugger she was. Unlike Dad, who always felt a little stiff, when Mom hugged you, she didn't hold anything back. And you just felt so warm and safe in her arms.

Like everything was going to be okay.

"Noah!" she cried, pulling out of the hug and staring at me, incredulous. She turned to Javier and the other man, who had introduced himself as David. "Where did you find him?"

"Oh, just wandering down One Hundred and Fifth Street," David replied. "I think Sonja here scared the snot out of him." He gave his dragon a disapproving look. The creature bowed her head, acting ashamed again. Was she like his pet or something?

Suddenly, it dawned on me. Was this guy one of Mom's dragon sympathizers? But then, why was Javier with him? He should be dead.

I was so confused it wasn't funny.

David gave Mom a salute. "If you guys are good, I need to keep training Javier with Sonja. We've got a lot of ground to cover today."

"That's fine," Mom said, smiling at him. "I'm going to take Noah straight back to campus as soon as I catch him up on some things." She turned to Javier. "Good luck on the training."

"Thanks," Javier said. He waved to me. "Come find me once you're settled. I've got quite a story to tell you. I'm guessing you have a good one for me, too."

I nodded wordlessly, not trusting myself to speak. I wanted to thank him for saving my life back in Times Square, but somehow the words wouldn't come. I watched as David playfully patted the dragon on her rear flank, beckoning her to follow him. Soon the three of them had disappeared, leaving Mom and me in the big empty garage that had once held fire trucks.

I gave a low whistle. "Wow. I can't believe Javier is alive. I mean, he got taken by a dragon when he was trying to save me. I saw it happen!"

"I know...." Mom bit her lower lip. "It's kind of a long story. But we're glad to have him here. He's going to be quite the asset, with all his tech experience." Her expression went grave. "Anyway, enough about him. Let's talk about you. What are you *doing* here? It's not that I'm not happy to see you. It's just...why aren't you belowground with the others?"

I shrugged guiltily. "I snuck away before they went underground. I wanted to help Dad look for you."

Her face darkened for a moment when I mentioned my father, as if a cloud had passed over the sun. Clearly I had struck a nerve. "Typical," she muttered under her breath. "He never said a word about you being up here."

"What?" I cocked my head in confusion. "Who didn't say a word? Dad?" I raised my eyebrows, a sudden spark of hope bursting inside me. "Wait, have you seen Dad?"

Mom sighed. She gestured to a nearby bench. "Sit down, Noah," she said.

I reluctantly obeyed, a shimmer of unease worming through me. Mom sat down next to me, reaching out to take my hands in her own. Her warm fingers stroked my icy palms, but it did nothing to thaw the chill seeping into my bones. She looked so serious. I had a feeling that whatever she was about to say couldn't be good.

"They found your father yesterday," Mom said, speaking slowly, carefully. As if she didn't want to use the wrong words. "He was wandering the streets in a daze, badly burned—from a dragon fight, I guess. In fact, at first I didn't even recognize him, he was so beat up." She pursed her lips. "Honestly, he's lucky to be alive."

"But he *is* alive? He's okay?" I asked excitedly, tears of relief slipping from my eyes. "When he didn't come back to the apartment, I thought he was…" I couldn't finish my sentence.

Mom reached up, gently swiping my tears away with her thumbs. She gave me a rueful smile. "He's alive," she confirmed. "But, well, it's too soon to know if he's okay. He suffered severe burns on a good portion of his body. Thankfully we've got a burn specialist at the hospital who's taking care of him. Your dad is in good hands."

"A burn specialist? Like an actual doctor?"

She nodded. "Yes, Noah. Like an actual doctor. Turns out there are still a few of them left in the world."

And evidently, they'd all joined a dragon-worshipping cult, I thought bitterly.

A swelling of anger rose inside of me. I'd been so happy to see Mom, I had almost forgotten the reason why we were out here, risking our lives, looking for her in the first place. If it hadn't been for her leaving the hotel, we'd all be safe, down below with the others. Dad wouldn't be fighting for his life. He wouldn't need some stupid doctor.

"Why did you leave us?" I demanded before I could stop myself. "Why did you have to go join some stupid cult?"

"A cult?" Her eyebrows shot up in surprise, then she shook her head. "Is that what your father told you, Noah? That I joined a cult?"

I shifted in my seat, feeling awkward. "He said you joined a dragon-worshipping cult," I admitted, suddenly not really wanting to talk about it. But still, it was like this big elephant in the room. She'd left us. Without a word. She had to know that wasn't cool.

She sighed sadly. "That sounds like something your father would say," she remarked. Then she gave me a stern look. "But I can assure you, Noah, we're not a cult. And we don't worship dragons—that's just ridiculous."

"But you like them, or whatever," I barreled on, unable to stop myself. "And you evidently hang out with them, too," I added, thinking about David and Javier and their big fiery friend. "They're like your pets or whatever."

"Not pets," Mom said. "More like...partners."

I stared at her. "How can you partner with a dragon? They're evil!"

"They're *animals*," Mom corrected. "They're not evil. Or bad. Or good even. They're just trying to survive on this earth, same as we are. If we treat them like enemies— like our government did when they first appeared—of course they're going to defend themselves. But if we treat them with the respect they deserve, they can become allies. We can conceivably live in peace with one another. Help each other out, even. Can you imagine what that would mean, Noah? No more hiding underground. No more living in fear."

I swallowed hard, my mind spinning. Partnering with a dragon? A couple days ago, I would have scoffed at the idea. But that was before I'd met Asha.

Asha, with her kind eyes. Who'd rather eat an apple than a person.

Who had tried to help me find Dad.

Who had told me her name.

But Asha was just one dragon, I reminded myself. Not to mention just a baby. And a few acts of kindness and mercy didn't exactly erase the entire history. Dragons had killed my grandparents, my friends, my teachers. Everyone I ever cared about, besides my parents. That was a fact, plain and simple. I mean, how could someone be aware of all they'd done and just want to wave it away like it was no big deal? To give these creatures—who had hunted us and destroyed our world—some kind of second chance?

No. Asha might be a good dragon, but her actions didn't excuse the rest of her kind.

"Look," Mom said. "We can talk more about this later. In fact, there's a lot you need to know. But right now I think it'd be a good idea to take you to your father. Maybe it'll do him good to see you. Lift his spirits. Give him something to fight for."

I nodded slowly, all thoughts of dragons fleeing my head as I remembered my dad. Here I was, blaming Mom for everything that had happened to him. But, the truth was, if I hadn't freed Asha from the trap, we'd never have been out there hunting her in the first place. And if I had just pulled the trigger on that dragon, instead of acting like a coward, I might have been able to take out the first dragon before the second arrived. And Dad wouldn't have been overwhelmed.

He wouldn't be in the hospital right now, fighting for his life.

A blanket of shame seemed to fall on my shoulders. This whole thing was my fault. If only I had just gone down to the subway tunnels like I was supposed to, none of this would have happened. I wanted to help my dad. To protect him and keep our family together.

Instead, I'd basically ripped it apart.

And if something happened to Dad? It would be all my fault.

CHAPTER SIXTEEN

Noah

I s that him?"

I stared through the doorway of the hospital room, squinting at the figure lying on the bed. I felt terrible having to ask—basically admitting I couldn't recognize my own father. But with all the bandages, he looked more like a mummy from ancient Egypt than my dear old dad. Only his face remained uncovered, and even that looked nothing like his own. Shiny, red, blistered—with no eyebrows or beard to speak of. Even his hair was gone, singed to the scalp. And he was lying so still, only the heart monitor he'd been rigged up to gave any indication that he was still alive.

"He suffered burns on approximately eighty percent of his body," Dr. Fisher explained, ushering Mom and me over to some plastic chairs outside the room. I took a seat, still a little in awe of being in an actual hospital. Sure, it wasn't up and running like in the old days, but there was electricity and machines and medicine. Not to mention actual doctors and nurses. Something I was told I'd never see again. Everything was so sterile and clean and smelled a little like rubbing alcohol.

I turned my attention back to Dr. Fisher, a tall Black woman in a white lab coat. She gave me a kind smile. "We've been cleaning and dressing his wounds regularly," she told me. "And he's still getting an IV of antibiotics to stave off infection. They're technically expired, but they should still contain some potency." She glanced back at my dad's room. "It's still too early to tell if any of it will work. There are no miracles when it comes to this kind of thing. Even back when we did have a full surgical staff here."

"Can I go in and see him?" I asked Mom. She shrugged, then looked to Dr. Fisher for permission. The doctor nodded.

"Yes. Just wash your hands and put on this mask first. We need to keep the room as sterile as possible," she said, handing me a surgical mask. "It'll do him good to see a familiar face, I think," she added. "He's been very depressed since he got here, and kind of angry. I don't think he quite understands how serious his condition is." She gave me a stern look. "Just...try not to upset him. We need him to remain as calm as possible."

I rose from my chair, drawing in a breath as I slipped into the hospital room. My heart was pounding in my chest, though I wasn't exactly sure what I was afraid of. Walking up to my father's bed, I peered down at him, cringing as I caught the anguished look on his blistered face. His eyes were squeezed shut and he was moaning under his breath.

My heart wrenched. It was so hard to see him like this. All helpless and fragile-looking and attached to machines. I knew how much he hated to appear weak. This had to be torture for him. To just lie there and be forced to have strangers take care of you.

Especially strangers who loved dragons. The same beasts who tried to murder him.

"Dad?" I tried in a low voice. "Are you awake? It's me, Noah."

His eyes flew open, and I couldn't help but give a small gasp at how bloodshot they were. I watched as he turned his head in my direction, releasing a loud groan, as if even this slight movement caused him excruciating pain.

But then his gaze locked on me. His mouth dropped open in shock.

"Noah!"

He struggled to sit up, but stopped halfway, his face contorting in agony from the effort. I shook my head, helping him back down onto the pillow.

"The doctor said you aren't supposed to get excited," I scolded him.

"Yeah, well, that doctor can shove it where the sun don't shine," he muttered. Then he grinned at me, revealing several missing teeth. His jaw looked bruised, too; the dragon must have hit him in the mouth at some point. "How can I not get excited to see my only son?"

"I'm happy to see you, too, Dad," I told him honestly.

He peered at me closely, shaking his head in wonder. "I gotta say, when I saw that dragon go after you, mouth full of fire, I thought for sure…" He stopped, making a face. "Well, it doesn't matter. You're here now. And apparently in a lot better shape than your old man," he added, laughing. Though it came out more like a wheezing cough.

I frowned, a little confused again. So he'd seen the dragon shoot fire at me, too. Just like I remembered. But then—had it simply missed its mark? Only burned my pants, but not me? I closed my eyes, desperate to remember what had happened. I saw the fire blasting down the street. I felt the flames licking at my skin. The blackness coming hard and fast.

But if I had been burnt, I wouldn't be standing here right now, perfectly fine. I'd be like my dad, or worse.

"I'm so sorry, Dad," I whispered, feeling the guilt threaten to consume me. It was so hard to see him in such pain and know I was responsible for it. "I'm so sorry I didn't take that shot. That I ran away. If I hadn't..." I trailed off, not knowing how to finish. There was nothing I could say to make things better.

"What? You'd have slain the dragon with your bare hands?" Dad demanded, surprising me with a impish smile. He reached out with effort, placing a bandaged hand over my own. "Noah, I don't want you blaming yourself for what happened back there. In fact, if anything, I should be the one feeling guilty. I should have never taken you out there like that. It was reckless. Dangerous. If anything had happened to you..." He shook his head, closing his eyes as if it hurt to even think about it.

"Dad..."

He opened his eyes. "I'm just glad you're okay," he said again, seemingly more to himself than to me. "I really thought..." He shook his head. "You didn't get burned at all? Nothing?"

I shrugged uneasily. "I mean, my pants were...," I confessed. "But I'm fine. And you're going to be fine, too," I added, as if saying the words out loud could help make them come true.

"Of course I am!" he bellowed, suddenly sounding a lot more like the Dad I knew. "There's no dragon in the world with the power to stop your old man. I'm going to recover and leave this bed and keep fighting the good fight till the bitter end." His eyes narrowed. "Those monsters will rue the day they ever dared to mess with me, that's for sure."

I took an involuntary step backward, the venom in his voice scaring me a little. My dad had always protected us from dragons in the past, and I knew he was proud of his three kills. But now he sounded as if he wanted to go out on a rampage, hunting them down and making them pay for what they'd done to him. Which maybe sounded good in theory but was really, really dangerous. He'd already almost died! If he went out there, guns blazing, the dragons were sure to finish the job.

But this wasn't the time to tell him this. Not while he was all fired up and furious. Maybe once he'd had a few days or weeks to think about it, he'd come to his senses. He was smart, after all. He'd kept us alive when so many had died. I had to trust he'd keep doing the right thing.

"I did get one of them," he said, staring up at the ceiling. "I'm sure I did. The female. I got her right in the sweet spot before her buddy blasted me." His hands squeezed into fists, as if he wanted to pound the second dragon right then and there. "Mark my words, his days are numbered, too. As soon as I get out of here..."

"I'm sure you'll get him, Dad," I said encouragingly, remembering I was supposed to be trying to keep him calm. "I know you will."

He smiled, seeming to relax a bit. "Darn right," he agreed. "Just as soon as I can spring myself from this jail cell." He glanced over at the doctor outside the room and rolled his eyes. "Which, unfortunately, might take some time. You gonna be okay without me for a bit?"

"Mom said I could stay with her until you're better," I told him hesitantly. Of course, she didn't actually say the "until you're better part," but I didn't want to start a fight.

"Well, that makes sense, I guess," he said gruffly. "But don't you let those people of hers brainwash you while you're in there," he added, wagging a bandaged finger at me. "If you suddenly become a dragon hugger on me— I'll be forced to hunt you down with the rest of them."

He said it as a joke, but it came out kind of bitter. As if he wasn't really kidding, deep down. It made me shudder a little. Also, when he said "the rest of them," was he still talking about the dragons...or the humans who had saved his life?

I decided it was best not to ask. He was just hurting, I reminded myself. People say ridiculous things when they're hurting. He'd be back to his old self soon—once he began to heal.

I hoped…

Dad winced as if in pain again. He waved his hand at me, dismissing me from the room. "Go tell that doctor to get me some more morphine," he grumped. "And come see me tomorrow if you can spare the time."

"I will," I promised.

"And remember, stay away from those dragons. Even the ones they say are tame." He snorted. "Tame. Of all the ridiculous…" He shook his head. "What do we say, Noah? The only good dragon…"

"…is a dead dragon," I finished, glancing awkwardly at the door, hoping Mom couldn't hear. "Right. I know. I'll see you soon."

Mom met me at the door. She looked down at me, her expression filled with concern.

"You okay?" she asked.

"Sure," I said. "I guess so. Just…exhausted, I guess."

She lay a soft hand on my shoulder. "Come on," she said. "Let me take you home."

CHAPTER SEVENTEEN

Noah

Asha was crying.

I could hear her before I could see her, and for a moment, I thought my mind must be playing tricks on me. A dragon that cried? It seemed ridiculous. But sure enough, as I rounded the corner of the alleyway, my eyes fell upon her crumpled little body beside the overflowing dumpster, trembling and sobbing uncontrollably.

My heart wrenched at the pitiful sight, and suddenly all I wanted to do was run over and give her a huge hug. Tell her everything would be okay. Instead, I hung back, not sure what I should do. She was a dragon, after all. I wasn't sure they appreciated hugging.

"Are you all right?" I asked softly, not wanting to startle her.

She whirled around, her once-glowing amber eyes now dull and defeated, her silver snout stained with tears. "My mother," she whispered. "She's gone."

"What?" I squinted at her. "Gone? Where?"

She seemed to flinch at my question but didn't answer. It took me a moment to realize why.

"Oh," I said. "You mean...gone."

She nodded slowly. Tears slipped from her eyes and splashed onto the cement. "I didn't even get a chance to say goodbye."

"I'm so sorry," I said, stepping forward. I reached out, laying a hand on her back. I could almost feel her emotions pouring out of her. Sad, lonely, afraid. Exactly how I had felt when I thought my father had been killed. Suddenly, I felt a little guilty that my dad was still alive. Fighting for his life, sure. But he had a chance.

While Asha's mother did not.

She looked up at me, her eyes filled with confusion and hurt. "Did you do it, Noah? Did you kill my mother?"

Startled, my hand jerked away from her, and I stumbled backward. "What?" I cried. "Of course not! I'd never—"

My mouth clamped shut midsentence as my mind

flashed back to the giant dragon coming in for a landing on Seventh Avenue. Me, a rifle in my hand, lining up my sights.

Had I almost shot Asha's mother?

Had my dad been the one to take her down?

I got her right in the sweet spot before her buddy blasted me....

"Tolkyn said there were two humans," she continued, her little voice cracking on the words. "A father and his pup. You were looking for your father when I found you." She stared at me, accusation in her eyes.

I winced. What was I supposed to say? I had just told my dad I was sorry I hadn't shot the dragon—and at the time, I had meant it. In my mind, it was a monster bearing down on us, ready to blast us to smithereens.

But in another world, it was Asha's mother. And she was only protecting herself from a man with a deadly weapon, aimed at her heart.

"I didn't shoot her," I said sadly. "I admit, I was supposed to, and up until the last second I thought I would. But then she got close and I saw her eyes, and she reminded me so much of you." I hung my head. "And I couldn't bring myself to pull the trigger. So I ran instead."

Asha regarded me with solemn eyes. "My mother would have killed you if you hadn't," she admitted quietly. "She was looking for you, you know."

My head shot up. "She was?"

"Because you freed me from the trap. I tried to tell her you weren't like the rest of your kind, but she wouldn't listen. She wanted you dead. And your father... Well, I guess he protected you, like she was trying to protect me."

I nodded slowly, a heavy weight settling in my stomach. "I'm so sorry, Asha," I whispered, not sure what else to say.

"Me too," she said simply, looking away. I watched as another tear slipped down her snout. And when I reached up to my own cheek, I realized it was wet, too.

It was funny—all my life I had been taught to fear dragons. That they were unthinking, brutal beasts, acting on instinct and out for destruction. But now it seemed that was entirely wrong. There was so much more to them—just beneath the surface. They had families. They loved one another. They protected one another.

Just as we humans did.

Asha snorted, bringing me back to the present. She looked suddenly uneasy.

"What is it?" I asked, worry rising inside of me again.

"It's just... the others," she admitted. "From my herd. They don't know you like I do. They won't understand. She was their queen. And they will do anything they can to avenge her."

I swallowed hard. "What are you saying, Asha?"

She shook her head, her silver scales rippling. "They're looking for you, Noah. And if they find you, well, I'm not sure there's anything I can do to protect you." She hung her head. "I'm sorry, Noah. I'm really sorry."

Sorry...

Sorry...

"I'm sorry, but are you planning to sleep all day?"

I startled awake at the sound of the voice. Looking up, I found my mother standing above me, a big tray of food in her hands. I sat up in bed, sucking in a shaky breath, mind still racing with visions of dragons and alleyways and death.

They're looking for you, Noah. And if they find you...

But of course, it had just been a dream. I wasn't in some alleyway talking to Asha. I was safe and sound in my mother's apartment. Asha was miles away. Dragons didn't go out and seek revenge. The whole thing was just my imagination running wild.

The food my mother was holding, however, was very real. I practically drooled as my eyes took in the mountains of scrambled eggs on the tray, the pancakes dripping with syrup, even what appeared to be a glass of milk.

"Where did you get all that?" I asked, amazed.

She smiled. "At the market. They were particularly

well stocked today, so I took advantage. I figured you'd be famished when you finally woke up."

I rubbed my eyes with my fists. She was right. My stomach was growling like a wolf. Though who could blame it—I hadn't really eaten anything since those cans of beans back at the apartment. And when I'd arrived at her place last night after going to see Dad, I'd passed out almost immediately from exhaustion.

"That's a pretty impressive market," I remarked, taking the tray from her and setting it on my lap. Maya's family's store consisted mostly of canned food and dried meats and powdered milk—basically anything they'd been able to scavenge. We hardly ever had anything fresh.

"Oh, we have a full-service operation here," Mom explained proudly. "We've planted fruit trees around campus. We raise chickens on the roofs. We have cows in Riverside Park for milk. We even mill our own flour to bake bread. Our ruling body, the group council, believes strongly in becoming completely self-sufficient, so we don't have to rely too much on all that nasty before times food with its preservatives and chemicals."

I thought back to the stale donuts I'd munched on the other day. I had to admit, this was a major step up.

"The maple syrup isn't real," she added, almost apologetically. "But Juanita does a great job faking it with sugar and butter. It actually tastes pretty good."

"Well, I'm impressed," I declared, picking up my fork, ready to dig in. "I was definitely not expecting breakfast in bed."

"Yeah, well, just this once," Mom said with a teasing smile. "I figured you deserved it after all you've been through these last few days."

I shoveled a bite of scrambled eggs into my mouth. They were fresh and delicious—so much better than the powdered kind I was used to. And Mom wasn't wrong about the maple syrup. It tasted just like what I remembered of the real thing.

"Once you're done eating, I'll show you around the place," Mom added, taking a seat by the side of the bed. "And introduce you to everyone. They're all dying to meet you."

"How long have I been sleeping?" I asked curiously.

Mom laughed. "It's about noon," she said. "So... roughly seventeen hours?

"Wow." I took a slug of milk. I hadn't had fresh milk in years. "That's impressive, even for me."

"You needed your sleep. I'm glad you got it."

I nodded, remembering how exhausted I'd been from everything. And the bed had been so comfy and soft. Mom's apartment had two bedrooms, so I didn't need to sleep on the couch like at Dad's place. It was clean and cozy, too, decorated with cheery old-time pictures of Disney World.

It was then that I realized the windows were open.

"Aren't you worried the dragons will see us in here?" I asked, my heart beating a little faster in my chest. I thought back to Mike's story about the family who didn't believe in dragons until they crashed into their living room.

They're looking for you, Noah. And if they find you . . .

But Mom only laughed. "Let's just say the dragons around here know how to mind their manners," she replied with a wink.

Oh. Right.

"So you're really friends with dragons now?" I asked, just to be clear. Even after witnessing Javier and David with Sonja, it still seemed hard to believe. Were the people here able to talk to dragons like I could talk to Asha? Maybe that was normal here.

"Well, friends might be stretching it," Mom said with a grin. "But we do have an arrangement, you might say, with this particular herd. We give them food and don't threaten to shoot them out of the sky, and in turn, they protect us." She snorted. "Turns out, simply not attempting to wipe them off the face of the earth goes a long away in winning their respect."

"Can I meet them?" I found myself asking. "The dragons here, I mean."

"Sure," Mom said, as if it was the most natural request in the world. "I'll take you out to the courtyard after you're done eating to see who's around. It's a little early for feeding time, but we may get lucky."

Lucky. That was a word I'd never associated with a dragon sighting before. But this was clearly a whole new world up here. A world that seemed almost too good to be true. With doctors and hospitals and fresh food and wide-open windows.

Suddenly, my father's words seemed to echo in my head.

Don't you let those people of hers brainwash you....

I swallowed hard. I needed to be careful. And watchful. Not take anything at face value. Just in case.

"What's wrong?" Mom asked, catching my look.

"Nothing. It's fine."

"Are you sure?" She looked at me a little closer. Of course, she would notice. Mom always noticed things like that. Dad used to joke that she was an empath. A person who could feel another's feelings as if they were her own. "Noah, you know you can always talk to me, right?"

"I know," I said automatically. But inside I wasn't so sure. She was being so nice. So kind. So welcoming. Which made me feel really good—but really confused as well. She seemed happy I was here, but was she really? After all, if she had wanted me here, why hadn't she just brought me here with her to begin with? Instead, she'd left—without even saying goodbye.

What was it about this place that made it so important to her? That she would leave everything behind—even her only son? Was it really a cult? Had they brainwashed her?

Would they try to brainwash me now, too?

CHAPTER EIGHTEEN

Noah

We headed out of the apartment building and into a large courtyard. To my surprise, it was packed with people. Men, women, and children out in broad daylight, seemingly without a care in the world, just hanging out and enjoying the day.

I watched as a girl around my age hurled a beach ball at her friend across the way. The wind picked it up and it flew off track, landing near my feet. The girl waved at me eagerly, obviously wanting me to throw it back to her. I leaned over and picked up the ball, tossing it in her direction. She smiled at me, then continued her game. She reminded me, suddenly, of Maya. I wondered what Maya was doing right now, down in the dark subway tunnels with their canned food and artificial light...

While I ate fresh eggs in the sunlight like it was no big deal.

I looked up at the sky but saw no dragons above. "Where are they?" I asked, a little disappointed.

Mom shielded her eyes with her hand, looking up with me. "Hm. I don't see anyone right now," she said. "They might be out on their patrols. Dragons are very territorial, you see. And each herd has a turf they work to protect. The dragons down in Midtown aren't from the same herd as the ones up here, and there are other herds in Queens and a few in Brooklyn as well."

I nodded, trying to take in her words. I remembered Asha talking about her herd in my dream, which must have been the Midtown one, since I'd only ever seen her down there. I wondered if she knew any of the dragons up here, too.

"Do the herds ever mingle?" I asked curiously.

"I wish," Mom said, shaking her head. "But unfortunately, dragons don't tend to get along with those outside their own families. Which limits the space we can spread out to. We have all of Columbia and the surrounding Morningside Heights area to live and scavenge in safely, thanks to our herd. But we can't go below One Hundred and Tenth Street without chancing running into another herd who might not react so favorably to our presence."

Before I could ask another question, an older woman in a colorful sari walked up to us with a big smile on her face. "Hey, Diana, is this your kid?" she asked. Her gray-streaked black hair hung in two long braids down her back. "I heard David found him and picked him up."

"Yes, thank goodness," Mom replied, greeting her with a warm hug. "This is Noah. Noah, this is Saanvi. She's a biologist and has been studying the dragons here for the last couple years."

"Nice to meet you," I said politely. Wow, a dragon scientist. Who would have thought?

Saanvi shook my hand, then turned back to my mother. "Have you taken him to the nursery yet?" she asked.

"No, but that's a great idea, actually," Mom replied. "Maybe you could come with us and explain it all to him? Obviously, I'm still learning myself!"

"Sure, why not? You know I love to show off my babies!" Saanvi replied with a grin. She slapped me on the back. "Come on, young man. You are going to love this."

We followed Saanvi across the courtyard, until we

reached one of the former university buildings and went inside. She led us down a long hallway, saying hello to various people we passed along the way. *Other scientists*, she explained. There sure seemed to be a lot of scientists and doctors in this place. Or at least people who called themselves scientists and doctors. I had no way of knowing if they had actual qualifications. We had one guy, back at the hotel, who liked to tell everyone he was a doctor. Until we had someone who suffered from a heart attack and we needed his help. It was then that he admitted his doctorate was actually a PhD in astronomy. Which was cool if you wanted to look at the stars. But not exactly useful in saving lives.

Finally, we reached a set of double doors. Saanvi stopped in front of them, turning to me with a big smile. "Here we are," she announced. "Our nursery."

She pushed open the door.

I waited, at first unsure of what I was about to see. A nursey sounded like a place for babies. We had plenty of babies back in our old group, too. They certainly weren't as rare as scientists. So why did she think I'd be interested in seeing them?

But once I stepped inside, I realized exactly why I'd be interested. Because there were babies all right.

Baby dragons.

I gasped, my eyes traveling across the room, hardly able to believe what I was seeing.

Baby dragons, around the size of puppies, all toddling around on the floor as if it were the most natural thing in the world. Some were wrestling with one another, others were lying down, gnawing on bones. Some sounded almost as if they were singing. Little, high-pitched chirps floating through the air like a happy melody.

"Dragon daycare," Saanvi joked. "It's a thing."

"I...don't understand...," I stammered, completely at a loss.

She smiled wide. "We have an arrangement with their parents. We take care of them during the day so the parents can go and patrol without worrying about leaving their little ones unprotected while they're gone."

"You're telling me the dragons trust you with their children?" I blurted out, hardly able to believe I was asking the question. But there it was, right in front of my eyes.

"It took a while to convince the herd. But their queen had a very difficult pregnancy last summer and couldn't look after her babies properly once they were born. We took them in and cared for them until she was back on her feet. After that, she seemed to give her approval for the rest." Saanvi replied.

"Did she tell you that?" I asked.

Mom laughed. "Um, dragons can't actually speak, Noah, smart as they are. But like with other animals, they are pretty good at making their intentions known."

I bit my lip, considering this. So the dragons had bonded with them—so much so that they trusted them with their children. Yet, they wouldn't talk to them like Asha talked to me.

Wouldn't... or *couldn't*?

I shook my head. It was all so strange. I thought about asking Saanvi—she was supposed to be an expert, after all. But before I could say anything, I felt a ruffling at my feet. I looked down, surprised to see the baby dragons had surrounded me and were chirping and sniffing my legs with great enthusiasm.

"I think they like you!" Mom exclaimed with a laugh.

Saanvi watched the scene with interest. "So strange," she murmured. "I've never seen them react like this to a total stranger. Usually, they're quite standoffish with new humans. A survival instinct, I'm sure. But you walked into the room, and it was like they'd just found their long-lost best friend!"

"That is strange," I replied, laughing as their little snouts tickled my legs. I wondered, suddenly, if they could somehow smell dragon on me.

On instinct, I dropped to my knees to check them out. They chirped excitedly, one of them trying to climb up onto my lap, which made me laugh. I petted his snout, which was much softer than I imagined it'd be.

I looked up at my mom. "Do you guys have any apples?" I asked, suddenly getting an idea.

"Um, I'm sure I can grab you one from the caf," she said. "Are you hungry?"

"Not for me," I explained. "For them."

"Actually, dragons are carnivores," Saanvi interjected. "They wouldn't like apples."

I thought back to Asha greedily slurping down her fruit. "Just trust me, okay?"

Mom shrugged and disappeared. When she returned a moment later, she had an armful of apples. She handed one to me. Sure enough, the dragons' eyes lit up and they all started yapping eagerly. I smiled, tossing an apple to the one who'd tried to climb into my lap. He chomped it down in one bite and then looked back at me for more.

"Well, I'll be a dragon's aunt!" Saanvi exclaimed, staring at me in disbelief. "We never even thought to try fruit on them. We just assumed... Wow."

I grinned, grabbing a second apple and tossing it to another baby. *If only Asha was here*, I thought as the dragon chomped twice then swallowed. *She'd love this place. Good food, lots of dragon friends...*

Mom glanced at her watch. "Ooh. We should head back outside. It's feeding time."

Excited, I followed her and Saanvi out of the science building and back out onto the main campus. We headed over to the courtyard, which was no longer filled with kids playing but rather several full-grown dragons, eating lunch.

"We can watch, but you need to stand on the sidelines. You don't want them to get confused and accidentally take a bite of you by mistake," Mom teased.

"Good idea," I said, taking a step back.

I watched in awe as several more dragons dropped down into the courtyard. A man in a plastic suit was throwing hunks of meat out into the center. No sooner did the meat hit the ground than it was scooped up by a dragon. Around the edges, people were watching as if it were a sporting event. Some even clapped and cheered certain dragons on.

"There you go, Daenerys! That's a good girl!"

"Another piece, Toothless? Save some for your friends!"

I shook my head in disbelief. "Where do you get all the food?"

"We grow most of it in a lab, if you can believe it," Mom explained. "It would be too expensive to raise enough cows to feed a herd of dragons weekly. Plus, many of our members are strict vegetarians and animal activists—they don't approve of slaughtering animals for food. So we take a few cells from chickens and cows and then pump them up with the nutrients they need to grow in our labs. Unlike a normal cow, who could take a year to reach full growth, this man-made meat can be harvested in mere weeks. Meaning we never run out of food for our dragons."

"That's incredible," I declared, impressed.

"Right? Who would have thought?"

Javier walked up to me with a friendly wave. He was carrying a bag of meat and wearing one of the plastic suits.

"They have you on feeding duty?" Mom raised an eyebrow. "Surely they can find something more productive for a guy with your talents."

"Nah. I volunteered. It's fun to feed the dragons." He winked at me. "You should try it sometime, Noah."

I watched as a big dragon came up behind him, sniffing his bag. He yanked it away, wagging a finger at the giant creature. "You need to wait your turn, Sonja," he scolded. But he reached into the bag anyway, tossing the meat to the dragon. Sonja caught it in her mouth and slurped it down without chewing. Then she started sniffing the bag again. I couldn't help but laugh.

Javier rolled his eyes, shoving her snout away. "She's so greedy," he said with a groan. "Never enough for this one." Then he grinned at me. "So what do you think of the place so far? Pretty cool, huh? Definitely beats sub-way summer, am I right?"

I shrugged, not sure how to answer. I mean, he wasn't wrong—this place seemed like a paradise. I looked around the courtyard. Everyone was happy. Everyone was safe. There was no shortage of food. Who wouldn't want to live here?

Well, my dad, of course. Suddenly his words rang in my ears.

If you suddenly become a dragon hugger on me . . .

"I know. It's all a bit overwhelming at first," Mom said comfortingly. "We've lived in fear for so long, it's hard to let go. But I promise you, Noah, these people truly want the best for mankind, and I believe they're the key to getting society back on track."

"Yeah," I said, nodding slowly. "That makes sense."

Suddenly, I felt something wet on my arm and nearly leapt out of my skin. But it was only Sonja, I realized, trying to get me to pet her. I hesitantly reached out and scratched her on the snout. Her scales were softer than I'd imagined them to be. Almost silky in texture. She chirped in plea-sure, nuzzling my hand.

"Watch out! She's going to want a belly rub next if you keep indulging her like that!" Javier joked.

"You truly are a dragon whisperer, Noah," Saanvi

remarked, looking impressed. "They all seem to take to you right away."

Javier grinned. "Hm. Maybe we'll finally get our first rider."

"Rider?" I asked, confused.

Mom rolled her eyes. "It's something everyone here's been hoping for. For someone to ride a dragon. You know, like in all the books and movies, people always seem to bond with dragons and ride them. But it's never happened here," she added. "They'll hang out with us and protect us and gladly eat our food. But no dragon has ever let a human on their back."

"Not yet," Javier said. "But you never know. Maybe you'll be the first, Noah!"

I smiled, kind of liking the idea. It was ridiculous, of course. But it sounded so cool.

Noah Miller, Dragon Rider.

"Well, we can always dream," Mom replied with a smile. "But now, if you'll excuse us, we're going to continue our tour."

"Sounds good. Find me later if you're bored," Javier said. "They've got me in the computer lab in the math building, and I've already rigged up a few old gaming consoles if you're in the mood for some *Zelda*."

"Always!" I exclaimed. I'd missed gaming with Javier. "I'll definitely come check it out."

We also said goodbye to Saanvi, who had to get back to work. Then we headed into another building, which turned out to be a large cafeteria, filled with people eating, even though it was the middle of the day.

"Are they eating lunch?" I asked in awe. Back at the hotel it had been considered greedy to eat a third meal. But clearly things were different here.

"Yes, lunch," Mom replied. "Are you hungry? I know you had a late breakfast."

"I will never turn down food," I said with a grin.

Together, we walked up to a window and were handed a tray with a cheese sandwich and a cookie on it. My mouth practically watered in excitement.

Fresh cookies. Still warm. This place was truly unbelievable. No wonder Mom wanted to live here.

But still...

As we sat down at a table, away from the others, something uncomfortable wormed through my stomach.

"Okay, what's wrong?" Mom asked immediately.

I considered lying for a moment, then decided to come clean. I mean, we had to talk eventually, right? Now was as good a time as any.

I cleared my throat. "Look, Mom, this place is great. I totally get why you'd want to be here. But..."

"But what, Noah?" She leaned across the table, giving me an encouraging look. "It's okay. You can say it."

"Why did you leave us behind?" I blurted out before I could lose my nerve. "Why didn't you want us to come with you?"

My voice cracked on the last part, and I could feel the tears threaten at the corners of my eyes. I stared down at my plate, not able to look at her.

"Oh, Noah," she said, her voice filled with sorrow. "Of course I wanted you to come with me. I wanted you here more than anything in the world."

CHAPTER NINETEEN

Noah

I stared at my mom. Her words ringing in my ears.

I wanted you here more than anything in the world.

Anger rose inside me. I set down my fork, meeting her eyes. "Then why did you just leave?" I demanded. "You didn't even say goodbye!"

For a moment, she didn't speak. The silence stretched out between us, long and agonizing. Then, at last, she sighed. "Your father wouldn't let me."

My head jerked up. "What?"

She shrugged uneasily. "When I first found out about this place, I thought it was a dream come true. A chance for us to make things better—to finally live a life without fear. But when I went to your dad, he was furious at me for even talking to the people here. Like you said, he thinks they're some kind of cult. Not to mention traitors to our country. I tried to reason with him—get him to change his mind, but you know how he can be. Especially about anything to do with dragons."

I nodded slowly. I knew all too well.

"It's not his fault. He bought into the propaganda that the government and media fed him back in the early days. That dragons were some kind of evil creatures out to destroy our world. That the only way to deal with them was to blast them into extinction." She poked her food with her fork. "But things have changed. We know more now. We understand more of what the dragons want and how to work with them. And we believe we can still build a bright future for mankind without wiping out an entire new species in the process."

She set down her fork. "But your father is still scarred from all he's been through—which is understandable. It was an awful time for everyone back then. You were young—you probably don't remember it too well. But it was so scary, not knowing what was going to happen. Your father protected us through that, and I'll always be grateful to him for doing so. But now..." She sighed. "Now we know more. And it would be going backward not to acknowledge that and use it to our benefit. At least, that's what I believe. Your father, on the other hand…"

She trailed off, and my mind flashed back to my dad in the hospital room, burned and battered. If he'd hated dragons before, it was going to be even worse now that one had almost taken his life.

The only good dragon is a dead dragon.

We'd made that joke a thousand times over the years. And I had always believed it, too. I mean, it seemed so obvious—dragons were the enemy, and everyone knew that.

Could we really trust them to become our allies?

"Anyway," Mom continued. "I told him I was going. And that I was going to take you with me. He could stay stuck in his ways, but you shouldn't have to suffer for it." She sighed deeply. "Let's just say he didn't like that idea very much. In fact, he flipped out on me. Told me I was a traitor. That I would break up our family over his dead body. He said if I even tried to take you away, he would leave with you and bring you somewhere I'd never find you."

"What?" I stared at her, horrified. "Dad said that?"

"Yes. And he meant it, too. He'd take you away from the safety of your group. Lead you into danger. I couldn't risk that. So I left alone, following his wishes. It was never meant to be forever, though. I thought once I got established here, I could try again. I could try to prove to your father that this would be a better place for you. A good, safe place to grow up without having to live in fear. That was my plan anyway." She shrugged. "But, as you know, best-laid plans and all that."

"But why didn't you just tell me all this?" I asked. "I mean, I'm twelve years old—I could have handled it! Trust me, it was much worse not knowing where you went. If you were even still... alive." My voice caught on the last word, and Mom flinched.

"Your father forbade me from telling anyone in the group. Especially you. I think it was a pride thing. He didn't want anyone to think he couldn't keep his family together. I tried to slip you a note that explained everything, the night I left, but he must have found it and torn it up if you never got it."

"I never got a note," I said dully, feeling sick to my stomach. Was she telling the truth? The look on her face told me she was, and my mother was not a liar. But the idea that my father would keep this from me. Pretend like he had no idea where she'd gone.

But he did know, I thought suddenly. *He knew exactly where she was this whole time. And he'd been planning to break her out of this place once the group had gone underground. Because he didn't want them to know.*

He didn't want me *to know.*

I wondered what it would have been like if I had gone underground like I was supposed to. Would Dad have come to this place and taken Mom back to the apartment against her will? He told me Mom was sick. That she needed help and that he was going to save her. At the time I believed him.

But looking at my mom now, she didn't look sick. In fact, she looked better. Happier than I'd seen her in a long time.

"How could Dad do this?" I asked, half to myself.

Mom sighed. "Honestly? I think he was afraid of losing you. I think he believed that if you knew where I was, you'd choose me over him. You know how important family is to him. He loves you, Noah. As much as I do. We just...have different ways of expressing it."

"No kidding," I muttered.

Mom bit her lower lip. "There's something else you should know."

"Oh?" I looked up at her, surprised. There was more?

"Before this all happened, I was working on a plan to get you back. I was going to travel to Midtown and try to find you when you were out and about, and explain everything and give you the choice of coming with me or staying with your dad. But then the dragons woke early, and it made traveling to Midtown impossible. At least for humans..."

"What are you saying?" I asked, confused.

She gave me a wry smile. "It was David's idea. He'd been working with Sonja for a while and believed he could train her to recognize your scent using some of your things that I'd taken with me when I left. Kind of like police used to do with dogs. His idea was to extract you right before everyone went underground. So no one would have time to look for you."

I stared at her, a sudden realization falling over me. "Extract me? You mean...?"

"Yes." Her cheeks colored. "I didn't like the idea, of course. I knew it would scare you half to death to have a dragon just pluck you off the ground and spirit you away. Also, as I said, I preferred to give you a choice whether you wanted to come or not. However, at this point we were running out of time. And David convinced me it would work." Her lips curled. "But in the end, you proved a little too resourceful. Which was impressive actually. But not so great for our plan."

My mind flashed back to the dragon Maya and I had encountered on the way to the library. I had assumed it was out to kill me. Was it really trying to rescue me instead?

"It tried to smoke us out of our hiding spot," I protested. "What if I had died of smoke inhalation before I could be 'rescued'?"

Mom winced. "Sorry about that. Sonja must have gotten a little...overly enthusiastic in her attempt. You know dragons..."

"Sure," I said, basically speechless. "I guess."

Mom gave me a rueful look. "Anyway, David tried again later that day. With a different dragon—someone had wounded Sonja on her way back, and she was forced to head uptown to heal. Unfortunately, the new dragon got confused when Javier jumped into your path at the last second and grabbed him instead of you. They don't have the best eyesight," she confessed.

My mind flashed back to the scene. Javier screaming as the dragon picked him up from the ground and flew away with him. I remembered feeling so sick to my stomach as I watched them go, assuming he was doomed. Imagine if I had known this dragon taxi had been meant for me.

I gave a small snort. "Javier must have been freaking out when he was dropped off here. I'm sure he thought he was dead meat."

"Oh yeah." Mom laughed. "It was a bit tough to explain. Thankfully, once he saw the place, he realized he wanted in. Which worked out well for us, since we were in need of someone with his tech expertise."

"And after that, you assumed I went underground?"

"Yes. Which I was fine with—I knew you'd be safe

there. And I could try again in the fall. But then you miraculously showed up—practically on our doorstep."

"And you got Dad, too," I said. "Two for the price of one!"

Her face tightened. "Yes. Like I said before, some of our scouts found him wandering around in a daze near the park. They didn't know who he was until they brought him back and I identified him. I wasn't so sure taking him in was a good idea, but we didn't really have a choice. He never would have survived if we hadn't."

"Right." I stared down at my plate. "Well, I'm glad you did. I mean, even after...you know." I sighed. Suddenly everything felt so complicated. Was this how kids used to feel back in the day when their parents got divorced? Like they were being pulled in two different directions at once?

Mom was silent for a moment. Then she sighed. "Look, your father and I may never see eye to eye on things. But we both love you. And who knows? Once he's feeling better, we can show him around. Maybe once he sees the place for himself, he'll change his mind about a few things. Even if he doesn't want to join us, maybe he'd at least let us share some of our methods with the hotel group when they come back aboveground. We could teach them to partner with their own heard. Maybe a satellite community down there that we can share resources with." She smiled wistfully. "I mean, that's always been the plan. Maybe this will be the opportunity to put it into action."

"Maybe," I said. But deep down I wasn't convinced. I mean, it sounded good in theory, and I did think maybe some of the others from the hotel might be open to trying. If for nothing else than the fresh eggs and plentiful food. Not to mention the fact that they wouldn't have to hide out for six months of the year anymore. I was pretty sure plenty of them would be down for that.

But not my father. Never him.

My mind flashed back to the hospital. His last words to me as I exited the room.

The only good dragon...

No, my father would never accept any of this. Nothing would ever convince him that dragons weren't evil monsters out to destroy us all. Even if he saw this place with his own eyes. He'd hate it all. He'd say the people were weak, not kind. Delusional, not open-minded.

And if I stayed, he'd believe I was, too.

CHAPTER TWENTY

Asha

"Who wants some apples?"

Asha startled at the oddly familiar voice, sounding as if it was coming from right around the corner. Curious, she rose to her feet, following the sound. She was inside a building, for some reason, which was strange in and of itself—dragons never went inside any of the monsters' buildings if they could help it. But what she found when she opened the door at the end of the hall was even stranger.

"One apple for you, and another for you."

It was Noah, the pup, sitting on the floor, surrounded by baby dragons, who were crawling all over him, croaking and squeaking excitedly as they tried to catch the fruit he was tossing into the air.

Noah's eyes brightened when he saw her. "Asha!" he cried. "I'm so glad you came! Would you like an apple?"

She stepped forward, still a little hesitant. The other baby dragons swarmed her in greeting, nipping at her feet, trying to get her to play. She felt a smile rise to her mouth as she teased them back with her teeth, tossing them playfully out of her path, only to have them scurry back in front of her for another round. When she reached Noah, he grinned at her, holding out the most beautiful apple Asha had ever seen.

"I saved the best one for you," he said.

She took it in her mouth, chewing and swallowing, rejoicing in the taste of the sweet juices sliding down her throat. She hadn't realized how hungry she was. But then, she didn't remember the last time she'd eaten a real meal. Her belly seemed to warm in pleasure.

"What is this place?" she asked Noah when she had finished the apple.

"It's where I've been staying," he explained. "It's a wonderful place. Like a paradise. Humans and dragons, living together in peace…"

She frowned. "But that's impossible. Dragons would never live with humans. And humans would never live with dragons."

"That's what I thought, too. But I've seen it for myself. The dragons here protect the humans. And the humans keep the dragons fed. Not just with apples. But meat—real meat."

Asha's mind flashed to the hungry dragons in her own herd. They'd lost two elders last week due to starvation. They wouldn't be the last, either, if they didn't find a better food source soon. This was something her mother always managed. But now it was all on Asha's shoulders.

Could there really be a place where dragons did not go hungry? It seemed too good to be true.

"Come see me, Asha," Noah said. *"Come see me and I'll show you myself."*

Asha . . .

Asha.

"Asha! My queen!"

Asha jerked awake at the sound of her general's voice. Tolkyn stood towering above her, his expression grave.

"What is it?" she asked nervously as she scrambled to her feet on the rooftop, embarrassed to be caught sleeping. Not that Tolkyn would mind. He'd been like a father figure to her most of her life, after her own father was killed in a battle between two dragon herds when she was just a baby.

"I have news, my queen," he said. "News of the young dragon slayer we've been searching for."

Noah. Asha tried not to wince. If only Tolkyn knew she'd been dreaming of Noah just moments before. And not just this time, either. Over the last few days, she'd had dream after dream about him. Each seeming realer than the last. She couldn't seem to forget about him, no matter how hard she tried.

Something Tolkyn would never understand.

"Did you find him?" she asked hesitantly, not sure she wanted to know the answer.

The large dragon snorted. "One of our scouts caught sight of a pup fitting his description up north near the edge of our territory. She followed him, preparing to strike when he ducked into a building. She tried to wait for him to come out again, but before he did, she was chased away by one of the traitors from the northern territory."

"The...traitors?" Asha queried, confused.

Tolkyn gave her a grave look. "Your mother never wanted to talk about this, but I think it's important you know. It seems the herd of dragons to the north have taken up with a group of monsters. They protect them inside the boundaries of their territory. Cohabiting with them. Eating their food."

Asha startled, her dream of Noah and his apples

rushing back to her. Hadn't he talked about a place where dragons and humans were living together? Was that where he was now? Up north living with another herd? A weird shimmer that felt a little like jealousy rippled through her as she imagined Noah hanging out with other dragons. Feeding them, taking care of them, while she and her dragons went to sleep with empty bellies.

Tolkyn huffed angrily, puffs of smoke shooting from his nostrils as he stared out over the rooftops. "How could any self-respecting dragon take up with humans?" he growled. "Betraying their own kind! And for what? What do they get from these humans?"

"Um, food? A chance to live in peace?" Asha suggested meekly, thinking about the baby dragons she'd seen in her dream. They'd seemed so happy, so content as they caught apples in their mouths. And their bellies had been so round—as if they hadn't ever missed a meal in their lives.

Tolkyn roared, almost knocking Asha backward with the force of wind exiting his throat. "It is an abomination," he declared. "They have hunted us, murdered us, and now they want to befriend us? I'd rather die than make peace with a monster."

Asha hung her head. Of course he would. And she should feel the same, right? After all, it was a human that had killed her mother.

But somehow she wasn't so sure anymore.

"And now the herd is harboring a dragon slayer," Tolkyn continued to rage, pacing the perimeter of the building they stood on. "They go too far. Perhaps we need to consider further actions against them."

Asha gulped at his words. War. He was talking about war with other dragons. Dragons who had befriended humans.

"No," she said after a moment. "We can't risk it. We're weak. Hungry. Our numbers are down. Our queen is dead. We can't afford to get into a battle with other herds. Especially herds in league with humans. We would lose, and we would never recover."

"But your mother must be avenged!"

"And she will be. But not like this. Too many lives have already been lost. I won't add to that number. My mother wouldn't want that. You know it."

Tolkyn let out a resigned sigh. "You're probably right," he said. "I'm sorry, my queen. I'm just...angry. Mostly at myself. I should have been there for your mother. I should have been able to protect her."

He sounded so lost, so sad. Asha cringed, wondering again what he'd think if he knew the truth. That, in a way, she had also betrayed her herd. By bonding with a human. What would the others say if they found out? Would they still want her as queen? Would they want her in the herd at all?

"What's done is done," she said firmly. "We cannot go back. We must look forward. Find a better future."

"And find the dragon slayer pup," Tolkyn grunted gruffly. "No matter how long it takes. He may be protected by them now, but if he ever dares stray back into our territory, we will get him. And, my queen, I promise. He will pay for your mother's death once and for all."

CHAPTER TWENTY-ONE

Noah

H ey, new kid! Want to hang out with us?"

I looked up from the book I was reading on a bench outside Mom's apartment building to see two kids—a boy and a girl—around my age approaching. They were dressed in baggy shorts and Columbia University T-shirts—which was pretty much the uniform around here for kids, thanks to the abundant supply of college wear from the shops around campus.

I closed my book. "My name's Noah, not 'new kid.'"

The boy grinned. "Sorry. I'm Hugo. And this is Lei." He gestured to the girl at his side. She was pretty, Asian, with long black hair that was tied up in a side braid and shiny brown eyes. Hugo, meanwhile, was skinny and freckled with messy, straw-colored hair and a peeling sunburn across his nose. "We're organizing a huge game of hide-and-go-seek around the neighborhood and need more people. You want in?"

I looked up at him, surprised. "You mean outside campus?"

"Sure. Why not?"

"Don't worry, it's perfectly safe," Lei added. "The dragons will be out on patrol. They'll keep an eye out for any danger."

Right. The dragons would protect us. That concept was still so weird to me, even after being here a week. Every time I looked up at the sky and saw a dragon, I would feel a pang of panic in my stomach, until I reminded myself I had nothing to fear. The dragons were what kept us safe around here. No one dared enter their territory without permission, which left us a neighborhood-wide playground.

"I don't know," I said, a little reluctantly. "I'm supposed to go see my dad this morning."

Dad was still in the hospital, still trying to fight off the infections he'd gotten from his burns. I tried to visit him every morning, but sometimes it was, well, difficult. Mostly because he was always complaining about the place and the doctors and nurses caring for him. These people were saving Dad's life, yet he held them in such contempt. As if they were keeping him prisoner and torturing him on purpose. And he wanted me to agree with him. Tell him how horrible everything was, how much I couldn't wait to leave.

The problem was, I was starting to not want to leave. This place was amazing. So much better than what we had in Midtown with the others. It was clean, it was nice. There was plenty of food, no danger. Yes, you had to be kind to dragons, but that seemed a pretty easy thing to do when the dragons were so cute and nice and well-behaved.

But anytime I even hinted to him that this place wasn't as bad as he thought, he would flip out on me, accusing me of letting these cultists brainwash me. And it made me feel so guilty. Like I was betraying his trust anytime I started to enjoy myself. I knew he wasn't trying to be mean. Like Mom said, he loved me and wanted to keep me safe.

He just had a very different idea about how to do it. And it was getting harder and harder to believe he was right.

I sighed, looking up at Hugo and Lei. Suddenly I was just so tired of it all.

"You know what?" I said. "I will join you. Just for a little while."

I rose to my feet, swallowing my rising guilt. Dad

could wait a few hours to rant and rave at me—it wasn't like he was going anywhere. In the meantime, I deserved some time off for good behavior. To act like a regular kid in a regular world for a few hours.

Lei and Hugo cheered. "Awesome," Hugo declared. "This is going to be epic."

I smiled. "Let me just go put my book away and I'll join you."

"What are you reading?" Lei asked curiously.

I turned the cover toward her. It was a new fantasy novel I'd found in the university library. It had taken some digging—mostly the place was filled with reference books and nonfiction. But it ended up being a good one.

Lei gave a thumbs-up. "Ooh! I read that one! It's really good. Though I warn you, it totally ends on a cliffhanger."

I groaned. "And of course I don't have the sequel."

"I do!" She grinned. "I'll let you borrow it if you want."

"Really? That'd be great!"

"I have tons of books," she told me. "You can come shop my home library anytime."

"And you can shop my mom's," I replied. "I swear she must have robbed a bookstore when she got here." I was so happy when Mom first showed me her collection, which included many of the same books she'd had to leave behind in the bunker. As well as some new additions, such as a special first edition copy of *The Hobbit*, our favorite book from the before times.

I ran inside and up the stairs to Mom's apartment. She was sitting at the breakfast bar when I entered and greeted me with a smile. "You ready to go see your father?" she asked.

"Actually, I'm going to go play with some of the other kids for a bit," I said. "If that's okay? I'll go see Dad later."

Her smile widened. "That's great, Noah. I'm glad you're getting to meet some of the other kids." She reached over to a nearby plate on the counter and grabbed a cookie wrapped in a napkin, then tossed it in my direction. I caught it and took a bite. Yum. Peanut butter. My favorite.

"Thanks, Mom!" I said, mouth full of cookie. Then I ran out of the apartment and down the stairs, my steps light and happy. This was going to be a good day—I could feel it.

It was funny, when I'd first made the decision to stay aboveground, all I'd pictured was a summer filled with danger and distress. Hiding out from dragons, barely scraping by, never finding enough to eat. I hadn't even been certain I'd be able to stay alive until November.

And yet, here I am. Eating cookies, playing hide-and-go-seek with new friends out in the warm sunshine of a summer day. If only Maya could see me now. I wondered what she'd think of this place. I was pretty sure she'd love it just as much as I did.

When I got outside, Hugo and Lei had been joined by a group of about twenty other kids, all dressed in Columbia University T-shirts and many with walkie-talkies attached to their belts. I needed to ask my mother if I could get one of those.

Everyone introduced themselves, then Hugo laid out the rules of the game.

"You can go anywhere west between One Hundred and Sixteenth Street and One Hundred and Twentieth," he explained. "All the way to Riverside Park. But you can't hide inside a building—you gotta find an outside hiding place. Somewhere the dragons can still keep an eye on you." He gave a salute up at the sky, where Sonja was circling dutifully. She dipped her wing in response. Hugo grinned, then turned back to us.

"Half of us will be seekers. The others will be hiders. If you're spotted, you run. But if you get tagged, you have to join the seekers. The last person to be tagged wins." He clapped his hands. "Then we switch and start again."

He tapped each person on the shoulder in turn, counting in twos. I ended up being a two, which meant I needed to hide. Lei was also a two and Hugo was a one. A seeker.

I walked over to the group of hiders, who were hopping

up and down in excited anticipation as they readied to take off. I studied their faces curiously; they all looked so happy. So healthy. So carefree. It made me a little jealous, actually. How come they got to have such cushy lives up here, while everyone else suffered below? I thought of Maya and my friends down in the subway tunnels right now. How dark it was down there. How boring. How little there was to eat. It wasn't really fair if you thought about it. Why should these kids have everything while we had nothing?

You could have everything, too, a voice inside me nagged. *If you choose to stay.*

It was a tempting thought. To agree to stay up here with Mom forever and never return to the hotel. Never again have to hibernate. Never again have to live in fear. But then, what about my friends? Maya? Not to mention my father. Could I just walk away—abandon—everything I knew and loved to start over again? I mean, sure, if they invited everyone from our group, that would be different. But I was pretty positive they weren't about to just open up their gates to whatever random survivor wandered in. I had an in through Mom. And Javier was a skilled tech guy. But what about Maya? Her family? What about Mike? What about grumpy old Griffin?

What about Dad?

Hugo's voice interrupted my troubled thoughts. "Okay," he announced. "You've got ten minutes. Go! Go! Go!"

We sprinted into action, running to the edges of campus, then out into the city proper. The streets were basically empty here, having been cleared out by the group to allow people to go jogging or biking safely. Which was great—except it meant there was less to hide behind.

"I've got a perfect spot," Lei announced, gesturing for me to follow her. She took off and I ran after her, until we came to an old playground in the middle of Riverside Park. We ducked behind a slide and Lei giggled a little, pulling a rock out of her shoe.

"Okay, now we wait," she said.

I nodded, my heart pounding in anticipation. It was strange to be hiding for fun, instead of hiding for my life. Above, I could hear the dragons calling out to one another as they flew in wide circles, making their patrols.

"I gotta say, it still feels a little weird knowing they're up there," I remarked. "And that they're not about to swoop down to attack."

"Yeah, I remember that feeling," Lei agreed. "My mom and I had been running from dragons for years before we came here. She's a doctor, so we'd travel from group to group, trying to help anyone we could. But when we got here and she saw the working hospital, she knew she'd found our forever home."

"So you like it here," I said. It wasn't really a question.

"What's not to like? It's safe, there's tons to eat. And the dragons are amazing! I'm even in this new study where humans are matched up with their own dragons to see if they can bond with them. I was matched with this baby dragon—I named him Bowie—and he's so cute!"

"Wow. That's really cool," I said, impressed. "Does he talk to you?"

"Well, not talk-talk, of course," Lei replied with a laugh. "But sometimes, I'm positive I can understand what he's thinking. Or feeling." She shrugged. "At least I think I can."

My mind went immediately to Asha. Did we have a bond, too? Was that why we could understand each other? But if so, our bond must be deeper somehow. Because I could completely understand what she said. As if she were speaking aloud.

What makes our bond different than the rest? I wondered.

I opened my mouth to speak, but at that moment, Hugo came barreling onto the playground. "I know you're here, Lei!" he called. "And I'm going to get you!"

Lei giggled, shooting me a mischievous look. "He won't," she confided. "I'm ten times faster than him." She gestured to me. "I'll lead him away. You go find a new hiding spot. Good luck!"

205

And with that, she dashed out from behind the slide, sticking her tongue out at Hugo and making a playful but rude gesture. Hugo squealed and gave chase, and soon they were both tearing down the street, laughing and jeering at each other.

Leaving me alone again.

Once they were gone, I emerged from the playscape, then made my way through the park, crossing the old Henry Hudson Parkway until I came to the running path along the river. I stared out at the water, watching the ripples lap against the shore. It was so beautiful here. So peaceful.

Suddenly, I felt like I was being watched. I scanned the river, my jaw dropping as my gaze fell upon a very familiar sight.

"Asha?" I whispered in awe.

Sure enough, it was her. There was no mistaking it. She'd grown since I'd seen her last. Not a lot, but she definitely looked bigger. Her silver scales seemed shinier, too, as they cast glittering rainbows across the water's rippling surface.

"What are you doing here?" I asked in disbelief.

She flapped her wings. "I was looking for you, actually," she admitted. "One of our scouts said they saw you enter the traitors' territory." She looked around nervously, as if maybe she wasn't supposed to be there. Which made sense; this was a different herd's land. Though I wasn't sure if the river was considered a neutral zone. I glanced up at the sky to see if any dragons were patrolling nearby. Thankfully the coast looked clear.

I turned back to Asha. "I've been dreaming about you."

"Yes." She flew in a small circle. "I've been dreaming about you, too. Though I'm not exactly sure they're only dreams. They seem...real." She peered at me with her glowing amber eyes. "Do you know what I mean?"

"Yeah." I nodded. "I think I do." Something jogged in my memory. "Is your mother...?" I trailed off, not sure how to bring it up.

But she caught my meaning. "Yes. She's gone," she admitted, hanging her head.

My heart wrenched. "I'm so sorry, Asha."

"I've learned to accept it. Being angry won't bring her back."

I sighed, knowing she was right. Once upon a time, things had seemed very black-and-white with dragons. Now, knowing Asha, and listening to my mother, it felt like a million shades of gray.

"I'm still sorry," I said.

She looked up at me. "Thank you. I appreciate that."

I bit my lower lip. "Can I ask you something?"

"What is it?"

"It's about our bond or whatever you want to call it," I said slowly. "How did it happen? And how is our bond so deep that we dream about each other? And understand each other when we speak? There are people here working to bond with dragons, too, but it's not the same. Why are we different?"

She spun in a circle in the air, her tail dipping into the water. "I don't know," she said. "The only thing I can think of is..." She trailed off, looking uncomfortable.

"What?" I pressed.

"I healed you," she blurted out. "Maybe it's because I healed you?"

I stared at her, shocked. For a moment, I didn't understand. Then, suddenly, it all fell into place. Like puzzle pieces clicking. Once again I saw the dragon fire blazing down the street. The flames licking at my legs. The excruciating pain. Falling to the ground.

"So I *was* burned," I realized aloud. "And when you showed up, you healed me." Now it all made sense. Why my pants had been burned but my skin had not. "How did you do that?" I added.

"Dragon saliva," she explained. "It has healing properties. I didn't know if it would work on a human, but I had to try. You looked like you were in such pain. And you had saved my life..."

"So you saved mine," I concluded in amazement.

"Wow. I can't believe I didn't know. That I didn't thank you."

She looked uneasy. "It wasn't a big deal."

I laughed. "Um, my life is kind of a big deal to me."

"Fair." She gave a small giggle. "You're welcome. And thank you for saving my life first."

I felt my face heat up. "Yeah, well, it was kind of my fault you were stuck in that trap to begin with, seeing as I had set it and all." I realized it was time to come clean.

Her eyes widened. Clearly she hadn't realized that. I cringed. "I know, I know. I'm a terrible person. Or I was. But I'm learning," I added. "Actually, I've been learning a lot from everyone around here."

"Oh?" Asha looked curious.

"Let's just say they have very different beliefs about dragons than they do in Midtown."

Asha nodded. "Tolkyn said the dragons up here have partnered with humans. Is that really true?"

I nodded. "It's pretty incredible, actually. The dragons protect the humans, and in turn the humans feed the dragons and take care of their babies."

"What do they feed them?" Asha asked, suddenly looking very interested.

"Oh, all the good stuff," I said with a grin. "Lots of nasty, gross meat product. And apples. They have an entire orchard of apples."

"So jealous," Asha said dreamily. "Especially of the apples. We barely have any food these days."

A sudden thought struck me. "Why don't you come back with me?" I asked. "I can get you some food, introduce you to the other dragons..."

But Asha was already shaking her head. "I can't," she said, sounding a little wistful. "Not that I don't want to. But it doesn't work that way with dragons."

"What do you mean?"

"Herds stay with their herds. They don't mix with one another. And especially not one that my herd sees as being traitors to dragonkind because of their involvement with humans. If they found out I was mingling with these traitors..."

I was beginning to get the picture. After all, wouldn't it be the same for me, if those from the hotel knew I'd been hanging out up here, feeding and playing with dragons? They might even decide not to let me come back to them, even if I wanted to.

"I get it," I said with a sigh. "But I wish things were different."

"Me too," Asha said. "Maybe someday." She did another little spin in the air. "At least we have each other," she said, her voice soft. "I mean, that's something, right? Before I met you, I thought you were all monsters. But now I know that's not true."

"And thanks to you, I know the same about dragons," I admitted. "And you know what? I promise you now, no matter what happens, I'll never hurt another dragon."

"And I won't eat another human," Asha said with a teasing smile. "Unless I'm really, really—"

I reached into my backpack and tossed her apple. She caught it in her mouth, chewed twice, then swallowed.

"Okay, okay," she said once she'd finished. "I get it!"

I opened my mouth to make another joke, but before I could, a loud screech filled the air. Asha's eyes grew wide.

"I've got to go," she said. "I shouldn't be here. If they see me—"

My smile dropped. "Asha—"

But she was already flying away. "It was good to see you again, Noah. I'm glad you found a good home. I would suggest you stay here where's it's safe. Don't cross back into our territory. No matter what."

A shiver spun down my spine. I remembered the words she had spoken to me in our shared dream.

They're looking for you, Noah. And if they find you...

And with that, she flapped her wings and flew away, skirting the river as she went. I watched her go till I couldn't see her anymore. I wondered if I'd ever see her again.

"Goodbye, Asha," I whispered. "Stay safe."

"Noah! There you are!"

I turned to find Hugo and Lei behind me. At first, I thought they were going to try to tag me in their game. Or maybe pronounce me the winner—I had been gone a long time.

But then I caught the looks on their faces.

"What is it?" I asked worriedly.

"My mother called me on my walkie-talkie," Lei explained. "She says you need to get to the hospital. Right away."

"Is it my father?" My heart pounded in my chest.

"Yes," Lei said, "And you need to hurry."

CHAPTER TWENTY-TWO

Noah

By the time I arrived at the hospital, I was completely out of breath, having run across what felt like half of New York City as fast as my legs could take me. As I burst through the front doors, I found Mom pacing in the lobby, wringing her hands. Her face was pale. She looked anxious.

"What's going on with Dad?" I demanded, without bothering to say hello.

She ran a hand through her hair, a frown etched on her face. "I won't lie to you, Noah," she said. "It's not good news. Some of his burns have started to suffer tissue necrosis."

I scrunched up my eyebrows. "What does that mean?"

"It means the infection has set in and his cells are dying. Unfortunately, the process is irreversible." She lay a hand on my shoulder, giving me a sorrowful look. "I'm so sorry, Noah. The doctors had really hoped to have it under control. But today…" She shook her head. "He just took a sudden turn for the worse. And I'm afraid there's nothing they can do." Her voice cracked on the last part. She turned away, as if she didn't want me to see her face.

My whole body went cold. Suddenly, I wanted to scream at her. To tell her she must be mistaken. Completely wrong. My dad would never let this happen to him. He was tough, a survivor. He was going to get through this and come out bigger and better because of it, like a superhero in a movie.

But the look in her eyes told me I was wrong. My dad might be strong.

But the dragon had been stronger.

Suddenly I felt like a huge traitor. Over the past week I'd been living it up, hanging out with dragons, petting them and feeding them. All while my dad was lying in the hospital literally dying from wounds he'd suffered from the very same types of beasts.

Dr. Fisher approached us, her face carefully neutral. The kind of face doctors wore when they wanted to break

214

the bad news gently. "Good, you're here," she said. "I've kept him awake so you could talk to him. But he's in severe pain, Noah. So, I need you to make it quick. Then we're going to attempt to make him as comfortable as possible, given our limited drug supply, for as long as he needs."

A long as he needs. She meant they were going to drug him up until he died. There was nothing else they could do.

I swallowed hard, not trusting myself to speak. Dr. Fisher gestured toward the room, and I headed through the door, my heart filled with dread. What was I going to say to him? He was my father! My rock! The one person who had always been there for me. Who kept me safe. Who never left me behind. No, he wasn't perfect. And yes, he'd done some things I was really angry at him about. But he'd always loved me. Fully, unconditionally. He'd sacrificed his own life to keep me safe.

How could I just walk in and say goodbye?

"Dad?" I asked cautiously, my eyes resting on the figure lying on the bed. He looked like a stranger to me. He'd lost so much weight since he'd been here, and now that he was unwrapped from his bandages, I could see his bones sticking out at weird angles, and his wounds had turned a sickening shade of black and purple—the rot setting in, I guessed. He was shivering, too, almost violently, yet at the same time he seemed to be sweating, his face wet with moisture.

But the worst part of all? He looked scared.

I'd never seen my dad look scared before.

"Noah!" he croaked, his voice barely more than a whisper. "You came."

"Of course I did, Dad!" I cried, guilt blooming in my chest. I should have been here earlier. I was supposed to come this morning. But I'd blown him off to play a game. A stupid game! What kind of son was I to do that to my own father?

I ran to the bed and threw my arms around him, but I quickly pulled away when he flinched in pain. I stared down at him, the lump in my throat threatening to choke me. Suddenly I had absolutely nothing to say.

"Well," Dad began, breaking the awkward silence. "From the look on your face, I guess you already know. It isn't looking so good for your old man."

I swallowed hard. "Dad..."

He waved me off. "You can stop with that look of pity. I don't need you feeling sorry for me. It's my time, and I accept that. I had a good run. Lasted longer than most people in this world." He choked out a hoarse laugh, then broke into a coughing fit. "But every streak's bound to run out eventually."

"Don't give up, Dad!" I cried. "You can still fight this! Maybe the doctors are wrong! Maybe you still have a chance."

He reached out with a shaky hand, gripping my arm with his fading strength. "Listen, son," he said, his voice so raspy it was hard to make out the words. "I need you to stay with your mother for the rest of the summer. I know she'll keep you safe. But then I want you to promise me you'll go back to the hotel in November when the others return. Find Mike, tell him what happened. He'll let you stay with them. We had an arrangement, he and I, if something ever happened to me."

I stared at him, horrified. "You want me to leave Mom?" I blurted out, before I could stop myself. But then, of course he did. He thought this place was poison. He'd rather have me leave my mother forever and become an orphan than stay here and become one of the dragon huggers.

Suddenly I felt a little angry. What happened to *family sticks together no matter what*?

He sighed deeply. "Well, maybe you can get your mother to come with you. That had been my plan, obviously. And perhaps it's not too late. Maybe once I die, you can convince her these dragons aren't the pet puppy dogs folks here seem to believe them to be." He cleared his throat. "You're a smart boy, Noah. You know the truth. These monsters must be wiped off the face of the earth if we can ever have any hope of coming back as a species. For mankind to once again rise to the top of the food chain."

I'd heard this speech before. It was one of his favorites. And in the past, I had always believed it to be true. Always cheered him on and wished for the death of the monsters right along with him.

But I could no longer do that, I realized suddenly. Not after Asha had saved my life—at the risk of her own. Not after the bond we shared. And it wasn't just her—she wasn't the exception to some kind of rule. Just as I wasn't the only good human in the world who would choose to save the life of a dragon instead of ending it. In fact, it seemed that humans and dragons weren't that different from one another after all. They'd both do what it took to keep their loved ones safe. And if you could bring them together, if you could work to understand each other's needs, there could be a real chance for a better future. One no longer filled with fear, but with love and respect.

We didn't need things to go back to the way they used to be before the apocalypse. We needed to find a way forward, to build a new future—a better future—together.

Because there were no *monsters* in the end. Just humans and dragons.

But I kept quiet. After all, he was dying. What good

would it do to argue with him on his deathbed? Better to let him go, thinking I was the good son who believed as he did. It was the last gift I could give him before he went.

My dad groaned, clearly in pain. He sucked in a rattling breath. "All right," he said. "I'll stop jabbering on. You're a good boy, Noah. You know what's right. I know you'll do me proud."

"I will, Dad," I said, scraping the words I didn't mean from the back of my throat. My last words to my dad, and they were a total lie. I laid a hand on his arm, tears rolling down my cheeks. I didn't bother to wipe them away. Instead, I turned and walked out of the room, hanging my head in shame.

It should have been me, I thought miserably as I took one last look back at him. He'd closed his eyes, but he was still shivering. *I would be on the bed, too. Right next to him. If it weren't for Asha...*

I stopped short, my heart leaping in my chest.

I'd been burned, too.

But Asha had healed my burns.

What if...?

WHAT IF!

I dashed out into the lobby, adrenaline spreading like wildfire through my veins. My mom caught me in the waiting room, her eyes widening at the look on my face.

"What is it, Noah?" she asked worriedly.

"I've got an idea!" I blurted out. "I know how to save Dad."

She shook her head. "No, Noah, I told you. It's too late. The doctors can't reverse the damage."

"The doctors might not be able to," I agreed. "But a dragon...What if a dragon could?"

CHAPTER TWENTY-THREE

Noah

Well, that's quite a story."

I shrugged, pulling my pant leg back down. I'd just explained the entire Asha incident to my mom and Dr. Fisher, and they were now wearing matching incredulous expressions.

"I know it sounds ridiculous," I admitted. "But I promise you, it's true. I was burned just like Dad. But a dragon found me and healed me."

Mom looked at me skeptically. "And you're just deciding to mention this now? You've been here a week, Noah. You didn't think to bring it up before?

"I didn't *know* before," I confessed, feeling like an

idiot. "But it makes perfect sense now when I look back on it. I got burned, I passed out. When I woke up, I was completely fine. And Asha was just standing there. She only told me about the healing thing today when I saw her down by the river."

Dr. Fisher waved her hands. "Wait, slow down. You say the dragon told you about the healing thing? What does that mean? How can a dragon tell you anything? They don't talk."

"Asha does," I corrected. "Or at least she can talk to me." I shrugged, not sure how to explain it so they would believe me. "It's like we're bonded, same as those dragons they're doing the study with. But in a deeper way. Maybe because of the healing? That's what she thinks anyway."

"Are you sure this wasn't a dream, Noah?" Mom ventured, looking a little uneasy.

"I'm positive," I insisted. "Though Asha and I have also met in our dreams...." I trailed off, realizing this little fact was not going to help my case. I needed them to believe me—and fast—if we were going to have any chance to save Dad.

"Look, I can explain it all later," I said. "But right now, Dad needs help—and he doesn't have much time. Can we at least try it? I mean, what's the worst that can happen? He dies? That's going to happen anyway. And maybe this way he still has a chance."

Mom turned to Dr. Fisher. "What do you think?"

"I'm willing to try anything," Dr. Fisher replied, holding up her hands. "And we've pretty much exhausted all other options. Why not a dragon?"

I could tell she was still skeptical. Not that I blamed her. But I was grateful she was willing to give it a try.

"All right," Mom said. "I guess we need to find Saanvi, then. She'll know which dragon would work best for this." She turned to me. "Unless you can call your dragon in?"

I shook my head. "She's from another herd. She can't enter our territory. And it'd be too dangerous to take Dad into theirs."

Also, Asha might not be super excited to heal my father, I thought, but didn't say, considering what he had done to her mother.

"Okay," Mom said. "Then we'll go talk to Saanvi."

"Sounds good," Dr. Fisher agreed. "But be quick. I don't know how much time he has left."

Mom nodded, rising to her feet. I scrambled after her, practically having to run to keep up as she headed to the door with quick steps. When we reached the main university campus about ten minutes later, Mom headed straight to the dragon nursery. There, we found Saanvi on duty, playing with her babies. She looked up and caught our faces, her smile dipping into a frown.

"What's wrong?" she asked, rising to her feet.

Mom told the story as quickly as she could, hitting the facts but leaving out some details. When she had finished, Saanvi nodded, surprisingly not looking as shocked as I assumed she would.

"This actually makes a lot of sense," she told us.

"Really?" I asked. I had expected we'd have to convince her, like I'd had to with Mom and Dr. Fisher. But no, she looked as if she believed every word.

"There was a day not long ago that I was in charge of the nursery," she explained. "One of the baby dragons cut her wing on a sharp piece of metal that a worker had left behind. It was bleeding pretty badly, so I ran to First Aid to get something to wrap it with. When I got back, she was cuddling with another baby dragon. And when I pulled that dragon off her to wrap her wing, I realized her wing was as good as new. As if it had never been cut at all." She picked up a baby dragon, holding it in her arms. "I have a theory that it's something in their saliva. Something with healing properties." Her eyes swung to me. "But I never considered it might work on humans, too."

"Well, there's only one way to find out," Mom said. "Do you have a dragon you think would do it?"

"Maybe Sonja," Saanvi said, after considering it for a moment. "She's the most docile and eager to please. The hardest part, though, will be getting her to understand what we want her to do. Maybe David can help. He's been working a lot with her."

"I bet meat would also help," I suggested. "That dragon is always hungry."

"It couldn't hurt," agreed Mom. "Noah, why don't you run to the feed house and grab something. Saanvi and I will get Sonja and David."

"Then we'll meet in the hospital courtyard," Saanvi added. "Seeing as our dragon's a bit too large to fit into the ICU."

I nodded, excitement surging inside of me. "Sounds good!" I said. "Meet you there!"

I took off, running out of the building and across campus, to the feed house, where they processed the meat they fed to the dragons. After some fast talking, I eventually managed to get them to give me a huge burlap bag of stinky dragon slop. I tried not to spill any as I raced back to the hospital, holding my nose the entire way.

It took me a while to find the courtyard. When I finally did, Sonja and David had already arrived and were standing side by side with my mother. Sonja's head jerked up immediately as I entered, her snout sniffing the air with great interest.

"Not yet, girl!" I apologized. "We need you to help us first."

Sonja snorted as if annoyed, which made everyone

laugh nervously. But our laughter soon faded when the door to the hospital opened and two orderlies wheeled my father out into the yard. He was lying on a hospital gurney unconscious, an oxygen mask on his face and his chest rising and falling rapidly, as if he was having trouble breathing. Fear rose inside of me all over again.

It's going to be okay, I attempted to reassure myself. *This is going to work. It has to!*

Sonja watched as the bed was wheeled in her direction. She sniffed the air again, then pawed the ground, almost anxiously, as if something was distressing her. Could she smell the infection festering inside of him? From what I understood, dragons had a very keen sense of smell, much like dogs. I stepped up to her, laying a gentle hand on her neck.

"It's okay, girl," I whispered. "I know you can do this."

"But how do we explain what we want her to do?" asked Dr. Fisher, looking from the dragon to my dad. "Can you talk to her like you can the other dragon?"

It was a good question. I turned to Sonja. "Can you understand me?" I asked, feeling a little silly.

Sonja snorted and turned away. Guess not.

"Let me try," David said. He placed a hand on her flank, then attempted to lead her over to my father's bed. But the dragon planted her mighty paws in the grass and shook him off. She clearly didn't like my father's smell and didn't want to get any closer.

David backed off, holding up his arms in surrender. Sonja began to unfurl her wings, as if she was ready to take flight. My heart sank in my chest. What if this didn't work after all? What if Sonja could heal him but wouldn't? We couldn't exactly force her...

It was then that I remembered the meat.

I stepped over to my dad, then waved the bag of meat. "You want this?" I asked Sonja. "Come and get it."

Sonja's eyes widened. She took a step in our direction. Hope rose in my chest. I reached into the bag, scooping up a bloody chunk of meat.

"Sorry, Dad," I whispered, then rubbed the meat all over his burns. He twisted in agony, clearly in pain, though still unconscious. My stomach rolled with nausea. So gross. So, so gross.

But Sonja had taken a step closer. Then another. And soon she was at my father's side.

Licking his wounds.

"Ugh. I think I'm going to be sick," David groaned. "That's so nasty."

"Nasty, but effective," Saanvi replied, giving me an approving look. "Way to think like a dragon, Noah."

I smiled warily. This was the moment of truth. Was it going to work?

We all waited as the dragon worked on my father. Slowly, methodically, taking her time and making sure not to miss a spot. I watched in fascination, trying to picture Asha doing the same to me. I'd been passed out at the time, of course, and never really understood how she'd done it. But now it was all becoming perfectly clear.

And so was my father's skin. Slowly, the black necrosis began to fade away, replaced by smooth, healthy tissue. His labored breathing began to relax. His whole body seemed to fall limp in relief.

Dr. Fisher shook her head in amazement. "This is incredible," she murmured. "Truly incredible."

"A miracle," David said in awe. "You go, Sonja!"

Sonja lifted her head. She glanced at me. I grinned and dumped the entire bag of slop onto the ground. Soon she was having her own dragon feast, while Dr. Fisher moved to examine my dad, listening to his heart with her stethoscope.

A moment later, she turned back to us. "I can't believe it," she said. "But he's stabilizing. I think he's going to be okay!"

I let out a cheer. Sonja lifted her head, snorted, then went back to her meal. Everyone laughed again, but this time the laughter wasn't nervous.

It was filled with joy.

My mom came over to me, hugging me close. I could

feel her tears dripping onto the top of my head, wetting my hair. "Noah, you saved him," she cried. "You really saved him! I'm so sorry I didn't believe you at first."

"It's okay, Mom," I assured her, hugging her back, my heart practically singing with joy. My dad was going to be okay! He wasn't going to die after all.

"This is wonderful," Saanvi declared, clapping her hands together. "I mean, just think what this will mean for our group! The fact that dragons can help us survive? This changes things. This changes *everything*."

I grinned widely, happiness flowing through me. Maybe she was right. After all, the reason our group back at the hotel feared dragons was because of all the bad they'd done in the past. But what if, when they came back up to the surface in November, we could show them something good the dragons were doing in the present? They'd realize that dragons didn't have to be their enemies after all. Maybe they would even be willing to befriend the Midtown herd when they came up from hibernation in the spring.

Asha's herd. If they were able to work together, they could both be safe.

Sonja raised her head, having finished her slop. She flapped her wings a couple times and I assumed she was planning to fly away. Instead, she surprised us, walking back over to my father and nudging him curiously with her snout. He groaned a little, shifting in his bed, but he didn't wake up, as he was still heavily sedated. Sonja cocked her head, glancing over at us with what looked like concern in her deep amber eyes.

"He's going to be fine," I assured her. "He just needs some more sleep."

Sonja snorted as if impatient, twin clouds of smoke puffing from her nostrils. She gave my father one last look, then unfurled her mighty wings and pushed off into the sky. We watched her go, until she'd disappeared from view.

"Interesting," Mom muttered under her breath.

"What?" I asked, turning to her.

Her gaze rested on me. "You said that after your dragon healed you, you developed a bond between you. Do you think the same thing could have happened this time?"

I stared at her, shocked. Sonja bonding with my father? The possibility hadn't even crossed my mind. But now that Mom said it, it made perfect sense. Especially after seeing the way Sonja had looked at my dad before she left. As if she cared about how he was doing.

I swallowed hard. Had I just accidentally bonded my dad to his number one enemy?

I looked over at my father again, sleeping peacefully, and a sudden guilt wormed through my stomach. Maybe

I should have asked him if he wanted a dragon to save him before I went through with this. Would he be angry at me when he woke up?

But no, that was ridiculous. He would have died. And now he was going to live. Surely the ends justified the means in this case. In fact, maybe this was the opening I'd been searching for. A way to convince my dad that dragons weren't all bad. Yes, one had almost ended his life. But another had saved it.

A flash of hope stirred inside of me. Maybe once he was up and better, I could show him around the university. Maybe I could even convince him to stay for the summer—it would be safer up here with this herd, versus going back to the one who was hunting us because of what he did. And maybe once he'd been here for a while, he'd start to realize he'd been wrong about things. Just as I had.

Maybe, just maybe, there was still a chance for us to be a family again.

CHAPTER TWENTY-FOUR

Noah

Your father's awake. He wants to see you."

I looked up from my book as Dr. Fisher stepped into the waiting room. Lei and Hugo had brought me a huge stack of fantasy novels from Lei's bookcase after I told them I wouldn't be leaving the hospital until I knew my father was all right. But while I normally had no problem losing myself in a book, I found I couldn't get into any of them. Not when I was constantly glancing up at the door to my father's room, waiting for him to wake up.

And now, three days later, he finally had.

I thanked Dr. Fisher, then put down my book and rose to my feet. When I stepped through the door, I was surprised to see that he was sitting up in bed, eating from a plate filled with steak and potatoes. He looked over at me and gave me a sheepish grin.

"Noah!" he cried. "How are you, kid?"

I ran over to him, happiness exploding inside of me. Leaning over, I tried to give him a gentle hug, but he set aside his tray and grabbed me fiercely, squeezing me tight. He was still weak, I could tell. But he was better. So much better.

"How are you doing, Dad?" I asked as our hug ended, my eyes roving over his body. He was still a bit skinny, of course, and was hooked up to a bunch of machines. But the burns he'd had—they were just gone. And his skin looked flushed and healthy. Even his beard had started to grow back. It was clear to me now that he was going to be just fine.

"Much better!" he declared, grabbing his plate and fork again and taking a bite of steak. "Just like I knew I would be. Those doctors, they think they know everything. Almost had me convinced I was on my way out. But they underestimated your old man." He patted himself on the chest like King Kong. It made me laugh.

"I wish you could have seen it, Dad," I cried, so happy to find him in such good spirits. Here I had been worried he'd be weirded out by everything. But instead, he seemed just fine. "It was like a miracle. None of us could believe it. To just watch her lick all your burns away…" I shook my head in amazement as I remembered Sonja at work. "I mean, just think what this could mean for…"

I trailed off, realizing my father's smile had faded. He set down his fork, looking at me intently. "What are you talking about?" he demanded, his voice suddenly gruff. "Who licked what?"

I swallowed hard, fear jolting through me. Had they not told him what Sonja had done to save him? I just assumed they would have explained everything when he first woke up. But maybe they hadn't had the chance. Or maybe they were waiting for the right time.

And I had just blurted it all out like an idiot.

I realized he was still glaring at me. I shifted uneasily from foot to foot. "Oh, uh," I stammered, not sure what to say. "I just mean, the burn treatment or whatever. Really miraculous." It wasn't technically a lie.

But my father's eyes only narrowed. "Noah." His voice was clipped. Sharp. "If you know something, you need to tell me. Now."

"Maybe you should ask the doctors—"

"I knew I couldn't trust them!"

CRASH!

My dad hurled his tray across the room, causing me to nearly jump out of my skin. The steak stuck to the wall for a moment before sliding down. The potatoes dripped like white glue.

And my father's hands had balled into fists.

I backed away, fear running through me. "Take it easy, Dad," I begged. "I'll get the doctor. She'll explain everything! And—"

"No." My father's voice left no room for argument. "You stay here. And you tell me exactly what they did to me. I want to hear it from you, not those traitors." His eyes leveled on me. "Tell me. Now."

I swallowed hard. "It was...a dragon," I mumbled, realizing I had no choice but to come clean. "Turns out their saliva has healing properties. She cured you, Dad. She healed all your wounds. Stopped your infection. You're going to be fine! Isn't that great?"

But even as I said the words, I knew he did *not* think it was great.

Not one bit.

"How dare they?" he growled, gripping the rails of his bed so hard his knuckles turned white. "You actually let them sic one of their monsters on me?"

"Dad—"

He dropped his gaze to his perfectly healed legs, glaring at them as if they were still festering with wounds. "I did not consent to this. They have no right to do something like this without my permission!" He started yanking out the tubes in his arms, the machines around him beeping furiously in protest.

"Dad, you would have died!" I tried, feeling tears spring to my eyes. This was not how this was supposed to go. Not at all. Why had I opened my big mouth?

"Better I had died," he growled, "then have my blood poisoned by one of those monsters."

He scrambled out of bed, his feet hitting the floor awkwardly and his legs, not accustomed to being used after more than a week in bed, collapsing under him. I leapt forward to try to stop him from falling, but once he'd righted himself, he pushed me aside angrily. I watched helplessly as he grabbed his messenger bag from the corner of the room and hobbled to the door, yanking it open. Dr. Fisher appeared on the other side.

"Sir, you really need to get back in bed," she protested.

"*You* really need to get out of my way," Dad shot back. "I refuse to stay here a moment longer."

"But, sir, you're not ready to leave yet. We still need to observe your—"

"The only thing you will observe is me walking out that door. Now I suggest you step out of my way before I make you."

Dr. Fisher did as she was told, rushing out of the waiting room looking half frightened to death. And for good reason, too. My dad looked positively murderous. I'd never seen him so angry in my life. I realized I needed to calm him down before he did something rash. But how? What could I possibly do or say to make things better?

He stepped toward the hall, beckoning me with a bruised hand. "Come on, Noah," he said gruffly. "We're getting out of here."

"But Dad, the doctors—"

"I don't care about the doctors. I care about you. And I need to get you out of this place—now!"

Oh no, I realized with horror. He didn't just want to leave the hospital. He wanted to leave the entire campus. To go back home to Midtown.

And he wanted me to come with him.

My heart sank in my chest as I realized the truth. I'd been a fool to think he would ever want to stay here. That he could ever accept that dragons were anything less than total monsters—even after one had literally saved his life.

But if he didn't stay…

My mind flashed back to Asha's warning. That the dragons of her herd were out looking for me after the death of their queen. It was going to be ten times worse for my dad, who had done the actual killing.

I decided it was time to come clean. "Look, Dad, you don't understand. We can't leave this place. If we go south of One Hundred and Tenth Street, we might as well be wearing targets on our backs. You killed their queen. The whole herd is out looking for us."

"Good. I hope they are," my dad shot back, not missing a beat. "Because I'm looking for them, too. One thing this whole mess has taught me? I'm not hiding anymore. Once I'm up and running at full speed again, I'm going to make it my life's mission to hunt down every dragon in this city, and I'm not going to rest until each and every one of them has been blown to smithereens. We're going to take New York City back, Noah. You and me. And whoever else wants to help. The way I figure it? There's got to be other people out there who are still loyal to our country. We can raise an army. We can take the dragons down once and for all."

I fought back a cringe, not sure what to say. The look in his eyes was almost terrifying. So much anger, so much hate. So much blind fury. So much so that it had wiped out his common sense. The survival instincts he'd always harbored to keep us safe. Now there was nothing left but an unquenchable thirst for revenge.

"I get it, Dad," I assured him, trying to sound calm, not wanting to fuel the fire. "I really do. But don't you think maybe we should wait? Not forever—just until the dragons calm down a little. Or till the hotel group comes back. They could totally help. I mean, Mike alone. I'm sure he could take down his fair share of dragons." I bit my lower lip. "I just don't think it's a good idea to go at it on our own right now."

Dad's eyes locked on me, suddenly suspicious. "What are you saying, Noah?" he demanded. "You're saying you want to stay here? With these traitors to our country? You want to live with them—and their dragons?"

"Would it really be so bad?" I asked, starting to get annoyed at his obstinance. "I mean, news flash, it's not exactly torture living here, Dad. There's some really cool stuff here. And the food's awesome. Also, they have this great gym. You could use it to get strong again. And, in the meantime, we would be safe."

I trailed off, giving my dad a pleading look. Silently begging him to open his mind. Just to consider the possibility. I knew he'd never agree to stay here forever. Become a dragon sympathizer. But if I could just keep him out of danger...at least until the dragons went to ground again.

"Wow." My dad gave a low whistle. "They really got to you, didn't they? This was exactly what I was afraid of." He took a step toward me, his expression grave. "They've messed with your head, son. They've confused you— made you want to think like them. Think living here is *safe*. But I can still help you," he added, almost pleadingly. "I can still save you. But we have to leave now."

For a moment, I couldn't speak. I couldn't even breathe. I wanted to defend myself. To tell him he was the one who was confused—not me. But I knew I would just be wasting my breath. Right now there was only one decision to make. And it was mine, not his.

I could stay with Mom. Or I could leave with him.

There was nothing in between.

Dad leaned down, placing both hands on my cheeks. They were rough and calloused and also trembling. Though I wasn't sure whether in anger or fear. "You're all I've got left in the world, Noah," he whispered. "Please don't make me lose you, too."

I closed my eyes, my stomach twisting. The last thing I wanted to do was leave this place. But at the same time, I couldn't just let my dad walk away alone. He was trying to act tough, but it was obvious he was still weak. In fact, it looked as if it was an effort for him to even stand. If I let him walk out that door alone, I knew he'd never survive the summer.

And it would be my fault for letting him go.

The only possible protection he had? My bond with Asha. Maybe if I was there, she could convince her herd to spare my dad. Maybe with her help, he'd have a chance.

It was a long shot. But the alternative...

I opened my eyes. "Okay, Dad," I managed to choke out. "I'll come with you."

His shoulders slumped in relief. He reached out, pulling me into a rough bear hug—the kind he never usually gave. I hugged him back, but it felt a little half-hearted. Mostly because I was still so torn. I didn't know if I was doing the right thing. But I didn't know what else I could do.

"I love you, son," my dad said, pulling away from the hug. "And I promise you, we're going to make you better. I've got those books, remember? The ones I was going to use on your mother to help her?" He sighed. "Well, she's a lost cause, I think. But you—I can still save you!"

Save me, I thought bitterly. Little did he know, I was the only one who could save *him*.

CHAPTER TWENTY-FIVE

Noah

We headed out of the hospital and onto the streets of Columbia University. It was evening, and the sun had just begun to dip under the horizon, meaning most people were inside having dinner, leaving the campus pretty much empty. Which was probably for the best. The last thing I wanted to do was run into Lei or Hugo—or even Javier—and have them start asking questions about where we were going.

The journey was slow. My dad was still very weak and had to stop every few minutes to catch his breath. At one point I dared suggest we go back to the hospital and wait until he was stronger before leaving. But he angrily refused. As far as he was concerned? He'd escaped from prison, and there was no way he was going back.

"Maybe we could at least say goodbye to Mom?" I begged as we passed her apartment building. I glanced longingly up at my bedroom window three stories above. I was pretty sure my days of fresh air and open windows were over for a while. "We could ask her if she wanted to come, too," I added. "Be a family again like we wanted."

But, predictably, my father only shook his head. "Not a chance. She'd only try to stop us from going. And she might call for backup. I can't risk it." He gave me a rueful look. "Sorry, kid. I miss her, too. But she's not the same woman we once knew and loved. She's one of them now."

I slumped my shoulders in defeat. I wanted to argue. Mom was still the same person we knew and loved. In fact, she was a better version of herself now. Happy, free. But Dad would never understand that.

A shadow suddenly crossed over our heads. I looked up, surprised to see none other than Sonja herself, hovering a few feet above. I frowned, uneasy. What was she doing here? It wasn't even close to feeding time.

My father's eyes followed my gaze. When they locked on the dragon, he screeched in alarm, retreating behind a large statue of Alexander Hamilton and dragging me with him.

"It's okay," I tried to assure him as the dragon came

in for graceful landing, settling down into the courtyard. "It's just Sonja."

"Sonja? You're telling me they actually name these vermin?" Dad looked disgusted. He also looked worried. He glanced out at Sonja, who was peering around the courtyard, sniffing the air curiously. Had she scented my father?

"Come on," I said, dragging my dad back out into the open. "She won't hurt you. I promise."

In fact, she saved your life, I wanted to add, but didn't. I was pretty sure it would only make him more anxious.

Sonja's eyes locked on us. They widened in delight. She opened her mouth, slurping the air with her long black tongue. I would have laughed, had I not been so nervous.

"Sorry, girl," I said. "I don't have any food for you today."

I could feel my father's sharp look. "Food? You've been feeding that thing?"

Oops. I felt my face flush. It might have been better not to mention that.

"N-not her specifically," I stammered. "Just the dragons here in general..."

I trailed off as Sonja eyes locked on my father's face. She stared at him for a moment, and I could almost see the gears turning in her head. Then she let out an excited squeal and started doing what looked like a dragon happy dance in the middle of the courtyard.

She was excited to see him again, I realized with surprise. I guess she hadn't seen him since she had healed him three days ago. Maybe she was pleased to find him up and walking again. Or maybe she thought she'd get some extra meat slop if she did some more licking.

It was then that I saw my father's face, which had gone stark white.

"No...," he whispered.

I felt a shiver of fear run through me. "Are you okay, Dad?"

"No, no, no!" He clapped his hands over his ears, his face now filled with terror.

"What's wrong?" I tried, but he wasn't listening. He was too busy staring down the dragon, a wild and frenzied look in his eyes.

"Get out of my head, you...you...monster!" he screamed, violently waving his arms in the air.

And suddenly I realized exactly what had upset him. He could hear her. Just as I could hear Asha. They were bonded.

And he didn't like it. Not one bit.

I sucked in a breath. "It's okay, Dad," I tried. "Just... relax, okay?"

He whirled around to face me. "Relax?" he spit out. "You're telling me to relax? This creature is trying to burrow itself into my brain!"

"She's just trying to talk to you!" I protested. "It's not a big deal...really!"

His face flamed with fury. When he spoke next, his voice was ice-cold. "You knew this would happen," he accused. "You knew about this the whole time, and yet you let them do it to me anyway?"

"Dad, you would have died!"

"She's the one who should die! They should all die!"

I heard a snort, and my eyes turned back to Sonja. She was pawing the ground anxiously, looking from my father to me. She looked so confused and hurt it kind of broke my heart. If only my dad could look beyond his hatred and see the actual creature standing before him. This beautiful, silly, life-giving animal who just wanted to live in peace. (And maybe get a little extra meat slop from time to time.)

I'm sorry, I thought. *You don't deserve this.*

But, of course, she couldn't hear me. She could only hear my dad. And I didn't want to know what kind of thoughts he was pushing inside her head.

"Come on, Dad," I said, realizing it was better to cut our losses at this point and go. He would never understand, and this would only get worse if we stayed. "Let's go home."

But my father didn't answer. Instead, he reached into

his messenger bag and, to my horror, pulled out a pistol. With shaky hands, he aimed it directly at Sonja.

"The only good monster," he mumbled, "is a dead monster."

The gun went off, but the shot was wild because my dad's hands were trembling so much. The bullet hit Sonja, but bounced off her scales—he hadn't managed to hit one of the soft ones. Sonja stood there for a moment, looking horrified and so, so hurt. As if she couldn't believe what had just happened. My heart ached seeing the pain and betrayal on her face.

She had saved my father's life.

And he had just tried to kill her.

She should have fought back. My dad was just standing there, completely unprotected and out of his mind. It would have been so simple for her to end his life.

But she didn't. She simply gave him a sad look, then unfurled her wings and leapt into the air. A moment later, she was gone.

But others would come. People and the other dragons would have heard the gunshot. They'd want to investigate. And when they found out what my father tried to do...

"Come on, Dad," I cried. "We need to get out of here. Now!"

CHAPTER TWENTY-SIX

Noah

We ran down the street as fast as we could. My dad was huffing and puffing and stumbling badly, and after a few blocks, I realized he couldn't go much farther. I dragged him into a nearby building, which luckily had a busted lock, and slammed the door shut behind us. Then I tugged him down so we couldn't be seen through the windows. We could hide here until it was safe to move again.

My father didn't say anything as we waited, listening to the shouts and footsteps just outside as my mom's friends scrambled to figure out what had happened. And soon he'd fallen into a troubled sleep. I kept guard the best I could, listening to the dragons squawking above, patrolling the air, probably looking for us. I wondered if Sonja could sense where we were hiding. Would she tell the others if she could? I wouldn't blame her one bit if she did. After what my dad tried to do...

Thank goodness he'd missed; I don't think I could have lived with the pain and guilt of seeing Sonja fall. It was hard enough seeing the smile slip from her face. To see the horror form in her eyes as she realized the truth. That the man she'd healed, the man she'd bonded with— wanted nothing more than to see her dead.

She saved your life! I wanted to scream at my dad. *How could you do something like that to a creature who saved your life?*

Sure, she hadn't done it out of the goodness of her heart. She had done it for food. But wasn't that the whole point in the end? That we could work with dragons?

But my dad would never understand that...

Eventually the shouts began to fade. The dragons stopped circling. The sun dipped below the horizon. And once again, we were alone.

Dad opened his eyes. "Are they gone?" he asked blearily.

"I think so," I said, helping him to his feet.

"Good." He smiled. "I knew we could outsmart them."

I nodded, though I didn't feel very smart as we exited the building, him leaning heavily on me as we walked down the street, keeping an eye on the sky for any danger. Instead, I only felt worried. Soon we would have to leave the safety of the Columbia herd and be smack-dab in Midtown territory. Where Asha's dragons would be patrolling.

Looking for us.

Hunting us.

And if they found us, we didn't stand a chance.

We moved into a new apartment. Dad had decided the old one was too small for the two of us and wanted something with more protection. The new place was on the other side of Times Square, closer to the old convention center. It was bigger than the last apartment, with two bedrooms this time, and nestled in a small courtyard with a tall iron gate. But it was still cramped and leaky and smelled like mold, so it wasn't exactly an upgrade. To make matters worse, Dad had blocked up all the windows with thick, gauzy fabric, and I found myself longing for the fresh air and beautiful views I had had back at Mom's place.

There were a lot of things I missed about Mom's place. The fresh food, hanging outside with actual friends my own age. And Mom herself, of course. I longed for the nights we'd spend curled up on the couch reading together, putting down our books only to talk about our day. Let's just say reading and talking weren't exactly Dad's favorite things.

In fact, these days Dad was spending most of his time trying to regain his strength and get back to his old self. He'd found some weights down in the building's gym, and he'd work out for hours on end while gulping down these powdered milk protein shakes that he'd dug up in an old health food store. I did my best to support him, cooking all our meals from cans of food I'd scavenged from the other apartments in the building. I'd also try to work out with him, mostly for something to do. It was the only time I had any human company at all.

I could have dealt with this kind of arrangement before, when I didn't realize things could be so much better. But now that I knew what life could be like? What life *was* like just a few miles north? It was almost unbearable.

I tried to remind myself that it wouldn't be forever. Eventually, our group would emerge from the subway tunnels, and I could bring Dad back to the hotel where Mike could keep an eye on him. Also, the dragons would be hibernating again, which would put him out of immediate danger. Once I knew he was safe, I could decide where I wanted to go myself. Stay with the group, hang out with Maya again, and take trips to the New York Public Library? Or go back up to Columbia and rejoin my mom, for good this time. I wondered if I could convince others in the hotel group to go with me. Or if they'd even be allowed. Mom had spoken about helping them form a satellite group down here, but she'd never actually suggested they come up and move in.

I guess that made sense. They had to really trust the people they invited in. I mean, look what happened when they made an exception for Dad. If he had killed Sonja, it might have set off a chain reaction with the others in her herd. And that would have been a disaster. They also didn't have unlimited food or supplies, so they could only invite those with certain skills. Like my mom, who was a teacher, or Javier, with his tech expertise. There was no way they could just take in a hundred random people, even if they wanted to.

Which meant once again I would have to make a choice between the people I loved...

But that was months away. In the meantime, I had to focus on keeping Dad safe...and sane. While he was definitely getting better physically, he seemed to be getting worse mentally. He was always mumbling about some plan or another, and drawing diagrams that he tried to hide whenever I entered the room. I knew he was up to something, but he wouldn't tell me what. I wasn't ready, he'd say. I was still sick.

And that was the worst part of all. Every night he'd sit me down to try to "deprogram" me and get me to hate dragons again. He'd show me old newspapers with articles about the dragons when they first came. Photos of the devastation they'd caused. Long lists of people who had been killed by dragons. And beautiful pictures of what the world used to look like—what New York City used to look like—before the dragons took over.

"I'll never forget the day the president of the United States came on TV," he said one evening while staring at a picture of the former leader of our country. "He was a strong man. He'd been in the military in his youth. He wasn't a wimpy politician like some of them were. But when he looked into those TV cameras that night, I could see the fear in his eyes. He knew how bad it was. How bad it was going to get." Dad laid a hand on my arm. "Do you know what he said to us, Noah?"

"What?" I asked dutifully. Even though I'd heard this story a thousand times by now. It was one of Dad's greatest hits.

"He told us that help wasn't coming. That it was up to us to make a stand against the dragons. To defend our country and take it back for its citizens." His hand tightened on my arm, a fierce look in his eyes. "This is still the

253

United States of America, Noah. And while our president is long gone, his command still holds. We need to rise up. Take back our world. Destroy those monsters once and for all."

Monsters.

Funny, that's exactly what we call you.

Something snapped inside me. I didn't know why. Maybe it was weeks of enduring these rants. Or maybe it was because I was missing Mom so much. Or maybe it was the fact that I'd dreamed of Asha the night before. Asha, whose mother had been slaughtered by my dad for no good reason—except his need to "rise up."

"Did you ever stop to think that dragons might feel the same way?" I demanded, jerking my arm away from him and rising to my feet. "You think they're monsters? In their minds, *we're* the monsters. We try to shoot them out of the sky. Blow them up. They think they're just defending themselves from *us*."

Dad's face twisted. He wasn't used to me talking back to him. "Oh! So you read dragons' minds now, do you?" he jeered, his voice thick with vitriol. "Is that something you learned from your mother's little cult?"

"Actually, no," I shot back. "I learned it from a dragon."

"What are you talking about, Noah?" His eyes had darkened to angry thunderclouds.

"News flash, Dad. You weren't the only one who got hurt that day. I was burned—probably just as badly as you were. But I got healed by a dragon—just like you. And now she and I can understand each other. Just like you can understand Sonja."

My father flinched. "I don't know what you're talking about."

I sighed. "Fine. Deny it all you want. But I'm telling you, it's true. Humans and dragons can form bonds with each other. We don't have to be at odds. We don't have to fight!"

I looked over at my father, swallowing hard as I waited for his response. But he said nothing; he just stared at the ground, as if his eyes were lasers that could burn holes right through the wood. His hands gripped the sides of his chair. His whole body seemed to tremble with rage. I watched, my heart beating fast, as he finally drew in a long, slow breath. Then he looked up at me.

"Oh, Noah," he said, his voice rich with pity. "They really got to you, didn't they?"

My heart sank. "Dad..."

"It's okay." He waved me off. "You're still sick. The books say it might take a while to reprogram your brain. But we have time. Don't worry, Noah. I won't give up on you."

He rose to his feet and headed to the door.

"Where are you going?" I asked, a sudden uneasiness welling up inside me.

He gave me a steely look. "I don't think you want to know."

Then he walked out the door, slamming it shut behind him.

CHAPTER TWENTY-SEVEN

Noah

I was reading in my bedroom when I heard a knock on the door.

This was unusual, of course. In the month my father and I had been in this place, we hadn't exactly had any visitors. And Dad wouldn't knock, obviously—he'd just come right in. Besides, I was pretty sure he'd already gotten home and was out in the living room, cleaning his gun.

He'd been leaving the house every day for the last week, now that his strength had returned. He'd go out every morning and not return until late in the evening. I'd pace my bedroom until I heard the front door finally squeak open, relieved that once again he'd managed to survive the day and not run into any dragons. I'd ask him, sometimes, where he'd gone or how he'd spent his time out there. But he'd never give me a straight answer. I knew it was because he didn't trust me anymore. Which made me sad.

It also made me worried.

I set my book down, straining to listen, my heart pattering nervously in my chest. I heard my father's footsteps, followed by his barking tone.

"Who's there?"

"It's us! Open up!"

I didn't recognize the voice. But a moment later I could hear the door swing open, so apparently Dad did. Curious, I slid out of bed, heading to the door of my bedroom, cracking it open and peering into the living room just in time to see two large men step into the apartment. They were dressed in camo gear and had large guns holstered to their backs. One had a wild, untamed beard streaked with gray and smelled like he hadn't bathed in a month, while the other seemed younger and a bit cleaner—maybe the older man's son? He was carrying a large tinfoil-covered package in his arms.

"Well, well, what do we have here?" Dad asked, observing the package with a toothy grin.

"Dinner," the bearded guy pronounced. "As promised—a gourmet feast."

Dad's eyes widened. "You didn't!"

"Oh, but we did!" cried the younger man. He lifted a corner of the tinfoil, and an overwhelming smell of roasted meat permeated the apartment. "Nabbed it in a trap over near Times Square. It's a little one, but it'll taste just fine."

"The young dragons are much more tender," added the older man as the younger set the package down on the kitchen table, and suddenly I felt sick to my stomach.

Oh no. No, no, no.

I backed away, horrified, accidentally tripping over my bed and stumbling to the ground with a loud thump. A moment later, Dad pushed into my room, giving me a stern look before gesturing for me to come out into the living room with him.

"Come on," he said, his voice leaving no room for argument. "I want to introduce you to my new friends."

It was the last thing I wanted to do. Especially with the overwhelming scent of roasted dragon now wafting through the apartment, making my stomach turn. But I knew I had no choice, so I reluctantly followed him out of the bedroom, forcing myself to glance over at the tinfoil-wrapped package.

Please don't be Asha. Please don't be Asha.

"Noah, I want you to meet Richard and his son, Brad," Dad said. "I found them holed up over on Riverside Drive a few days ago."

259

"Yeah, when you almost shot my head off!" Richard barked out a laugh, as if he wouldn't have minded being accidentally murdered. He slapped my dad on the back hard, and my dad laughed heartily. I hadn't seen him in this good a mood in a while.

"Um, nice to meet you," I sputtered, not sure what else to say.

"You too, kid," Brad replied, thrusting a grubby hand in my direction. When I reached out my own hand to shake his, he squeezed it so hard I felt like my bones would break. I yanked my hand back, wincing in pain, and he broke out laughing. "Sorry. Guess I don't know my own strength."

"So, you got any silverware in this place?" Richard asked, walking over to the cabinets and rummaging around like he lived here. His dirty hands left fingerprints all over the wood. Dad joined him and together they managed to produce four plastic forks, tossing one in my direction. I didn't make a move to catch it in time, and it clattered to the ground.

Dad sighed, reaching down to grab the fork. He held it out to me. "Noah, you gonna eat with us?"

My gaze drifted over to the tinfoil package, then I quickly looked away. "I'm...good," I muttered. "I'm actually not that hungry."

"Suit yourself," Dad said, walking over to the package.

He began to unwrap the tinfoil, lowering his head to breathe in the meaty smell. I felt my stomach lurch as I caught a glimpse of silver scales.

"I'll be in my room," I muttered, then quickly abandoned the living room for the safety of my bedroom, slamming my door shut behind me.

"What's up with him?" I could hear Brad ask in the next room. "He okay?"

"He's fine," Dad said with a long sigh. "Let's just eat. White meat or dark?"

"I'll take a little of both."

I lay on my bed, trying not to listen to the foil being pulled back. My heart ached in my chest. Was it really her? Had they found her and butchered her?

It was too much to think about. I leaned over and threw up in my trash can, trying to do it as quietly as possible, so as not to draw attention. But thankfully the men were laughing loudly, and I could hear them pouring drinks. They didn't care what was happening in here.

I tried to pick up my book again and read, but the words blurred on the page through the tears in my eyes. Setting the book down, I closed my eyes, hoping that maybe I could sleep. But the voices rose from the next room, even louder once drinks had been consumed. And I couldn't help but listen.

"Okay, here's what I'm thinking. Kind of like a lobster

trap," my dad was saying. "We place the devices here and here. That should block off these two ground routes. Once they're trapped, we go in for the kill."

"Yeah, but what about this area over here?" asked Brad. "It's still wide open. They could escape out that way."

"True." Richard grunted. "And we only have enough material to make two bombs."

I shot up in bed. Bombs? Did he just say *bombs*?

"Okay then, how about this?" my dad suggested, not sounding at all surprised about the bomb mention. Had he had a part in making them? "We put out a big trap, filled with meat. Then we attach both bombs to the trap. We wait until all the dragons come to eat and—BOOM! Detonate!" He pounded his fist on the table. The other two men cheered.

"Ooh! Or maybe we could trap another young dragon," Brad broke in. "Instead of eating it, we could use it as bait. That would work, too."

I felt like I was going to be sick again. Here I'd left Columbia with my dad in hopes of protecting him from the dragons. But now it seemed the dragons would need protection from him. His rage had only gotten worse. And now he'd found friends to help him carry out his plans.

Friends with bombs.

"Poor dragons!" Richard declared. "I almost feel sorry for them!"

"Sorry enough to skip seconds?" teased his son.

"Not a chance. In fact, I'm fixing for thirds of this sweet baby boy!"

They broke out into more laughter, and I heard the tinfoil being pulled back again. I lay in my bed, breathing heavily, Richard's words echoing in my ears.

Baby *boy*, he'd said. Which meant...

It wasn't Asha.

It wasn't my dragon.

For a moment, my shoulders slumped in relief. But then I felt sick all over again. Maybe it wasn't Asha, but it was someone else. Someone's brother. Someone's son.

And now it was nothing more than dinner.

The men started talking again. Going over their plans. Plans to take out the entire herd.

Asha's herd.

I swallowed hard, making up my mind. She'd risked her life to warn me about the danger from her herd.

Now it was my turn to warn her...before it was too late.

CHAPTER TWENTY-EIGHT

Noah

The men left soon after discussing their plans, slamming the front door behind them. I waited for Dad to come to my room to say goodnight, but he only bustled around the kitchen for a bit, then headed straight to his bedroom. Probably not interested in facing my questions.

I waited a half hour more, then tiptoed to my bedroom door, trying to be as quiet as possible as I pulled it open. But when I stepped into the living room and heard my dad's loud snores, I realized I was in no danger of him waking up. Feeling bolder, I grabbed my shoes and headed out of the apartment and into the courtyard.

As I exited, I glanced up at the sky nervously, suddenly

having second thoughts about my plan to sneak out and find Asha. It was all well and good in theory, but in reality, it was a bit more complicated. New York was a big city, after all, and she was only one small dragon. How would I be able to find her? Especially without accidentally alerting the rest of the herd—who wanted me dead—to my presence.

Asha? I pushed out with my thoughts. Maybe if she was somewhere nearby, she could hear me. *If you're there, I need to talk to you. It's important.*

But there was no reply.

Sighing, I continued down the dark street, thankful for the full moon to light my path. I stayed close to the buildings, too, to reduce my chance of being seen. And I kept an eye on the dark sky above—until I tripped over a huge pile of debris and almost fell straight into an open manhole. I watched the ground more carefully after that, longing for the clean streets of Columbia.

I wasn't sure where to go, but in the end, I decided to head toward Times Square. That was where I'd first met Asha—maybe she had made her home somewhere nearby. Perhaps if I got close enough, she'd hear me and come find me. I could warn her of the danger, then get back home before my dad had any idea I had been gone.

Just a few more blocks—

Thrump.

I froze in my tracks at the sudden sound above, breaking through the silence of the dark night.

Thrump.

Thrump

Thrump.

Heart in my throat, I dared to look up, praying the dragon wasn't as close as it sounded. Sometimes sound carried in a weird way in the city—maybe the creature was miles from here and therefore no threat at all. Maybe I'd get lucky.

But no, my heart sank as I caught sight of the giant, menacing shape flying through the sky above. It was right over my head.

Thrump.

Thrump.

Thrump.

Mind racing, I pushed my body as flat as possible against a nearby brick wall, trying not to move. It was dark, I reminded myself. There was no way the dragon could see me down here—not if I stayed perfectly still. Their eyesight was bad enough during the day; it was likely even worse at night. If I just waited, it would fly away soon, and I could continue my journey to Times Square.

Please go away, I begged it silently. *Please! I just need to find Asha.*

Suddenly the dragon stopped. It turned on a dime, craning its neck to stare down at the earth below. I watched breathlessly as it began to lower itself to the ground. Had it seen me? Scented me? I suddenly remembered the cooked dragon smell that had permeated the apartment earlier. Did I still smell like roasted meat?

Dragons' eyes might be bad, but their noses worked just fine.

The ground shook as the dragon landed with a heavy thud. I watched as it turned to face me, lowering its head and staring straight into my eyes. I tried to determine if I recognized it—could it be one from the herd uptown, here to rescue me? But there was nothing familiar about this dragon, as far as I could tell, and the icy look in its eyes made me lose hope that it was here on a friendly mission. I cringed, paralyzed with fear. What to do? What to do?

Please leave me alone, I thought as hard as I could. *I just want to warn Asha.*

But the dragon only stepped closer. So close I could feel the steam from its nostrils heating my skin. I broke out into a cold sweat. Pressed up against the wall with nowhere to run, there was nothing I could do.

Asha. Where are you, Asha? I could really use your help!

But still, there was no answer.

I closed my eyes, waiting for the fire to come. Knowing in my heart that this was the end. After all I'd been through the past few weeks, all the danger I'd faced, this was how I would die. All alone, in the dark, with no one even knowing where I was.

And Asha and her herd would soon follow, with no one to warn them.

I'm sorry, Asha. I tried. I really tried.

But, to my surprise, the dragon didn't attack. Instead, it reached out with its heavy front leg, curling its paw around my body and yanking me close to its chest. I screamed, struggling to get free, but, of course, it was no use. I was trapped in its vicelike grip. There was no getting away.

Once I had been secured, the dragon grunted as if satisfied, then pushed off the ground with its mighty hind legs, shooting us both into the sky. I yelped in surprise, my stomach dropping to my knees as the ground fell away beneath me. The wind whooshed in my ears, pulling tears down my cheeks as we rose higher and higher.

I was flying. I was flying with a dragon.

But where was it taking me?

And what would it do to me once we got there?

CHAPTER TWENTY-NINE

Asha

My queen! There you are!"

Asha lifted her head to see Tolkyn come in for a landing a few feet in front of her on the rooftop she'd been hiding out on for the past few hours. She yawned uneasily, rising to her feet. She should have known they'd find her eventually, but she'd hoped for a little more time alone before being called back to her official duties.

She spit out the remains of the rat she'd been chewing on; it was mostly guts and bone anyway, and not all that satisfying. But food had become even more scarce these past few weeks, and though the other dragons always offered her the best cuts of meat they could find, with her being queen and all, she had largely refused them, telling them they should instead distribute it among the older dragons who had difficulty hunting.

She sighed, thinking of Noah and the territory to the north. To the dragons who allowed themselves to be fed by humans. Tolkyn had called them traitors. But she wondered, deep down, if maybe they were on to something. They might be traitors, but they had full bellies. And they weren't dying of starvation. It seemed a pretty good trade-off to her.

But she knew the others would never agree. They'd rather die than take food from the monsters.

"What is it?" she asked wearily, looking up at her dragon captain. She hadn't accepted his resignation after her mother's murder—she knew he had done his best and didn't blame him for what had happened. Besides, she needed strong, older dragons on her side to win the trust of the herd. Not everyone, she'd learned, was thrilled with having such a young dragon in charge, especially during these tough times.

But at least she could be assured that Tolkyn had her back.

"Don't worry, it's good news for once," the older dragon declared, his voice rich with excitement. "We found him. Your uncle finally tracked him down."

Asha cocked her head, confused. "Who?" she asked.

Tolkyn shook himself, shimmers of silver flickering down his sides. "The young pup, of course," he replied, as if stating the obvious. "The one who helped kill your mother."

Oh no. Asha swallowed hard. *Noah. They found Noah?*

"You found him?" she asked, trying to keep her voice neutral. Meanwhile, everything inside her wanted to scream. Why hadn't Noah listened to her and stayed up north? Stayed with the other dragons who could protect him from her herd? She'd told him it was dangerous to come back here.

Evidently, he hadn't listened.

"Yes. And we have him contained on the high tower," Tolkyn replied. "As you requested." His mouth dipped into a frown. "Though I'm still not sure why you wanted to bring him here, Your Grace. Your uncle could have easily taken care of the problem on sight."

Asha shifted uneasily. *Taken care of the problem.* In other words, blast Noah with dragon-fire, no questions asked.

"I want to look him in the eyes," she said at last. "I want to see the facts written on his face."

"But, my queen," the older dragon argued. "We already know the facts. The pup and his father murdered your mother in cold blood."

271

She set her eyes on him. "Did you see him do it?"

Now it was Tolkyn's turn to look uncomfortable, and she immediately felt bad. She knew he still felt guilty about not arriving in time to save her mother. She shouldn't poke at the wound.

Still, she knew for a fact that Noah hadn't been the one to hurt her mother. Though she couldn't explain that to Tolkyn. If she told him she had bonded with a human, he probably wouldn't even believe her. And if he somehow did, well, that would be the end of her reign. She would be the one called a traitor.

"Everyone deserves a fair trial," she said. "Even the monsters. Tomorrow, we will hold a tribunal and he will appear before all our dragons. There, I will decide what shall be done with him."

Tolkyn gave her a dubious look. She supposed it was for good reason. She could pretend all she liked that she had the ultimate say in this matter. But there was no way the other dragons would agree to mercy. In their eyes, Noah had killed their queen. In return, he must die.

Except Asha wasn't going to let that happen.

"Why do you seem to care so much about this pup?" Tolkyn asked softly, as if he didn't want any other dragons that might be nearby to overhear. His eyes narrowed on her. "Is there something you're not telling me, my queen? For I cannot help you if you keep things from me."

She gave him a sorry look. She knew he meant well. And he cared about her, probably more than anyone else in the herd. But, in the end, he was still loyal to the ways of her mother—to the herd. And she risked him turning on her if he knew the truth.

If he knew what she was about to do.

CHAPTER THIRTY

Noah

At some point during the flight, I must have passed out. Maybe it was the altitude, the thin air way up high making it difficult to breathe. Or maybe it was just pure fear—my brain unable to take it anymore. When I woke up, I found myself high in the sky on the narrow ledge of a large skyscraper, the ground looking like it was a thousand miles below.

My heart sank. This was not good.

Gripping the sides of the building with white-knuckled fingers, I averted my gaze, forcing myself not to look down. Instead, I trained my eyes on the sky, searching for the dragon who had dropped me here. But he was nowhere to be seen. I supposed I didn't need guarding up here. It wasn't like I could run away.

I slumped down on the ledge, my back pressed hard against the wall. Hugging my knees to my chest, I wondered what I was supposed to do. The sun had risen, which meant I must have been knocked out for a while. My dad had probably woken up by now and realized I was gone. Did he think I ran away? That my mom had come to get me? Would he go out looking for me? Or was he too wrapped up in his dragon-killing plan to waste the time?

Oh, Asha, I thought miserably. *I'm sorry. I tried…*

"Noah!"

I startled, almost falling off the ledge at the sound of the familiar voice. After regaining my balance, I looked up just in time to see a dragon flying toward me. A dragon with shimmery silver scales and big amber eyes.

Eyes I'd recognize anywhere.

"Asha?" I breathed, hardly able to believe it.

She was now as big as a large truck, her tail long and elegant as it wrapped itself around the skyscraper's spire. The rising sun's rays seemed to catch her scales, casting rainbows across the side of the building.

"Oh, Noah…" I heard her voice whisper through my mind. "I told you to stay away."

I hung my head. "I know," I said. "I should have

listened to you. I was worried about my dad. What he'd do. Asha—he's planning something big. I needed to warn you. Him and his friends, they're going to go after your herd! With guns and bombs. You're in danger."

The expression on Asha's face grew grave. "So are you, Noah. My herd still believes you killed my mother. And even if you didn't, they don't seem to care about the truth. They're planning to execute you tomorrow in front of the entire group. And there's nothing I can say to change their minds."

I slumped back against the building. Of course. They would kill me. Then my dad would kill them. The cycle would go on and on forever. "This is never going to end, is it?" I asked, suddenly feeling exhausted.

"Actually...," Asha replied, flicking her tail. It smacked against the building with a loud, sharp snapping sound. "It ends now."

I looked up at her, confused. "What do you mean?"

"I'm not going to let them kill you."

"But you said—"

"I know what I said. But you're my friend, Noah. We share a bond. I can't just fly away from that, even for my herd. I love them, but they're wrong to do this. You shouldn't have to pay for your father's crimes."

Hope rose up inside me. Maybe all was not lost. I had come here to save Asha. But maybe she would end up saving me instead. "So what are you going to do? Are you going to try to convince them to let me go?"

"No. They won't listen." She sighed sadly. "I know they won't. Just as your father wouldn't listen to you. The only thing left is to help you escape."

I swallowed hard, relieved. Escape. She was going to help me escape! Then a worrying thought came to me. "But won't you get in trouble?" I asked.

She snorted, puffs of smoke pluming from her nostrils. "Let me worry about trouble. Right now, we have to get you somewhere safe, where my herd can't find you." She peered down at me. "Where do you want to go?"

I realized there was only one answer to that question. "Can you take me to my mother?"

She hesitated for a moment, then slowly nodded her head. "Yes," she said decidedly, as if coming to a conclusion. "Of course that's the best place. The safest place. Though..." She stared off into the distance, her eyes clouded with concern. "Do you think your dragons will be okay with me bringing you there? I'm not supposed to enter their territory, you know...."

I frowned. I forgot about that. Also, what if Sonja had told the herd that my father had shot at her while I was with him? How was I going to show them I was on their side?

I shook my head. No. I couldn't show them. But maybe

Asha could. After all, they might be from different herds, but at the end of the day, they were still one species. Surely Asha could assure them that we meant no harm.

"Just tell them the truth," I said. "Explain that I need to see my mother. Hopefully that'll be enough."

It had to be, because we had no other options.

"It'll be interesting to meet them," Asha mused. "To see this better life you've talked about for myself. To see if there might be some way..." She shook herself. "Well, I'd just like to see it is all."

I nodded, suddenly feeling a little excited. This was a step, I realized. Maybe a baby one, but a step all the same. If Asha met the other dragons—if they impressed her—maybe it would give her hope. Maybe it would give her strength to fight for change in her own herd.

To stop this endless war, once and for all.

"Great. Then it's a plan. Except..." I glanced over the side of the building, at the ground seeming a thousand miles below. "How are we going to get there?"

A smile crossed Asha's face. "Isn't it obvious? We're going to fly."

CHAPTER THIRTY-ONE

Noah

Whoa! This is awesome!"

The wind rushed at my face, bringing tears to my eyes, as we shot up into the sky like a rocket, the tall buildings falling away beneath me as we rose higher and higher until we were above them all and they looked like little toys. My fingers clung to Asha's long neck while my legs pressed against her sides, just above her wings, which were flapping rhythmically up and down with the thrumping sound that had always terrified me in the past.

But now it filled me with joy.

This was amazing. Absolutely amazing. Like something out of one of my fantasy books. Not real life. I wondered, suddenly, if I was the first person in the world to ever ride a dragon. Javier had said none of the dragons with them had ever allowed human riders. *Maybe you'll be the first*, he'd said.

If only he could see me now.

Asha turned her head to look back at me, the sudden shift in weight almost knocking me off-balance. I squeezed her neck hard, trying desperately to hold on.

"Don't choke me!" she teased, but I could tell she didn't really mind. In fact, she looked pretty proud of herself as she swam across the sky. She was so graceful, even if the air currents did make things a little bumpy.

I loosened my grip a bit, allowing myself to look around. We'd climbed high into the sky by this point, and I now had a dragon's-eye view of the city skyline. It was beautiful—breathtaking and huge. I had no idea just how big New York City really was until I saw it from above. It seemed to stretch on forever.

"Are you okay?" Asha asked, careful not to turn her head this time.

"I'm amazing," I assured her. It was funny. I'd spent almost my entire life being afraid of dragons. But now, literally flying on the back of one, I felt completely fearless. Like nothing could hurt me.

Until we ran into more dragons.

They came up quickly. One minute we were flying

free, and the next, we were surrounded. Asha stopped short, and the sudden deceleration nearly caused me to fall off her back. Clinging to her neck, I looked around fearfully from dragon to dragon as they hissed and snarled, their bellies warming with fire.

Oh no. This was not good.

"Asha, say something to them," I begged. "You're their queen! They're your herd!"

But Asha only looked from one dragon to the next, her whole body trembling. "Actually," she whispered, "I think they're yours."

Wait, what? I looked up at the dragons again, my eyes locking on the fourth one, flying quickly in our direction. To my shock and amazement, I realized it was none other than Sonja. I let out a shuddering breath.

We'd made it!

"Sonja!" I cried, waving one hand in greeting. "It's me, Noah!"

Sonja approached cautiously, peering at me with a curious look in her eyes. I could tell that she recognized me, but she was also confused. Why was I riding a dragon from another herd? Why was I riding a dragon at all?

It was then that I remembered what my father had done. I had been with him at the time. Did she blame me, too, like Asha's herd did for her mother's death? If only I could talk to her!

But maybe Asha could.

"Asha!" I hissed. "Can you speak to these dragons?" I had no idea, I realized, if dragons from other herds spoke the same language.

"I don't know. I'll try."

Asha lowered her head as if in a sign of submission. The dragons watched her closely, and I could tell they were communicating with one another, though I couldn't understand what they were saying. I held my breath as I waited to see what would happen next, praying they'd be friendly to Asha and not see her as a threat.

"Okay..." Asha's voice suddenly returned to my head. "They're going to let us down. I told them I was bringing you to your mother, and they've given me special permission to land."

I let out a breath, relieved, as the other dragons broke ranks, leaving us a clear path forward. Asha gave a respectful nod to Sonja, then dipped her wings, dive-bombing the ground. A moment later, we landed safely in the courtyard.

"Noah? Is that you?"

I whirled around to find Lei and Hugo running up to me, stunned looks on their faces.

"Hey!" I cried, slipping off Asha's back and rushing over to greet them. I hugged each of them in turn, my heart overflowing with excitement at seeing them again.

It hadn't been long, but I'd missed them a ton. "It's so good to see you!"

"What are you doing back here?" Hugo asked, looking me over. "I thought you took off for good with your dad." He gave me a bit of an accusing look. I wondered what people had been saying about me. It couldn't be good.

"Yeah, well, that didn't exactly work out," I confessed, feeling sheepish.

"And who is this?" Lei asked excitedly. She started toward Asha.

Asha squawked in fear, backing up quickly out of her reach. She ducked behind me as if trying to hide, even though she was about five times my height by now. I reached out and gently stroked her neck, calming her down.

"It's okay, Asha," I assured her. "This is Lei. She won't hurt you."

It was funny; I'd been so concerned with Asha meeting the other dragon herd that I hadn't even considered how afraid she might be of the other humans here. All her life, she'd been taught that they were the enemy. It was going to take a little time for her to get used to them being friends. Just like it took me a while to get used to the dragons hanging out around here.

Asha snorted uneasily but stepped out from behind me again. Lei peered at her, then me, looking puzzled.

"Asha?" Lei repeated. "Is she new or something? I don't remember seeing her around."

"She's pretty skinny, too," Hugo pointed out. "Is she, like, a stray?"

"She's from the Midtown herd," I informed them.

They raised their eyebrows and glanced at each other. "I heard the Midtown dragons were mean," Hugo said. "And violent."

"But she doesn't seem mean," Lei added, observing Asha with great interest. "And even better, she lets you ride her." She sighed dreamily. "We've been trying to get my dragon, Bowie, to let me ride him for weeks now. But he seems totally freaked out by the idea. I was beginning to give up hope."

Asha snorted, and I turned to look at her, but her eyes were focused on something behind me. I turned to see Hugo had pulled out a giant piece of beef jerky from his messenger bag.

"That smells…so…good…" Asha began sniffing hard, pawing the ground excitedly.

"You want this?" Hugo asked, waving the meat in the air. Asha snorted eagerly, smoke puffing from her nostrils, causing us all to laugh.

"Don't tease the dragon!" Lei scolded, grabbing the meat from him. She turned to Asha. "Sorry, girl," she apologized. "He's the worst."

She tossed the jerky in Asha's direction. It landed by her feet, but the dragon made no move to eat it; instead, she glanced at me worriedly. As if she thought it might be a trap.

"It's okay. I told you," I reminded her, using the bond we shared. "They take care of dragons here. Feeding them is kind of a normal thing."

Asha's lips curled. She dropped her head, slurping up the jerky hungrily, as if she hadn't eaten in a week. I smiled at Hugo. "You sure know the way to a dragon's heart," I joked.

He smirked. "Yeah, well, no matter what herd they're from, dragons are pretty much the same. Food first, everything else later."

"Sounds about right," I said, glancing over at Asha, who was still chomping down on her food. I stepped away, giving her some space, then turned back to Hugo.

"Look, do you think you could go find my mom?" I asked him. "I would go myself, but I don't want to leave Asha alone."

"Of course. Be right back!"

I watched as he handed the meat satchel to Lei, then took off running in the direction of the apartment building where my mom lived. I turned back to Asha, wondering if she was still eating. But, to my surprise, she now had her eyes on the sky. Carefully watching a new dragon come in for a landing.

"Uh, oh. I think he saw me giving out food after hours," Lei joked. "We're in trouble now."

A moment later, a young male dragon about Asha's size dropped down a few feet in front of us. His gaze narrowed on the new dragon as he took a step toward her. Asha watched him warily, stumbling backward a bit to keep the distance between them. My heart started beating a little faster as I watched the scene unfold, the air between the two dragons seeming to spark with electricity. What was going on here? Had Asha made him mad by eating his food? Had she overstayed her welcome and they were signaling for her to leave?

Should I get between them? Or let this play out?

Before I could make a move, Lei jumped in front of the male dragon, waving her arms as if scolding him. "Bowie!" she snapped. "Be good! These are our friends!"

To my surprise, Bowie backed off immediately, bowing his head respectfully to Lei. She gave him a stiff nod, then threw him a piece of jerky from Hugo's satchel. As he gobbled it up, she turned back to Asha and me.

"He says he's sorry," she told us. "He didn't mean any harm. He just thinks she's cute." Lei giggled. "Well, he didn't actually use the word *cute*, but I'm pretty sure that was what he meant."

"You can talk to him?" I stared at her, amazed. "Since when?"

"Oh yeah!" she said, her eyes brightening. "You don't know, do you? A lot has changed since you've been gone. Saanvi's been doing all sorts of experiments after what happened with your dad and Sonja. So when I got a papercut, she had my dragon heal it. After that, he and I could talk back and forth just fine." She smiled at Bowie, reaching out to stroke him on the neck. "He still won't let me ride him, though," she added sadly. "Stubborn little guy. But lots of the others are riding their dragons now. It's pretty amazing."

Bowie snorted, then turned to Asha. He stepped forward, lightly nipping Asha's leg then dashing away. I knew from my time in the dragon daycare that this was how they liked to get one another to play. At first, I worried Asha wouldn't know this; maybe they didn't have the same games where she came from. But to my relief, she launched after him almost immediately, nipping at his heels. A moment later they were both in the air, locked in a wild game of aerial tag. I couldn't help but grin. How cute was that? Asha had found a friend!

"Noah!"

I whirled around. My gaze fell on my mother, who was running toward me with long strides. My heart leapt with joy at the sight of her face. I hadn't realized until that very moment just how much I had missed her.

"Mom!" I cried.

Before I knew it, she was there, throwing her arms around me in the tightest hug known to mankind. I hugged her back just as hard, feeling the tears springing into my eyes. It was just so good to see her. How could I have ever thought leaving her was a good idea? I buried my head in her shoulder, breathing in her warm, earthy scent.

"Oh, Noah!" she murmured in my ear. "Thank goodness you're back! I was so worried!"

"I'm so sorry, Mom," I said, pulling out of the hug. "I shouldn't have just taken off on you. It's just...I didn't know what else to do. I was worried about Dad leaving alone, and I didn't want him to get hurt."

"I know. It's okay," she assured me. "You're a good son, Noah. You care about your family, and that's important." She frowned for a moment. "But where's your dad now?" she asked. "Did he come back with you?"

Something in her voice told me it wouldn't be a great idea for Dad to return. Which made sense, of course, after what he'd done before he left. This group had saved his life, and he'd basically spit in their faces by trying to hurt their dragon. And if they knew what he was up to now...

"Look, Mom," I said quickly. "Dad found these new friends. They're really bad guys. And they have bombs. They're planning to blow up the Midtown dragons." My voice caught in my throat. "Which is Asha's herd. They're in trouble, and I don't know what to do."

Mom nodded stiffly. If Dad's plans were surprising to her, she didn't show it. "We need to bring this up with the council," she decided. "We'll call an emergency meeting, and you can explain to them what he's planning. I'm sure they'll be able to come up with some way to help."

"That's a good idea," I said, feeling relief wash over me. Maybe if we got everyone to agree to help, we'd have a chance to stop Dad after all.

Mom turned and headed out of the courtyard, presumably to let everyone know. Meanwhile, Hugo picked that moment to return, his hands filled with bags of meat and apples. "A truly delectable, dragon-licious snack!" he declared, tossing a bag to me with a grin. It stunk to high heaven, and I laughed, then waved at Asha in the sky. She dropped down in front of me, her eyes shining with eagerness as she eyed the fruit in my hand.

"Apples!" she crowed.

"I told you," I said, dumping the contents of the bag onto the pavement. "And there's meat, too. All you can eat."

Asha's eyes bulged so widely that, for a second, I thought they might pop out of her head. Then she dove in, devouring the feast, barely even chewing as she slurped up every bite. When she had finished, she let out a loud, satisfying burp.

"Wow," she exclaimed. "I can't remember a time I ate so much. Maybe never. How is it possible?"

"They grow their own meat here," I explained. "It's pretty cool, actually. Science."

Asha nodded thoughtfully. "I have to say, this place is all that you said it was, Noah. A true dream come true. I'm really impressed..."

"But...?" I asked, sensing the word before she could say it.

"That's all it can ever be. A beautiful, impossible dream."

I frowned. "Why can't it be real? It's real for the dragons here."

She dropped her head. "Yes. But my herd would never accept this kind of life—even for all its benefits. Because it would mean trusting humans. And that's something they will never do."

I sighed. Of course. Just like my dad. Some people—and dragons, it seemed—were so lost in the world as it was that they could never see what it could become, if they'd just give it a chance.

"Well, then, why don't *you* stay?" I blurted. "I mean, just don't go back. What do you have there? An empty stomach. Threats against your life? Why don't you stay here? With me."

Asha gave me a sorrowful look. "You know I would

290

love to do that, Noah. Maybe more than anything in the world. But I can't. I'm their queen. If I don't return, they will come find me. And I would not put this beautiful place in danger." She paused, then added, "Also, I must warn them of your father's threat. They don't know what he's planning. And they could walk right into his trap."

I shifted from foot to foot. I didn't like it, but I knew she was right. "Maybe you *should* go back," I agreed. "At least to warn them of the danger. They need to lay low and hide out until we can come up with a plan to stop my dad and his friends."

And maybe if we did, I thought but didn't say aloud, *maybe we could prove to them we aren't the monsters they believed us to be...*

Asha seemed to brighten at this. She flapped her wings, sending shimmers down her scales. I reached out, rubbing her snout with my hand. "Just be careful, Asha," I whispered. "I couldn't bear it if anything happened to you."

Asha nuzzled my hand with her snout. Then she looked up at me with her big amber eyes. "Goodbye, Noah," she whispered. "Thank you for showing me all this. It is good to know that things can be better. It...gives me hope."

And with that, she spread her wings, lifted off the ground, and disappeared into the sky. I watched her go, my heart aching.

"Stay safe, Asha," I whispered.

But even as I said the words, I wondered if it was possible. Because my dad and his friends would soon be on the move.

And they wouldn't stop until Asha and her entire herd were dead.

CHAPTER THIRTY-TWO

Asha

Once she was back in her own territory, Asha headed straight to the park where she knew the dragons would be gathering, preparing the tribunal for Noah. Of course, Noah wouldn't be there. She wondered how angry they would be when they realized he'd escaped. Would they suspect her involvement? Or blame the other herd?

They were all assembled when she arrived. Tolkyn and her uncle and aunt at the front, pacing back and forth. When Tolkyn saw her approach, his face shone with relief.

"My queen!" he cried. "There you are!"

"Where have you been?" her uncle demanded, looking less pleased. "You were supposed to be here at sunrise."

She landed gracefully, though her whole body was sore from allowing Noah to ride on her back. She tried to imagine what the others would think if she admitted to what she'd done. They'd probably think she wasn't fit to rule.

"We have a problem," Tolkyn broke in, before she could answer her uncle. "The young pup has disappeared."

She considered feigning surprise. But what good would it do? If she was going to get them to listen, she had to start being honest, no matter the consequences.

"I freed him," she stated flatly, lifting her head with what she hoped looked like a regal air. But her body betrayed her, trembling fiercely, her legs buckling beneath her. She tried to tell herself it was due to sore muscles, but she knew, in her heart, it was fear—pure and simple. Fear of the very same dragons who had raised her and kept her safe her whole life. Fear of what they'd do to her now.

Her uncle glanced at her aunt. Then he let out a roar of rage so loud it echoed across the park, causing some of the younger dragons to scatter in fright. "Why would you do something like that?" he demanded. "What right did you have?"

She swallowed hard and forced herself to look him

in the eye. She was afraid, but she refused to show it. "My right as your queen. And because he did not kill my mother," she said calmly. "He is innocent."

"That is a lie! Tolkyn! Tell her!"

Tolkyn shook himself, clearly uneasy. "You know I arrived too late to see what happened," he reminded her uncle. "I had assumed he'd had a hand in it. But if our queen believes something different, shouldn't we hear her out?"

"She is a child!" her uncle bellowed. "What does she know?"

"I know the truth," Asha shot back. "I know he did not kill my mother. His father did. And what's worse is his father did not die as we thought in the fight. He is very much alive, and he is planning an attack on our herd as we speak." She swallowed hard, trying to keep her voice steady. "We are all in danger. They have something called bombs. Which are worse than rock sticks. They plan to wipe dragons out of the city for good."

But her uncle only laughed heartily. "I'd like to see them try," he boasted. Some of the other dragons in attendance cheered at this. Asha felt her stomach sour.

"This is serious!" she cried. "You have to—

Her uncle stepped toward her, almost threateningly. "How do you know any of this?" he demanded. "How would you know of a monster's plan?"

Asha cringed. And…there it was. The question she had been dreading most of all. She could feel the eyes of the entire herd on her, waiting for her answer. Half of her wanted to just flee the scene. Never return. Let them fend for themselves if they were so sure they could do it.

But then she saw the older dragons who could barely fly. The baby dragons who had never had a full meal in their lives. She was their leader, like it or not. She could never walk away.

And she owed them the truth.

"It seems I have bonded with the young pup," she announced to the group. "His name is Noah. I can understand him. And he can understand me."

The other dragons broke out into excited chatter, drowning out anything else she might have wanted to say. Until her uncle let out another fierce roar, silencing them all instantly.

"This is unacceptable," he declared. "You have betrayed your herd. You have sided with a monster over your own family."

"That's not true!" Asha protested. "Noah isn't a monster. And he's on our side. He risked his life to warn me what his father is up to."

"A trick. A trap, most likely," her uncle muttered.

"No." She shook her head. "A real threat. One we need to take seriously. Do what you like with me, but please heed my warning. They are coming for us. We need to get somewhere safe."

"Are you kidding?" her uncle bellowed. "We are dragons! We do not hide from humans!"

She hung her head. Of course. They would fight till their dying breaths. And, like Noah said, nothing would ever change.

She could feel someone watching her. She turned to see Tolkyn gazing at her with an unreadable expression on his face. Did he believe her, deep down? If so, why wouldn't he stand up for her? Why would he let her uncle just take over like this and put the herd in danger?

"Tolkyn," she pleaded. "You believe me, right?"

But, to her dismay, he turned his head, looking away. Her heart sank. She would have no support from him. And the rest were all too blinded by their hatred and arrogance. Just as Noah's father was. And now more dragons and humans would die. Each believing they were in the right.

A war that would never end. Peace that would never come.

She lifted her eyes to the sky. What good was being queen if she couldn't protect her herd? What good was waiting around for a chance to say she told them so when the monsters finally came? Then it would be too late.

No. She couldn't just sit back and watch it happen. She had to do something.

"Very well," she said. "If you do not believe my words, let me prove it to you. I will find evidence that the threat is real…and deadly. I will not return until I do." She unfurled her wings, shaking them out one by one before lifting into the air. She was the queen. She would help her herd, even if they didn't want her to.

Even at the cost of her life.

CHAPTER THIRTY-THREE

Noah

"Come on, Bowie. You can do this. I know you can."

I watched, amused, as Lei gave her dragon a pep talk before trying once again to climb onto his back. She'd been at it for hours, ever since she'd learned that I'd been able to ride Asha. But Bowie clearly wasn't so sure about the whole thing. And every time Lei tried to mount him, he quickly bucked her off.

"Ow!" she cried, rubbing her butt as she scrambled back to her feet. "You're the worst dragon ever, you know that?" But her eyes danced merrily as she scolded him, and I could tell she didn't really mean it. And Bowie knew it, too. He had nuzzled her with his snout, and she hugged him tight before giving him a piece of beef jerky and trying again.

It was cute. But it also made me kind of sad. Because I should be sharing the same kind of closeness with Asha right now. Asha should be enjoying beef jerky.

Instead, she was still in danger.

I sighed, my heart feeling heavy. It had only been a few hours since Asha had flown away, yet I couldn't stop thinking about her. Worrying about her. What would her herd say when they realized she'd helped me escape? And would she be able to convince them of the danger they were in? I didn't know when my father planned to act— maybe my disappearance would buy the dragons some time while he went out to search for me. But eventually the attack would come.

Would they be prepared?

"They're ready for you, Noah."

I whirled around to find Mom on the steps of what used to be the grand Columbia University library, now turned into a meeting place for the group's elected council to discuss important matters. My mom had requested that they schedule an emergency meeting to hear about my dad and his friends' plan. And now they were gathered inside, waiting for me.

I followed Mom into the building, my earlier excitement dissolving into nervousness as my steps echoed through the marbled halls. So much was riding on them being able to help. What if they refused?

But of course they won't, I scolded myself. *They care about dragons. That's one of the reasons they founded this group to begin with. They won't just stand back and watch them get hurt.*

We entered the large meeting room where the elected council members were waiting, sitting behind a long table that was covered in papers and books. There were twelve of them seated, all of various ages and races, wearing matching black robes and white shirts. Mom had told me that a few of them had been founders of the group and on the council since the beginning, while others had joined later, wanting a bigger role in making decisions for the community. One had been a doctor. Another, a farmer. One had run a construction company. All of them had different backgrounds and experiences, but they shared the role of governing the group.

They looked up as I entered. A few of them smiled encouragingly, which made me relax a little. I stopped in front of them, waiting for their instructions.

"So," the man at the center of the table, the speaker of the house, boomed as I stepped forward to address the group. He was a large Black man with graying locs that tumbled off his broad shoulders. "Your mother says you have something to tell us."

I drew in a shaky breath. "My father...," I said. "You remember him—he was the one who came here, burned by the dragons."

I saw a few of them exchange knowing looks, and I wondered what they were thinking. Did they blame me for letting my father escape? Or were they glad he had gone—certainly they hadn't wanted someone like him in their group over the long term.

I swallowed hard, forcing myself to continue. "He's... better... now. Which is... good. But, well, I found out he and his new friends are planning an attack on the Midtown herd of dragons. Which is... bad." I hesitated for a moment. "They've got bombs and guns and traps," I added quickly, my face heating up. "They're going to ambush them and take them all out."

The council erupted in murmurs. I shifted from foot to foot, feeling hot and stressed.

"This is most unfortunate," declared a woman to the speaker's right. She was older and wearing a black hijab in addition to her robe. "This continued violence against dragons will only hurt our cause. How can we get other dragons from other herds to trust us if they are constantly being threatened by humans?"

"Yeah, well, maybe you all should have thought of that before you went and saved that dude's life," jeered a young white man with copper-colored hair who was sitting at the end of the table. "I told you we were just asking for trouble, bringing him back here. We should have just left him out on the streets to die like the dog he is."

I cringed. While I understood what he was saying—if my dad had died, we wouldn't be in this predicament— it was pretty harsh to wish him dead. Did they truly feel this way about anyone who didn't agree with their beliefs? That they should be wiped out because they were on the other side? Wasn't that, in some ways, just as bad?

But now was not the time to argue. Not when I needed their help.

"Regardless of your feelings for my husband," Mom broke in, her voice strong and loud as she stepped up beside me, "the problem remains. There is a herd in Midtown that is about to be violently exterminated for no reason. And if we can help, we should."

"There are good dragons there!" I broke in. "They don't deserve to die!"

A woman around my mom's age gave me a pitying look. "Do you know where they plan to carry out this ambush?" she asked quietly. "Or when they plan to do it?"

"No," I said, apologetic. "They didn't say."

"Well, then, how are we supposed to stop them?" demanded the man at the end of the table. "If we don't know where or when this attack will take place?"

It was a good question. And I had no answer. I glanced at my mom. She shrugged, a look of unease on her face.

"Look, son, we want to help," the council leader assured me. "But we need to be careful if and when we decide to act. If we send people down there, we would be putting them in danger from the Midtown herd. The dragons there wouldn't understand that we were trying to help them and they would attempt to kill anyone they saw." He focused his gaze on me. "You're from there. You know this is true."

I hung my head. I knew it all too well. There wasn't a dragon down there that didn't want me and every human on earth dead.

Except, of course, Asha.

"Then send the dragons," I tried, feeling desperate. "They can communicate with one another. Maybe they can let them know we want to help."

"If we send in our dragons, then we risk them falling into the same ambush you're trying to save the others from," the council leader explained sorrowfully. "Also, we're not their masters. We can't order them to do something against their will. And what do they care about the plight of another herd? A herd they don't even get along with."

My heart sank. They kept talking, but I could no longer listen. I didn't need to hear any more excuses on why they wouldn't lift a finger to help Asha and her herd. Even if they were good excuses.

"Please," I begged the group, trying one last time. "You have to do something! You can't just sit around and let them be slaughtered!"

"I'm sorry," the council leader said in a firm voice. "We would love to help these dragons. But unless they waltz in here and ask for our help themselves, I don't see how there's anything we can do."

I nodded stiffly, feeling defeated. I glanced at my mom. She sighed, then put an arm around my shoulder, leading me out of the room. I could feel the council watching me as I left, their gazes filled with pity.

Anger rose inside of me. I'd never felt so helpless before. I couldn't just sit around and let Asha's herd be killed. But what could I do on my own? I was just a kid! I could try to talk to my dad again, but there was no guarantee I'd even reach him in time. Like the council said, if I entered the other herd's territory, I'd have a target on my back.

Because they didn't want me to save them. They wanted me dead.

CHAPTER THIRTY-FOUR

Asha

Asha flew low across the city, her eyes glued to the ground below. She wasn't sure exactly what she was looking for, and now she regretted not getting enough details from Noah as to what his father's plan could be. But she was determined to find *something*. Something to prove to her herd that there was danger they couldn't ignore.

She turned left, heading toward the large open area where she'd first met Noah. It seemed to be a human place—maybe she would find something there. She was almost upon it when a strange smell began to waft through the air. It took her a moment to figure out what it was. The smell of meat. But not a good smell, like most meat. Instead, it smelled rancid. Horrible. Dead.

It was then that she saw the source. Some kind of small bony carcass, lying in the center of the square. Confused, she flew a little closer, trying to determine what kind of animal it had been. It was so picked over it took her a moment to figure it out. But when she did, her stomach wrenched and she almost fell from the sky.

It was a dragon. A baby boy dragon. There was no mistaking it.

It was then that she felt it. A small prick at her neck. It didn't hurt exactly. But it felt strange and hot. And a moment later, everything began to go blurry. The ground seemed to weave under her feet. Scared, she tried to ascend again, to get up to a rooftop to figure out what was going on. But her wings felt heavy and slow. And soon she found herself falling.

Falling.

Until everything went black.

Asha woke to find herself in a cage. A monster cage, made of ugly bars of metal. She tried to stand, but the cage was too small and she couldn't uncoil herself to reach the door, which she assumed was locked anyway. Panicked, she tried to bite through the bars with her teeth, but she only managed to hurt her jaw. Finally, she collapsed onto the floor of the cage. A low, desperate cry escaped from her throat as she accepted the truth.

She was trapped. Trapped by the monsters once again.

How could she have been so stupid? She was looking for a trap, and she'd walked right into one. She'd been so concerned about the dead dragon that she'd stopped paying attention to her surroundings. They had shot her with something—she didn't know what, but it was enough to take her down. And now she was their prisoner.

She tried to summon up a small blast of fire, but it was useless. She was too drained.

She watched as three burly men walked up to the cage, keeping their distance and talking loudly. The first one looked at her then said something to his friends that she couldn't understand. She wondered which one of them was Noah's father. She wondered what they were planning to do.

It was then that she saw the bucket of blood in the second man's hand. They must have drained it from her when she was out cold—no wonder she felt so weak. She watched as he started smearing it all over the streets. It took her a moment to realize why. But when she did, her body went cold.

They were using her blood to scent the square. They

knew the others in her herd would smell it and come looking, just as she had when she'd smelled the baby dragon.
And when they came, the humans would attack.

Oh, Noah. I tried. I really did.

The men left soon after, still jabbering to each other
in a language she couldn't understand. Not that it would
likely do any good if she could. Knowing what they were
saying was not going to free her from the trap. Her only
hope was to try to warn any dragons that came near
before it was too late. They might kill her, but at least she
could die saving her herd, like a true queen.

"Asha!"

She startled at the sudden sound of her name. Her
gaze shot to the sky, but it appeared empty. There were
only puffy white clouds and a bright yellow sun.

"Tolkyn?" she whispered back, her heart pounding in
her chest. "Is that you?"

"Yes, my queen. I'm hiding out on a nearby roof. I'm
going to come down and set you free."

"No!" she cried, her eyes darting around the city
square in horror. "Don't come any closer! It's a trap.
They'll kill you if you do."

"I am not afraid of death," he replied stiffly. "And I
refuse to fail you as I failed your mother."

Tears slipped from her eyes at his words. He was so

strong. So loyal. Out of all the other dragons, she knew he cared about her the most. Which is why she couldn't let him do this.

"Please don't!" she begged. "As your queen, I command you to stand down!"

He grunted, annoyed. "Then what am I supposed to do? Just leave you here to die?"

She hung her head. She knew he'd never do that. He'd never walk away from his queen. But the humans were close—lurking in the shadows—she could feel them. Once he showed himself, it would be too late.

Oh, Noah, she thought miserably. *What do I do now?*

Noah! Her head jerked up. Maybe *he* could help them somehow. It was his father who had set the trap, after all. Maybe if she could get him down here to talk to his dad...

But how? She couldn't exactly call to him when he was so far away.

"My queen. What do I do?" She could feel the dragon captain's rising frustration. And suddenly an idea began to form in her mind.

"Tolkyn," she said, "I need you to do something for me." She paused, then added, "Though I'm afraid you're not going to like it."

His reply came instantly. "I'll do anything, my queen. You know that."

"Good," she said. "Then I need you to go find the pup—Noah. He's the only one who can help us now."

"What?" Tolkyn didn't even try to hide his horror. "How could you even—"

"You have to! Or I will die. And others will, too." She sighed loudly. "Look, you once said you couldn't help me unless I told you what was going on. Well, I'm telling you now. Noah and I share a true bond, Tolkyn. I trust him with my life. And if you want me to survive this—for all of us to survive this—well, then you're going to have to trust him, too."

CHAPTER THIRTY-FIVE

Noah

Mom walked me out of the council room, down the hall, and out of the library, only stopping once we got to the bottom of the front steps. She turned to me, a regretful look on her face as she reached out to touch my arm. "I'm sorry," she said softly. "I know they want to help. They're just being practical."

"I know," I said, staring at the ground. "I get it. I don't want anyone to get hurt, either." I stubbed my toe against the pavement. "Anyway, it's not their fault. It's Dad's. He's the one doing all this." I raked a hand through my hair, frustrated. "I should have just tried to talk to him in the first place when I found out what he was planning.

Instead of sneaking out and going to warn Asha. Maybe I could have talked him out of all this. I'm his son—he might have listened to me."

Mom gave me a pointed look. "Do you really think he would have listened?"

"I don't know." I groaned. "Maybe not. I just wish he could open his mind a little. If he could just see what I've seen."

"Me too," Mom agreed. "I wish that more than anything. But you can't change people, Noah. You can only show them the door. It's up to them to walk through it."

"And he never will."

"Probably not," she said honestly. Then she sighed. "You've gone through so much, Noah. No kid should have to deal with what you've been dealing with. And I'm really sorry for my part in it all."

I looked up. "What do you mean?"

"The thing between your father and me. It's not about you. It never was. And I'm sorry you've been caught in the middle of it over and over again. I never wanted that for you. I love you, Noah. I just want you to be safe and happy."

She wrapped her arms around me, holding me close. I buried my face in her shoulder, feeling the tears drip down my cheeks. At least I had her back. That was something, at least.

She pulled out of the hug, giving me a sympathetic smile. "Come on. Why don't we go and get some ice cream? I hear they have chocolate chip tonight at the market. We can eat it straight out of the tub and read some books. Get our minds off everything. How does that sound?"

"Maybe later," I replied. I knew she was trying to make me feel better, but at the moment, I kind of wanted to feel rotten. "Right now, I just want to be alone."

"I understand. Take all the time you need. But I'm here for you, Noah. If you ever want to talk, just find me, okay? You're not in this alone."

"Thanks, Mom. I appreciate that," I told her.

My mother headed back to the apartment. I watched her go, then slumped down on a nearby stoop, wondering what I should do. It wasn't like I was going to be able to focus on anything right now. Maybe it was best to just sit around and be miserable.

Oh, Asha, I thought, though I knew she couldn't hear me. *I hope you're okay.*

And maybe she would be, I told myself. Maybe she had already told her herd about the danger and they'd listened. Maybe they'd already gone into hiding. Maybe they were safe.

Maybe...

Suddenly, I heard a screeching noise from above. For

one brief second, my heart leapt, thinking maybe Asha had heard me after all. But no, it was just several large dragons from our herd circling above, screeching wildly.

"What are they freaking out about?" Lei asked, approaching with Bowie following close behind her. Her dragon had an ear to the sky. "It's not feeding time." Then her face went pale.

"What is it?" I asked.

"Bowie says there's a dragon approaching," she told me. "Not one from our herd."

"Is it Asha?" I cried, before I could stop myself. Maybe she had come back! Maybe she'd even brought her herd.

Lei turned to Bowie, silently asking the question. But the dragon shook his head.

"No," Lei said. "It's a bigger dragon. And they say he's asking for you."

What?

Sure enough, a moment later, a full-grown dragon with flashing silver scales appeared above us, flanked by several members of our herd who were clearly keeping a close eye on him, not trusting him completely, even if he was outnumbered.

I watched warily as he hit the ground. He was a huge dragon, bigger than any I'd ever seen up close, with massive wings that were now folded to his sides and horns that curved in a perfect spiral. His silver scales seemed to shimmer in a lightning bolt pattern down his back as he shook himself before settling down and lowering his head in a sign of submission that I'd seen Asha do when she first came here. His eyes were solemn, and I thought I caught a hint of moisture in the corners, as if he'd been crying. My fear intensified.

"What's happening?" I asked Lei. "Can you please ask Bowie to interpret for me?"

She turned to her own dragon, instructing him. Bowie stepped up to the new creature, a little timidly—he was about three times the size of the young dragon—then lowered his head.

"He says his name is . . . Tolkyn," Lei translated, after a pause. "He needs our help. Something about . . . a queen? His queen?" She shrugged. "I guess she's in danger or something?"

My heart leapt in my chest. "Asha!" I cried.

Tolkyn's head jerked in my direction. His somber amber eyes narrowed on me.

"He's asking if you're Noah," Lei said. "I had Bowie tell him you were. I hope that's okay."

"Where's Asha?" I blurted out. "Did something happen to her?"

My stomach twisted as Lei translated his answer. My worst fear coming true. Asha trapped—being used as bait for the other dragons.

316

And there was nothing I could do about it.

"He says Asha believes you might be able to help them," Lei finished. "He says she trusts you and that you'll know what to do."

I raked a hand through my hair, frustrated. "Look, I want to help. Believe me—I want Asha safe as much as you do. But I don't know what we can do. I tried to talk the council into helping, but they say it's too dangerous." I hung my head, feeling useless.

Tolkyn sighed deeply as Lei translated through Bowie. I could sense the disappointment radiating from his body. Asha had sent her one last hope to find me. And I was letting him down.

What to do? What to do? I paced back and forth, trying to think.

"Are you okay?" Lei asked, speaking for herself this time.

I whirled around to face her. "No. I'm not okay. I'm worried about my dragon. My father's going to kill her, and I'm stuck up here unable to help her."

Lei nodded slowly, a look of pity on her face. She reached out and placed a hand on her dragon's neck.

"Bowie says he's sorry," she said. "He really liked Asha. He wishes he could help."

I nodded vacantly, at first too wrapped up in my own thoughts to absorb her words. But then they slowly settled into my brain.

317

"Maybe he can," I said slowly, glancing over at the dragon.

Lei looked at me quizzically "What do you mean?"

My heart fluttered in my chest. I drew in a breath. "Tell him to gather as many dragons as he can. I want to talk to the herd."

She nodded, wide-eyed, and relayed the message to her dragon. Bowie danced around excitedly, then lifted his head and let out a loud, wailing cry.

A moment later, the skies above darkened with dragons. The herd heeding the call. One by one, they dropped down into the square. Big dragons, small dragons, male and female dragons all coming in for a landing. Tolkyn watched, looking warily at the crowd. I didn't blame him—he was vastly outnumbered.

But that was the whole point.

I leapt onto a nearby pedestal in front of a statue. Then I motioned for Bowie to join me. The young dragon hopped up beside me, looking rather excited at the opportunity to have the spotlight.

"I need you to have Bowie keep translating for me," I told Lei. "Can he do that?"

"Yup. He's ready when you are!"

I bit my lower lip. "Um, hello?" I tried. "Sorry to bother you all. But we have a bit of a situation here. And I need your help."

The dragons listened as I explained what was going on, with Lei and Bowie interpreting in turn. When I had finished, I looked up at them, trying to judge their reactions. But they were only staring at me blankly. My heart sank.

"What are they saying?" I asked Lei.

She gave me an apologetic look. "They want to know why they should help this other herd. Their situation has nothing to do with them."

I sighed. Right. Of course. Dragons only cared about their own families. They considered other herds their rivals—why would they want to risk their lives to save them? I glanced at Tolkyn, who was shifting from side to side, looking more and more uncomfortable. Maybe this wasn't going to work after all. . . .

No. It had to! Asha's life depended on it. I couldn't let her down.

I turned back to the herd. "Look, I get it," I said. "I grew up hating dragons. I thought they were monsters who had destroyed my world. But then one day I came across a baby dragon stuck in a trap. She was going to die if I didn't help her. At first, I considered walking away—it wasn't my problem, right? But then I realized I couldn't do that. Because she was no longer some faceless monster, but a creature who needed my help." I paused, then added, "We're all creatures here, living together, sharing New

York City. And at times we all need each other's help. Yes, we're in different herds and we have different beliefs. But at the end of the day, we all want the same thing. And I believe we'd be stronger together than apart."

A few dragons snorted. A few others pawed the ground. I wasn't sure if this was a good sign or not, but I couldn't stop now.

"If we're going to survive this apocalypse, we're going to have to start working together. You've already done this with humans—that's huge! You took a risk, and it gave you a better life. Now I'm asking you to take another risk. To rise up and defend your enemy. An act of kindness. A leap of faith. But imagine what could come of it."

I closed my eyes, completely spent. I had nothing else to say. I'd laid it all out the best I could. Made my case. Now it was up to them.

Silence stretched across the square, and my heart pounded in my chest.

And then, suddenly, the dragons roared in unison— one joyful, ferocious, yet amazing roar. My eyes flew open. I glanced over at Lei, hardly able to breathe.

"Are they saying yes?" I asked.

She turned to me, grinning from ear to ear. "Yes! They're going to help!" she exclaimed excitedly. "They're going to help save the queen."

My heart soared. *Oh, Asha. Hang on! We're coming.*

Bowie leaned toward Lei again, whispering something in her ear. Her grin widened. "They do have one condition," she added.

"What's that?" I asked.

"That you and the other humans join them."

Of course only a handful of people at Columbia had bonded enough with their dragons to be able to ride them down to Times Square. But it was better than nothing, and the other dragons would come along as riderless backup, giving us a small dragon army. Even my own mother had mounted her new dragon, whom she'd named Mickey, and was ready to go.

I was ready to go, too—except I was still on the ground. Because my dragon was the one we were saving. I frowned, suddenly a little worried. I couldn't be left behind. I was the one Asha trusted. I was also my father's son—if anyone had a chance to talk him out of this, it would be me.

"Do you think someone's dragon will take two?" I started to ask the group. But before I could finish, I felt a blast of warm air at my back. Turning around, I found Tolkyn standing behind me. He leveled his big eyes on me, then slowly dropped to his knees, bending a wing in my direction.

"You want me to ride you?" I asked, astounded.

The dragon closed his eyes and lowered his head to the ground. I could tell he was nervous. But he didn't flinch when I took a step toward him. A moment later, I scrambled up onto his mighty back. He was much larger than Asha, so I couldn't wrap my arms around his entire neck. But I latched on to two of his thick, leathery scales and managed to get as comfortable as I could.

"Thank you," I whispered to him. I knew he couldn't understand me, but I felt I had to say it anyway. I could tell how much Asha meant to him. If only I could explain how much she meant to me, too.

Guess I'd be proving it soon enough.

"Okay," I said, drawing in a long breath. I leaned forward, touching Tolkyn's neck. "Take us to your queen."

CHAPTER THIRTY-SIX

Asha

Asha paced in her cage, feeling restless and scared. It had been so long since Tolkyn had gone to find Noah, and there had been no word from him since. What if he'd run into trouble? What if he'd been intercepted by her uncle or some other dragon and had been forced to confess his mission? While she never doubted Tolkyn's loyalty to her, she couldn't say the same about everyone else. And if they learned of his plan...

No. She shook her head. Tolkyn wouldn't fail. She had to trust in him as he trusted in her.

She just hoped he'd hurry.

Suddenly, a large shadow crossed over her from above.

She looked up, her heart pinging with hope. Was it Tolkyn? Was he back at last?

But no. Her hope sank like a stone. It was her uncle. And he looked angry.

"Well, well," he growled, circling the sky above her, weaving in and out between buildings. "Hanging out with the monsters again, I see."

She watched in dismay as he descended into the square. "Please!" she begged. "Don't come any closer. It's a trap. They'll kill you if you try to save me! Just wait for Tolkyn! He'll be back any minute!"

But her uncle ignored her, landing a few feet away, the ground quaking under his massive weight. She imagined her captors, lurking in the shadows, grinning with glee over this new arrival. They wouldn't act right away; they'd wait for the others to come, too. So they could get them all—including her—in one fell swoop.

Her uncle approached her cage, dropping his head to nudge his snout against the trap's steel jaws. "It seems to be stuck," he muttered, sounding annoyed. "I'll need to get some of the others to help."

"No!" she cried. "Please don't! Please don't bring anyone else—"

But her uncle had already released his mighty roar. The kind of roar that brought dragons near and far. Inviting them straight into the trap.

Tears began to form in Asha's eyes. "Please, Uncle. I beg of you. Don't let them come here! I don't want anyone to get hurt." She tried to sense whether Noah's father and the other men were still near, but she couldn't tell for sure. But even if they weren't, they'd be back soon, she was sure of it.

Her uncle laughed. "How will they hurt us?" He tsked dismissively. "There are far more of us than there are of them."

"You don't understand," she tried, even though she knew he had no interest in listening. Any second now, the others would arrive. It was already too late.

"Asha!"

Or was it?

Her eyes shot up to the sky. "Noah!" she cried as she looked up to see the most beautiful sight in the world. Noah, *her Noah*, flying on Tolkyn's back! And behind them were even more dragons, each with a human rider, as if it was the most natural thing in the world.

She let out a sigh of relief. Maybe it wasn't too late after all.

Her uncle followed Asha's gaze, his mouth dropping in horror at the sight of the army of dragons above. "What are they doing here?" he demanded. "This is our—"

He broke off when he spotted Tolkyn, his face twisted with rage. "Is that Tolkyn?" he cried. "With a monster on his back?"

"Not a monster," Asha corrected solemnly. "A human, and he's here to save us all."

CHAPTER THIRTY-SEVEN

Noah

I looked down in horror at the scene unfolding in Times Square. A huge cage my dad and his friends had set up in the center, probably acquired from the old Central Park Zoo, with Asha trapped inside. The bars are made of iron, and there was a huge padlock on the door. Surrounding the cage were smears of blood, streaking the street. Asha's blood, I assumed, and winced.

But that wasn't even the worst part. My eyes traveled to the two complicated-looking devices on each side of the cage. Guess they hadn't been bluffing about the bombs.

If they detonated them...

There was also another complication. A very large dragon,

with mighty curved horns, was standing in front of the cage. Was it one of Asha's herd? Would he be friendly to us, like Tolkyn, or would he attack if we tried to fly down to help?

I reached out to Asha. "We're here!" I told her. "But I'm not sure it's safe to land with your big friend standing there. Is he going to be okay with this?"

Asha's voice rose in my consciousness. "I'll tell him to stand down. But he's not going to like it. Hopefully Tolkyn can deal with him." She paused, then added, her voice thick with worry, "Just...hurry, Noah. The others are on their way. If they show up, I won't be able to deal with all of them at once."

"Right. We'll do our best." I turned to Javier, who was riding a dragon named Zoe, and the others behind him. "Okay. I need some of you to land and surround the cage. The rest keep watch for any approaching dragons and try to keep them away. Javier, you work on dismantling the bombs."

"But what if they go off?" asked another man on his dragon as he eyed the nasty devices below.

"My dad won't detonate them with humans nearby," I assured him. "That's why some of us need to be down there on the ground. He's a dragon hater, but he would never hurt another person." At least I hoped not. Otherwise, all of this was going to fail.

But we had to take the chance—there was no other

way. So I urged Tolkyn to land, and together we dropped to the ground right by the cage. Then I slid down his wing, landing on my own two feet. I watched as some of the other dragons and riders joined us one by one, until we had a rather large crowd surrounding the square. Javier dashed toward the cage to work on dismantling the bombs while my mother started organizing our group to lock arms and stand around it as a human shield.

Now—time to find my father. Not that I was sure what I was going to do when I found him. Maybe try to talk him out of this madness—one final plea? Or maybe I could at least distract him—keep him from triggering the bomb before we had Asha out and safe.

It was then that I felt something behind me. I turned slowly, coming face-to-face with Asha's big friend, who was staring me down, a fierce expression on his face. Frightened, I stumbled backward, almost crashing into Tolkyn in the process. The dragon took a menacing step forward, his lips curling back into a nasty snarl.

"Uncle, stop! I told you, he's here to help!" Asha's voice rang out from the cage. "We need him—and his friends! As your queen, I demand that you stand down."

But the dragon only snarled in my direction. He did not back down. Instead, he took another threatening step forward, slashing his claws through the air. I ducked just in time to avoid being skewered.

"Uncle, please!" Asha's voice took on a desperate tone.

Suddenly, my ears were being blasted by a deafening roar. Tolkyn had leapt in front of me, between me and Asha's uncle, shielding me from his next attack. The two dragons faced off, staring defiantly at each other and wearing matching snarls. Bellies building with fire.

I scrambled to my feet, breathing heavily. I turned toward Asha. She looked so pitiful in her cage, so cramped and twisted up. But her eyes were alight with hope. She believed we could do this. Which made me want to believe, too.

"Tolkyn will deal with my uncle," she told me. "You go find your father!"

"What is the meaning of this?"

Or maybe my father would find me.

Suddenly, my father burst out from behind a building, brandishing his rifle in his hands. He looked horrible. His eyes were bloodshot and ringed with dark circles. His hair was wild and uncombed. It looked as if he hadn't slept in a week.

"Noah! What is the meaning of this?" he repeated. His gaze shifted from me to the humans surrounding the cage. "Who are these people? What are they doing here?"

I took a small step forward. My knees threatened to buckle, but somehow I forced myself to stay upright. I squared my shoulders, lifted my chin.

Time for a face-off of my own.

"It's over, Dad," I declared. My voice sounded strangely calm and even, at odds with the twisting fear inside. "We're dismantling the bombs. We're not going to let you hurt these dragons."

My father's jaw dropped. He stared at me with wide eyes that almost didn't look human. "Are you insane?" he demanded. "Why would you do that? You want these creatures to live? After what they did to me? After what they did to the world?"

His eyes fell on my mother, who'd stepped up to stand by my side. His face twisted into a scowl. "Brainwashed! They've brainwashed you both!" he declared. "They've turned you against your own family! I was there for you! I saved you when everyone else was dying! And this is how you repay me? By siding with the monsters?"

"It's not about choosing sides, Dad," I pleaded. "It's about ending all this violence and war. Don't you see? This will go on forever at this rate. You'll destroy them, they'll destroy us, and over and over it'll go until everyone's gone." I glanced over at Javier, wondering how he was doing with the bombs. "But it doesn't have to be this way."

"You're all fools," Dad growled. "You think you can trust a dragon? Who's to say they don't turn on you the second you look away?"

"I do," I proclaimed. "And so do all the people here

who have bonded with their dragons. We know them now, and they know us. We can hear their thoughts, and we know they don't wish us any harm. You could know this, too, if you just allowed yourself to listen."

"I don't have to listen to anything!" my dad snapped. He reached into his pocket, pulling out a small silver device and palming it.

I gasped. It was the detonator.

"What are you going to do, Dad?" I demanded. "Are you going to kill all of us? All these people? Your wife? Your son?"

My dad's hands shook. He gripped the detonator tighter. I closed my eyes for a moment, trying to regroup. Whatever I said next, it had to be good. It had to be perfect. Or all of this would be for nothing.

I opened my eyes again. "Look, Dad, I know it's been horrible for you. Ever since the start of this whole thing. You were the one who protected us. You kept us safe. You did what you had to do back then. But don't you see? You don't have to do it anymore. We're no longer in danger! We're safe. We're happy. Wasn't that your goal from the start? And you did it, Dad. You got us through the bad part. And now it's time to rest. To step into the next chapter of our world. A better chapter, where we don't have to fight for our lives anymore."

For a moment, Dad said nothing. He just stood there

as if frozen in place, his hands white-knuckling the detonator. I could practically see his thoughts whirling through his brain, but I had no idea what he was thinking.

Dad, I thought. *Please, Dad. Let go of your hate.*

I felt the tears leak from my eyes, but I didn't bother to brush them away. Maybe he'd see me as weak, but I no longer cared. I was done apologizing for who I was. He could accept me or not. That was his choice in the end, not mine. "Please, Dad," I said, reaching out a hand in his direction. "Just give us a chance. A chance to be a family again."

I watched in surprise as a lone tear slipped down my dad's bearded cheek. He looked from me to Mom and then back to me again. Slowly, the hand holding the detonator began to drop to his side. I let out a sigh of relief.

"Oh, Dad—" I started to say.

But I couldn't finish, because at that moment Richard and Brad burst onto the scene. They stopped short when they saw us, their jaws dropping in disbelief.

"What is going on here?" Richard demanded.

My dad shrugged uneasily but didn't reply. I wondered if he didn't trust his voice to speak.

Brad let out a disgusted noise, pulling the rifle from his back. "You weak, pathetic fool...," he muttered. Then he lifted the gun and aimed it directly at Asha's cage. His face was twisted in rage, giving him the true look of a monster.

A monster who was about to kill us all.

CHAPTER THIRTY-EIGHT

Noah

I didn't think. I just moved, diving toward Brad in a desperate attempt to push the gun skyward before he pulled the trigger. But the shot rang out before I could reach him, the sound clapping at my ears, followed by a hot sting of pain as the bullet pierced my side.

I collapsed to the ground, gasping. My vision blurred. The pain was literally blinding. I looked down in horror at the blood seeping from my stomach.

"Noah! Oh no! Noah!"

My dad was at my side in a second. Mom dropped down beside him, yanking up my shirt to examine the wound. It was gushing blood—the bullet had evidently gone straight through me. They exchanged looks. The expressions on their faces told me it wasn't good.

Dad rose to his feet, a horrific expression on his face. "How dare you hurt my son?" he screamed. He began to charge at Brad, but Brad only raised his weapon again, pointing it at Dad.

"You're crazy!" he screamed. "You're all freaking—"

His voice cut short as if slashed by a knife.

I craned my neck to see what was happening. Tolkyn and Asha's uncle were no longer locked in a standoff. Instead, they were stalking side by side toward Brad and Richard. Their huge bellies burning with fire.

Richard and Brad looked at each other, their faces filled with dread. Brad tried to shoot, but the bullets bounced harmlessly off of Tolkyn's tough scales, missing the soft ones on his underbelly. Asha's uncle let out a mighty roar, and the two men started screaming and running down the street as fast as their legs would take them, two giant dragons in hot pursuit.

For a moment, I felt almost bad for them. But then, they had made their choice. Now they would pay for it.

I wanted to keep watching, but the pain hit me again, hot and blinding. I let out a soft moan, and Dad dropped back down to my side. I looked at my stomach, horrified at how fast the blood was soaking through the shirt Mom had been using to put pressure on the wound. I started to feel dizzy. Faint.

"Noah! Stay with me!" Mom commanded.

But I couldn't. My breath was coming in shallow gasps. My body was growing numb.

"Oh no," Mom whispered. "Noah..."

"The dragon!" My dad suddenly exclaimed. "Could the dragon help?"

Without waiting for a reply, he leapt to his feet, racing to Asha's cage and dropping to his knees in front of the lock. He pulled out a set of keys from his pocket and popped open the padlock. Asha bolted out, straight to me, burying her face in my wound. It felt weird—her wet, rough tongue, licking me—but not entirely unpleasant. And soon I could feel the pain slowly slipping away. The bullet hole closing before my eyes.

I was going to be okay.

We were all going to be okay.

At least for today.

"Oh, Noah," Mom whispered, her shoulders slumping in relief. "Thank goodness."

"Thank the *dragon*," Dad corrected, looking at Asha with appreciation radiating from his eyes. For a moment I thought he was actually going to hug her.

Asha looked warily at him, then back at me. "What is he saying?" she asked.

"He's thanking you," I told her with a weak smile. "For saving my life once again."

She winked at me. "It wasn't a big deal."

I smiled up at her, meeting her glowing amber eyes with my own. "Um, my life is kind of a big deal to me."

She grinned. "Fair."

I sat up, wrapping my arms around her neck and burying my face in her silky silver scales. Then I broke away to hug Mom, then Dad. Dad held me so tight that for a moment I almost lost my breath. Maybe I'd turn him into a hugger yet. Soon, the others had crowded around us, too. Human and dragon. Hugging each other. Sharing the moment. For once all on the same team.

A family, in a sense. A real family at last.

CHAPTER THIRTY-NINE

Noah

November 1

And they all lived happily ever after!"

I closed the book, glancing over at Asha, who had been curled up at the bottom of the stoop, listening with sleepy eyes. She raised her head in question.

"Is that it? That can't be the end of the book!"

I grinned. "What else do you want? They defeated evil! They saved the day!"

"But then what? What happens next?"

"You'll have to use your imagination. Or let me read you the sequel."

I set the book down on the stoop, reaching out to pet my dragon on the snout. She snorted, annoyed, puffs of white smoke billowing from her nostrils. She had grown so big since that first day we'd met in Times Square, but she'd always be little Asha to me.

Asha the apple lover.

"But we don't have time for the sequel!" she argued. "It's hibernation day."

"I know. But I promise to save it for you when you get back, okay?"

She gave me a pouty look. "So unfair."

"Agreed." I said. "But what can we do?"

It was still hard to believe that Asha and I had been together for almost half a year now. Ever since the showdown with my father and his friends, she and some of her herd, including Tolkyn, had moved up here to join the others to give living with humans a try. They'd realized, after watching me almost die to try to save their queen, that maybe we weren't all the monsters they'd thought us to be. And after many discussions with the other herd, they'd worked out an agreement between them. To combine some of their land to the south with the herd's up north, creating a larger territory for all dragons to share. And, thanks to a suggestion from Asha, they'd agreed to create a joint council with elected members from each herd to solve any problems that might arise.

Not everyone was in, of course. There were several dragons, including Asha's uncle and aunt, who just couldn't swallow the idea of regular human interaction. They chose to stay in Midtown to form a smaller herd on a smaller parcel of land in a neighborhood once known as Chelsea. Asha allowed it, making her uncle king of the new group, but made them promise they would never harm a human unless they were specifically attacked by one. In return, the northern herd would share their food. It still remained to be seen if it would all work next summer, assuming we could talk the hotel group into staying aboveground. But I had a good feeling Tolkyn could keep Asha's uncle in line, especially after seeing him in action.

As for my dad? We had invited him to come live with us, too, but in the end, he declined, saying he wasn't cut out for life in large groups. I think he still wasn't comfortable with the idea of being this close to dragons. We did meet up weekly, though, to spend time together. Which was a little awkward at first, after all that had happened. But my father did seem truly apologetic for all he put me through and had been dutifully working through a series of self-help books my mom had acquired for him, just as he'd once planned to do with her. He'd never love dragons—I knew that for sure. But he'd agreed to live and let live, just like Asha's uncle. That would have to be enough for now.

And at least I still had Mom. She and I had grown so close over the past few months. She was always telling me how proud she was of me. Even if she did harass me a little too much about my math studies. I'd enrolled in the community school she taught at and was currently working my way through seventh grade with Lei and Hugo and the others. It wasn't always easy—Mom was a tough teacher—but I didn't mind too much. After all, one didn't become a dragon scientist by failing to hit the books.

The days and weeks and months had flown by. Literally at times, now that we were riding our dragons on a regular basis, which definitely cut down on transportation issues around the city. Saanvi had even set up a bonding program to help match suitable humans with new dragons, based on all sorts of complicated algorithms I didn't understand. Not every dragon wanted a human, and not every human wanted a dragon. But those who did grew very close, and you'd often catch them soaring through the skies, happy and free.

But for me, there was no dragon but Asha.

We'd spent the entire summer together, she and I. Flying, exploring, playing. And reading, of course. Turned out Asha liked stories almost as much as I did, and we'd spent hours curled up, lost in a good book. She preferred the ones with dragons.

But now, summer was over, and the dragons were preparing to go into their six-month hibernation again. Usually this had been a time of celebration for me and my friends, who had been stuck down in the subway tunnels for months. The beginning of six months of freedom above. But now, it was kind of sad. I was going to miss Asha and the other dragons a lot.

And they were going to miss us, too.

Asha sighed. "I wish I didn't have to go."

"Me too," I assured her. "But you'll be back soon. And we'll spend the time you're away making things even more awesome for when you come back."

She smiled. "Make sure you save me some apples...."

A shadow crossed over us from above, and I looked up to see Sonja coming down for a landing. She had been hanging around a lot lately, always making sure Asha had everything she needed. It was really cute—like she'd taken her under her wing as a mother figure. I knew Asha liked her a lot.

Sonja was still technically bonded to my father, but since he wasn't interested, she'd gone back to hanging out a lot with David. He was good to her, always making sure she had enough to eat, and was always willing to scratch her belly when it was itchy. In turn, she let him ride her around the city as he scavenged for parts Javier needed to build a new technology network. It wasn't as complete a bond as I had with Asha, but it was something, at least. And they both seemed content with what they shared.

Sonja nudged Asha gently with her snout. Clearly

letting her know it was time to leave. Asha sighed, then gave me a half smile.

"Thank you again," she whispered. "For everything."

"I'll see you in the spring," I told her, feeling a lump form in my throat. "I'll have all new books to read to you then."

I watched Sonja lead Asha away, toward the circle where all the dragons stood. One by one, they pushed off on their hind legs, launching into the sky while the humans on the ground cheered them on. I wasn't the only one, I noticed, with tears rolling down my cheeks.

"Goodbye, Asha," I murmured. "Stay safe."

And just like that, they were gone. But they would return, I reminded myself. We would be together again.

A shadow crossed over me then. I looked up to see my mom standing above me, an excited smile on her face. "Are you ready, Noah?" she asked. "I think it's time."

"More than ready," I declared with a grin. "Let's do this."

A few hours later, I found myself standing there, just as I'd promised back in April. In front of the subway exit in the middle of Times Square, my eyes locked on the heavy vault door as my mother and father stood on each side of me, waiting for it to open.

This was it. The moment of truth.

My breath caught in my throat as the door began to move. It was slow at first, then it just seemed to burst open, with people streaming out and up the stairway, laughing and cheering as they stepped into the square and witnessed their first glimpse of the sun in months. They were dragging suitcases and carts and all sorts of stuff. Wanting to get back to the hotel in time to score the best room for the winter. A few of them saw me and my parents and greeted us excitedly. My mom gave out a ton of hugs.

But I just stood there, waiting. And finally, after what seemed like forever, Maya emerged from the tunnel, too, her arms full of boxes—probably leftover supplies from her family's store. She was thinner than she'd been before, and her clothes were old and stained, but she was there. And that was all that mattered to me.

I stepped forward, my heart swelling with joy, although I felt a little nervous, too, for some weird reason. But Maya's eyes only lit up as they fell on my face, and she let out a cry of excitement, dropping her boxes and running toward me at full speed.

"Noah!" she cried. "You're okay! You're really okay!"

"I'm more than okay," I said with a smile. I reached into my pocket and pulled out an apple, tossing it in her direction. "And I've got so much to tell you."

She caught the apple and took a bite, then grinned. "I can't wait to hear."

ACKNOWLEDGMENTS

Writing a book can be a dragon-sized adventure, and I'm so fortunate to have such a fantastic team at Little, Brown Books for Young Readers at my side. Especially my talented and amazing editor, Liz Kossnar, who always asks exactly the right questions to level up my manuscripts. This book would not be where it is today without you.

Thank you also to the marketing and publicity folks, who work tirelessly to get these books into readers' hands, including Emilie Polster, Marisa Russell, Stefanie Hoffman, Cheryl Lew, Cassie Malmo, Mara Brashem, Victoria Stapleton, Christie Michel, and Amber Mercado. And thank you, Janelle DeLuise and Hannah Koerner, for so enthusiastically representing my book around the world. And to Alvina Ling, editor-in-chief, who made me feel so welcome and valued from day one.

Special thanks to Diana Peterfreund, one of this book's earliest readers and my favorite plotting buddy. Our brainstorming retreats are legend—let's do another one soon! And to my daughter, Avalon, who insisted I read her this book chapter by chapter as I was writing it—never letting me slack off and skip a day! I don't know if this book would have ever been finished without you, and I still cherish all the artwork you made of little dragon Asha.

Thank you also to agent Mandy Hubbard who has always been such a wonderful advocate and cheerleader of my work.

And to my husband, Jacob—my biggest supporter and true love. I wouldn't want to face a dragon apocalypse without you by my side.

And last, but definitely not least, to all the readers out there. Thank you for allowing me to introduce you to Noah and Asha and their world. You make this entire dragon-sized book-writing adventure so worthwhile.